AFRICAN WRITERS SERIES

...ebe

PETER ABRAHAMS
❋ *Mine Boy*

CHINUA ACHEBE
❋ *Things Fall Apart*
❋ *No Longer at Ease*
❋ *Arrow of God*
❋ *A Man of the People*
❋ *Anthills of the Savannah*
100 *Girls at War**
120 *Beware Soul Brother†*

THOMAS AKARE
241 *The Slums*

T. M. ALUKO
70 *Chief, the Honourable Minister*

ELECHI AMADI
❋ *The Concubine*
44 *The Great Ponds*
210 *The Slave*
❋ *Estrangement*

I. N. C. ANIEBO
206 *The Journey Within*

KOFI ANYIDOHO
261 *A Harvest of Our Dreams†*

AYI KWEI ARMAH
❋ *The Beautyful Ones Are Not Yet Born*
154 *Fragments*
155 *Why Are We So Blest?*
194 *The Healers*
218 *Two Thousand Seasons*

BEDIAKO ASARE
59 *Rebel*

KOFI AWOONOR
108 *This Earth, My Brother*

MARIAMA BÂ
❋ *So Long a Letter*

MONGO BETI
13 *Mission to Kala*
77 *King Lazarus*
88 *The Poor Christ of Bomba*
181 *Perpetua and the Habit of Unhappiness*
214 *Remember Ruben*

STEVE BIKO
❋ *I Write What I Like§*

OKOT P'BITEK
193 *Hare and Hornbill**
266 *Song of Lawino & Song of Ocol†*

DENNIS BRUTUS
115 *A Simple Lust†*
208 *Stubborn Hope†*

SYL CHENEY-COKER
221 *The Graveyard Also Has Teeth*

DRISS CHRAIBI
79 *Heirs to the Past*

❋ Four colou...
* Short Stori...
† Poetry
‡ Plays
§ Biography/...

WILLIAM CONTON
12 *The African*

BERNARD B. DADIE
87 *Climbié*

MODIKWE DIKOBE
124 *The Marabi Dance*

MBELLA SONNE DIPOKO
57 *Because of Women*

AMU DJOLETO
41 *The Strange Man*
161 *Money Galore*

T. OBINKARAM ECHEWA
❋ *The Crippled Dancer*

CYPRIAN EKWENSI
2 *Burning Grass*
9 *Lokotown**
84 *Beautiful Feathers*
185 *Survive the Peace*
❋ *Jagua Nana*

BUCHI EMECHETA
❋ *The Joys of Motherhood*

OLAUDAH EQUIANO
10 *Equiano's Travels§*

NURUDDIN FARAH
252 *Sardines*

NADINE GORDIMER
177 *Some Monday for Sure**

BESSIE HEAD
❋ *Maru*
❋ *A Question of Power*
❋ *When Rain Clouds Gather*
182 *The Collector of Treasures**
220 *Serowe: Village of the Rain Wind§*

LUIS BERNARDO HONWANA
60 *We Killed Mangy-Dog**

OBOTUNDE IJIMÈRE
18 *The Imprisonment of Obatala‡*

EDDIE IROH
189 *Forty-Eight Guns for the General*

KENJO JUMBAM
231 *The White Man of God*

CHEIKH HAMIDOU KANE
119 *Ambiguous Adventure*

FARIDA KARODIA
❋ *Coming Home and Other Stories**

AHMADOU KOUROUMA
239 *The Suns of Independence*

MAZISI KUNENE
211 *Emperor Shaka the Great†*

ALEX LA GUMA
❋ *A Walk in the Night**
110 *In the Fog of the Seasons End*
❋ *Time of the Butcherbird*

DORIS LESSING
131 *The Grass is Singing*

HUGH LEWIN
251 *Bandiet*

HENRI LOPES
❋ *Tribaliks*

NELSON MANDELA
❋ *No Easy Walk to Freedom§*

JACK MAPANJE
236 *Of Chameleons and Gods†*

DAMBUDZO MARECHERA
207 *The House of Hunger**
237 *Black Sunlight*

ALI A MAZRUI
97 *The Trial of Christopher Okigbo*

TOM MBOYA
81 *The Challenge of Nationhood (Speeches)§*

THOMAS MOFOLO
229 *Chaka*

DOMINIC MULAISHO
204 *The Smoke that Thunders*

JOHN MUNONYE
21 *The Only Son*
45 *Obi*
94 *Oil Man of Obange*
153 *A Dancer of Fortune*
195 *Bridge to a Wedding*

MEJA MWANGI
143 *Kill Me Quick*
176 *Going Down River Road*

JOHN NAGENDA
❋ *The Seasons of Thomas Tebo*

THE POOR CHRIST OF BOMBA

Mongo Beti

Translated by Gerald Moore

HEINEMANN

Heinemann International Literature and Textbooks
a division of Heinemann Educational Books Ltd
Halley Court, Jordan Hill, Oxford OX2 8EJ

Heinemann Educational Books Inc
361 Hanover Street, Portsmouth, New Hampshire, 03801, USA

Heinemann Educational Books (Nigeria) Ltd
PMB 5205, Ibadan
Heinemann Kenya Ltd
PO Box 45314, Nairobi, Kenya
Heinemann Educational Boleswa
PO Box 10103, Village Post Office, Gaborone, Botswana
Heinemann Publishers (Caribbean) Ltd
175 Mountain View Avenue, Kingston 6, Jamaica

LONDON   EDINBURGH   MELBOURNE   SYDNEY
AUCKLAND   SINGAPORE   TOKYO   MADRID   PARIS
HARARE   ATHENS   BOLOGNA

First published in France as *Le Pauore Christ de Bomba* 1956
© Editions Robert Laffont 1956
This translation © Gerald Moore 1971
First published 1971

ISBN 0-435-90088-9

Reproduced, printed and bound in Great Britain by
Cox & Wyman Ltd, Reading, Berkshire

93   94   95   15   14   13   12   11

I don't wish to deceive the reader. There has never been a Reverend Father Superior Drumont in African experience, probably there never will be one — not if I know my Africa. That would be too much luck for us.

The Africans who swarm in these pages have been taken straight from life. And there is no incident here which is not strictly and demonstrably authentic.

M. B.

FIRST PART

– So, what happened, then? said Ivanov with his satisfied air. Don't you think it's marvellous? Has anything more marvellous happened in all history? We tear the old skin off humanity and give it a new one. This is no job for weak nerves, but once the whole idea filled you with enthusiasm. What has happened to make you suddenly as fastidious as an old woman?

Arthur Koestler *Zero and infinite*

Catholic Mission of Bomba

Sunday, 1 February 193–

Surely it isn't any blasphemy . . . oh, no! It even fills me with joy to think that perhaps it was Providence, the Holy Ghost himself, who whispered this advice in the Father's ear, 'Tell them that Jesus Christ and the Reverend Father are all one.' Especially when our village children, looking at the picture of Christ surrounded by boys, were astonished at his likeness to our Father. Same beard, same soutane, same cord around the waist. And they cried out, 'But, Jesus Christ is just like the Father!' And the Father assured them that Christ and himself were all one. And since then all the boys of my village call the Father 'Jesus Christ'.

Jesus Christ! Oh, I'm sure it's no blasphemy! He really deserves that name, that simple praise from innocent hearts. A man who has spread faith among us; made good Christians every day, often despite themselves. A man full of authority. A stern man. A father – Jesus Christ!

A stern man, certainly. But when you know him well, he often makes you want to laugh. It happened this very morning, at Mass.

The Vicar who was in charge, my friend and I who were serving the Mass, had just sat down to hear the Father's sermon. Instead of going straight up into the pulpit, the Father walked right down the nave, sweeping it with a suspicious glance. Whenever he saw a man sitting down, he said:

'So you are so tired, you can't wait a few seconds before sitting? Jesus carried his cross right to the end, and he wasn't tired. Get up at once!'

They know well enough that the Father hates to see them sitting when they should be standing, or standing when they should be kneeling. But there are always some people, especially men, who

3

never conform if they can help it, as if they just wanted to put him into a rage.

Then he went back down the aisle, looking particularly at the women's side. At least women generally behave well. But what was my surprise this morning to see the Father plunge right in among the women, striding over the wooden benches furiously. Then he came back up the central aisle, dragging a woman along by her left arm. He pulled her before the table and forced her down on her knees. I've no idea what she had done. Only then did the Father decide to climb the wooden staircase to the pulpit, but very slowly, and casting heavy glances all around the church.

At last he was in the pulpit. But instead of beginning his sermon he stood there silent, in a most unexpected manner. I was worried and I'm sure the new Vicar, Father Le Guen, was too, for our glances met and I could see he was wondering what was going on. The man is terrible, sure enough, but the scene itself was comic, and I almost burst out laughing. There were the converts standing up, all turned attentively towards the pulpit. And there was the Father, tall as a tree and quite silent. And then those coughs which began rustling here and there. You'd have thought you were in a forest attacked by an army of frantic woodcutters. It's amazing how a crowd can cough! I soon understood that only those coughs could explain the Father's strange behaviour, for it wasn't the first time it had happened. The faithful must have understood it too, for all at once the tide of coughs ebbed away, and the Father, who up till then had kept a frozen silence, said in a dull voice:

'Yes, I'm waiting. Some day perhaps you'll stop coughing, and then I'll be able to begin my sermon.'

Immediately a silence cold as a forest river flooded the church. The Father cleared his throat and was just about to start when a baby let out three long wails right across the aisle and he froze again into an attitude of rigid disapproval. The church beadle came hastening forward and whispered something in the ear of the baby's mother, waving his cane about the while. The mother took her baby with infinite slowness right down the wall of the nave and out at the west door, for the Father had recently ordered all other doors to be closed at the time of Mass, so as to stop people from sliding out before the sermon, which had frequently happened before.

4

Even so, the Father still couldn't begin his sermon, for an indignant murmur now rose from the women's side in sympathy with the expelled mother. They seemed to feel that it wasn't the mother's fault if her baby decided to cry, and that the same fate might befall all of them sooner or later, when they became mothers in their turn. Whether the Father appreciated this reasoning I don't know. At any rate, he didn't begin his sermon until everything was calm again and the Vicar Le Guen had expressed his relief with a long sigh.

This sermon took me by surprise. Having read from the Evangelist, the Reverend Father said:

'My children, here is important news for you. I am leaving the mission for two weeks. I am going to tour the Tala country which, as you know, I haven't visited for three years. If there are any Tala people here, especially catechists, let them tell their fellow Talas that I am coming amongst them once more, offering them another chance to repent, to abandon their vices and return to Christ. Their punishment has certainly been hard, but it was necessary. It arose from their bad conduct, from their refusal to recognize him who came down to earth for them and died on the cross to save them from sin. Now he stretches out his arms to them and offers pardon, on condition that they renounce their past errors and take a firm decision to become good Christians.

'The Good Shepherd leaves his flock to go in search of a lost lamb. But I am not leaving you alone. There is a new priest in the mission with you. He is not yet used to the country, but you must obey him as you would myself. I speak particularly to the girls of the sixa.[1] I am leaving tomorrow, and I trust that my absence will not be felt in Bomba. . . .'

I didn't follow the rest of the sermon.

[1] In every mission in the southern Cameroun there is a building which houses, in principle, all the young girls engaged to be married. This is the sixa. All our girls who want to be married in the strict Catholic way must stay in the sixa for two to four months, except in special cases, which are always numerous. The defenders of this institution praise its usefulness, if not its necessity. Doesn't it prepare these girls to be mothers of Christian families? But this justification is disputed by others. What is certain is that the inmates of the sixa are compelled to do manual labour for more than ten hours every day.

I thought we would make a tour this month. It's already been rumoured, and our tours always begin from February onwards. But I didn't guess it would be so soon, and in Tala country too! The famous tribe of Tala!

It seems that this country we are going to visit is vast in extent and that the Christians there behave very badly. It was because of this that the Father refused to set foot there for three whole years, although normally he or his Vicar make an annual tour of each of the six regions which depend on the Bomba mission. And since I've only been at Bomba for two years, I have never had the chance to visit the Tala country.

Three years! He has abandoned them for three whole years!

Zacharia claims that it won't have changed them a bit. He says they'll be only too happy not to be badgered every year. That's just like him! But all the same, he doesn't say such things in front of the Reverend Father.

I still don't understand one thing, though. Why does the Father want to make this tour himself, instead of sending his Vicar?

I keep thinking of the conversation they had after dinner, over their coffee. It was Father Le Guen, the new Vicar, who talked most. He said such strange things about our country, about the forest. And from time to time he threw me a meaning look, as if taking me to witness. I was serving them on that occasion, because Daniel was busy packing the Father's boxes.

Le Guen the Vicar was still talking. Father Drumont replied little, except for an occasional uneasy laugh. He had the air of a man who is listening to two voices at once, each telling him different stories. But he was looking at his Vicar with an expression compounded of astonishment, irony and perhaps admiration.

Of all that conversation, I remember especially what was said over coffee. Father Le Guen was stroking his cup, without ever lifting it to his lips. He said:

'Listen, Father. Do you know what I felt when I first arrived in this country? Guess what the forest reminded me of? Why, the sea! Yes, just so! Not the Mediterranean, of course. But a real ocean, misty, boiling, savage and frightening – the Atlantic, for example. The last place where you expect to find men, isn't it, Father? However, just get into a boat with the fishermen and put out to sea. Then

6

you'll be astonished to see little boats scattered all about you, each one clinging desperately to the side of a huge wave. The very image of resignation and despair. So, you can imagine that I seemed to find the same vision in looking at this landscape by moonlight. The static forest which nevertheless seemed to billow, the dark menacing mass of the bushes, houses hung here and there in a forest full of wild beasts. . . .'

'Ah, ah!' laughed Father Drumont. 'Are you sure you're not exaggerating, Father?'

'In what way?'

'There are no wild beasts here, you know.'

'No wild beasts? And what about the gorillas, pray?'

'Yes, all right. But so few of them left that one can really only speak in the past tense.'

'They still exist, all the same.'

'Father, you have been here almost a year now. Have you seen a gorilla since you came?'

Then they both laughed, for it was impossible that Le Guen could have seen a gorilla already.

'All the same, Father,' he replied, 'didn't the forest produce the same impression in you when you arrived?'

'Er, no. . . . I can't say I ever thought of comparing trees with the sea.'

'But I'm not talking about trees!'

'Of what, then?'

'Of the forest, Father.'

'What's the difference?'

'Listen, Father. The forest isn't just a whole lot of trees side by side. It has a personality of its own, quite apart from that of the trees taken one by one.'

'Perhaps, but I've still never thought of making the comparison. Maybe I should have made it, if only I had ever seen the ocean.'

'Oh, it's true that you've only seen the Mediterranean! All the same . . .'

And again they laughed together.

Then Father Drumont, wanting to tease his Vicar, said to him: 'Your coffee's getting cold, Father.'

So they laughed once more. But all the same, the Father Superior was sad, unshakeably sad. He is always pensive like this when he hasn't some great task on hand, especially since the new church was finished. Or when he isn't out and about, and when he finds himself amongst other priests. But this time he was certainly anxious and even sad. I'm sure it's because of the tour we are about to make. It's obviously very important to him, otherwise he would have left it to his Vicar.

'It is certainly strange,' he said after a pause. 'The forest has never struck me in that way. I suppose a clump of bushes has always seemed to me like a block of houses at home. And a striking baobab – why, it simply reminds me of the spires of our cathedrals. To tell the truth, I just don't see the forest.'

'But you went hunting, Father?'

'Oh yes, like everybody else. All the new arrivals here go hunting. But I never really saw the forest. I came here to convert the blacks; I thought of nothing else. I still think of nothing else. I think of it more and more.'

I had finished serving dinner and I left them.

It's funny how I like Father Le Guen, the new Vicar. However, I also love the Father Superior, but it's not the same thing at all. The Father Superior is like a real father to me, while Father Le Guen is more like a friend, a crony even. He's only been here a year, and already he speaks our language better than the Father Superior, who speaks it so strangely that people say they only understand him next day, after thinking all night about what he said the day before.

Of course, people say that in time Le Guen will become just like Father Drumont, pig-headed, quick to anger, deaf to everything that is said to him, doing everything according to his own ideas. They say everyone becomes like that after a while here, and Father Le Guen will be no exception. But that isn't my opinion.

Whereas the Father Superior, heavens above! I'm sure he'll blow up again tomorrow, at our very first stop, over his old subject of unmarried mothers. That business will really drive him mad one day, poor Father Drumont! Sometimes I really feel sorry for him. He's tried everything to arouse our bewildered villagers to a sense of the situation of the unmarried mother. He reminds me of our monitor, keenly explaining to us a problem in arithmetic that we are incapable of understanding. For myself, I can't see why he attaches so much

8

importance to this question. After all, don't all the unmarried Christian girls bring their babies for baptism, paying a special fee fixed by the Father himself? Isn't that an extra source of money for the mission coffers? And we need so many things – an organ for the new church, a tractor for ploughing our fields, a generator for electric light, a motor-car, and so forth.

But the Father will surely kill himself over these girls. To think that we blacks are all damned simply for loving children too much! After all, my father is a catechist, yet I'm certain he'd be the happiest of men if my sister Anne had a baby before marriage, especially a son. That would be one man more in the household. The only thing is, my father might be excommunicated by Father Drumont over a thing like that, especially as he's a catechist. However, fortunately he's got his wits about him.

He's found something else to fume with rage about, my poor father. He keeps complaining that at nearly fifteen I'm only in the first year of middle school, whilst Zomo, Bella, Medzo and lots of other boys of my age from our village are about to take the primary leaving certificate. I really don't understand him. After all, as a catechist he ought to know how things are here. Is it my fault if I have to spend more than half the school year touring with one of the Fathers? He was warned about that when my mother died and he handed me over to the Father Superior to look after. He was told that the mission boys never had time to go to school. He simply said that to see the white priests at close quarters would be the best education I could have. Either he should leave me in peace, or take me out of the mission, if he's so keen on seeing me get the certificate. But he'd never dare do that, he's too scared of the Father Superior, who certainly wouldn't understand it. Anyway, I want to stay at the mission now . . .

Yes, there are two of us boys here at Bomba. But Daniel is more than four years older than me, and in any case he's been here longer. He doesn't go on tour any more, he's beyond that. Touring is my department, as Father Le Guen says.

The one who was really delighted after Mass was Zacharia. He embraced everybody and kept saying:

'We're going on tour! We're going on tour! Tomorrow! To-morrow!'

I know why he's so pleased. He's sure to be the one who goes with us on this tour. The assistant cook, Anatole, only goes with the Vicar. Zacharia is the Father Superior's constant companion, a bit like St Peter with Jesus Christ, sticking with him even after he'd betrayed him. And Zacharia is always betraying the Father. He's always full of tricks when we're on tour. Unknown to the Father, he's always demanding girls, palm-wine, goats and other things from the faithful, by promising to support them with the Father if things go badly, or to keep an eye on their children in the school at Bomba.

Lots of complaints have been made to the Father about Zacharia, but he refuses to believe them. Besides, he's so keen on his blessed cook that it would take the intervention of Christ himself to separate them. Yet, strangely enough, Zacharia is far from indispensable. Here at the mission it's Anatole who does all the work, while Zacharia spends his time drinking palm-wine or arguing with the bricklayers and carpenters. If he isn't at the brickyard or the sawmill, then he's sure to be wherever the girls of the sixa are working. Only when the bishop comes to the mission will you find Zacharia in the kitchen. The Father knows all this perfectly well, but he refuses to believe that Zacharia is really bad.

At Bomba everyone says that Zacharia has grown very rich since he came to the mission, but I can't be certain of that, because his home village is about fifteen miles off, and it's there that he's supposed to keep his wealth. I only know that the Father has had a house built for him there, with brick walls and a tiled roof.

But if Zacharia is really rich, why is he always demanding a rise from the Father? Is it really true that he wants to grow so rich that he can leave the mission and marry more wives? His real wife, the one he married in church, has just born him a fine baby son, their second son already! Would she really agree to live with a husband who became a polygamist? This Zacharia really upsets me.

I keep wondering why the prospect of this journey is so disquieting. Fifteen days on the road!

For fifteen days, nothing but forest. Forest wherever you look, instead of our fine new church with its big towers, its coloured glass, its clock chiming harmoniously at noon and evening, with the girls of the sixa singing the Angelus. Instead of the long, high house of stone, surrounded by flower-beds, and with white walls shining even whiter in the sunlight, instead of the familiar noise of the schoolchildren at play, nothing but endless forest, all day and every day.

So long we are on the road, it's not too bad. But it seems that in Talaland there's nothing but a little track, on which a lorry might just squeeze its way. And we won't even have a lorry!

Ah, there's the clock sounding twelve strokes. So it's midnight! I must try to sleep. Daniel is snoring already. It's true he's been working all day. He didn't even go out this evening, as he nearly always does. Poor old chap, they're going to work you to death! And I can't give you any help. Either I'm on tour or else I'm at school. Tomorrow morning you must be up before five! As for me, I'm going on tour, so there's no need for me to get up at that hour.

Mombet, First Stage

Monday, 2 February

– Oh! now I begin to understand. I begin to understand the meaning of the Father's sad expression at dinner last night, when he was talking to Le Guen, the Vicar. Yes, he was listening at the same time to another, invisible, speaker. And that other voice was the prospect of this vexing journey. The Father must really have a . . . *sixth sense*, as Father Le Guen says. For last night, he already knew!

I pity him more and more; it's as if he was really my father. My feeling for him is so strange – exactly as I felt for my mother during her birth-pangs.

I have never seen the Father in such a painful situation. I have always seen him triumphing over obstacles, building, hustling men along, leading them like a drummer. Now, it is so different, and I love and admire him more and more. It seems to me that I stand in his very shoes and that the two of us form a single man.

It is midnight and the Father is still working in his hut, along with the local catechist whom he is questioning, haranguing and tearing apart just as he pleases. Then suddenly he will wrap himself in a stormy silence; presently he will gaze up at the ceiling or begin writing. He can't help flying into a rage when things don't go exactly as he wants.

And here at Mombet they have gone so badly that he can scarcely contain himself. I went to bed early because I couldn't bear to watch him.

He says it's all his own fault, for abandoning these poor wretches for three whole years. I think he judges himself too harshly, though, as everyone does when they're angry and in despair. He only abandoned them for their own good; so that they would recover themselves and become better and return to the true faith. Oh, the stratagem has failed too dismally. How could it be otherwise in this

Tala country, this kingdom of Satan, this Sodom and Gomorrah? And he expected so much from his stratagem!

Now he says if it's the same in the other villages he can only ask the bishop to attach Tala to another mission. He will have done everything he can. He says this is far the largest and most populous district under Bomba and if, after twenty years of effort, they have made no progress in religion, then he can only admit his helplessness and give someone else a chance.

Many of these converts have taken a second or even a third wife. Only the little children still come to catechism on Wednesday morning. The whole place is rotten. No one but the older women now pays the church dues.

And the cocoa they've sold this season! It seems the more money they have the less they think of God. A bicycle, a gramophone, china plates and leather shoes, that's all they ever think of. But in God's name, what use will all that be to them?

He has said this so many times, beating the table with his fist.

Personally, I think God should send a sign to these people to bring them into the right path, a general misfortune or . . . I don't know, but something that will teach them.

What a beginning to our tour!

It was the Father who reached Mombet first. I wonder how they received him?

It was nearly nine when Zacharia and I left the mission. We were in such a hurry that we followed the road, despite the heat. The palm trees are so scattered that there's scarcely any shade. After ten kilometres on the road, we took a footpath which buried itself in the forest like a corridor. It was so cool and pleasant there. Zacharia knows every bit of the country. Sometimes we burst out into a clearing in full sunlight; these were fields or villages, but we hadn't yet reached Tala country. Zacharia talked all the time but I wasn't listening; I was gazing at the forest and drinking in all its strange noises.

The Father joined us later, dismounting from his bicycle and walking with us for a while, speaking gently like a father to his children. He had hoisted up his white soutane and we saw the flapping of his khaki shorts above the knee, with his long stockings turned back below them. He also turned back his sleeves to the elbow and we saw his great hairy arms. Like that, he gave an impression of great force,

13

but softened by the black beard which surrounded his face and gave him a paternal look.

Then he jumped on his bicycle and went ahead of us, saying that he would scarcely gain much ground because the road was so terrible: 'I've fallen off twice already!' he cried with a great laugh.

We also laughed and he disappeared round the corner, turning back once more to laugh back at us.

Then Zacharia began humming the song of the sixa girls:

> *Work with a will,*
> *Then strive harder still.*
> *And never give up,*
> *But work till you drop.*

Then he said thoughtfully:

'That song, didn't Father Drumont make it up himself?' And as I didn't reply, he added: 'I shall find out. But there's no doubt he must have made it up. He taught it to the girls to make them work harder, and they've passed it on from year to year. It must be so.'

Typical Zacharia! Devil-may-care and irreverent as ever. No doubt he was just the same when he was cook to a Greek trader in the town. In fact, I suspect that to him the Reverend Father is just another sort of trader. Conceited ass, thinking himself superior to the Father! And in what is he superior? Success with women, perhaps? Zacharia knows that they all admire him and is always striving for still more admiration. He dresses sharply and walks in a haughty manner that suits his tallness. And then he feeds his pride on the swarms of girls who run after him. It's maddening to think how little you need to attract them. I remember my mother coming home from market in the town, after selling her vegetables and cocoa. How indignant she was: 'It's so shameful,' she cried, 'our best-looking and most respectable girls go to town and throw themselves at strangers as ugly as sin, speaking the most outlandish tongues. Men I can scarcely look at without shuddering! And why? Just money! Money! Ah, what a world!' And my father replied in a buried voice, 'It's the times!' 'The times!' shouted mother, 'can you imagine my child Anne with creatures like those?'

But perhaps the girls who chase Zacharia aren't drawn by his tallness or his leather shoes. Perhaps they're only after childish things, a bit of bread or a pot of jam, knowing that he's a cook. My father often says women are like children in their desires. And after all, I too can boast a little. Plenty of women turn to look at me, especially when I'm dressed all in white! But I'm not vain enough to fuss over a little thing like that. Not like Zacharia, who doesn't know women are simply children.

What does Zacharia see in the Reverend Father? An organizer? A builder? A man of business, as Father Le Guen called him the other day – but he was only joking, of course. Certainly not the representative of God on earth.

One day when he was pestering the Father with his demands, the Father turned on him with: 'Can you not labour for the love of God?' Then Zacharia smiled in a way I didn't like, as if to say: 'Whoever heard of someone who worked just for the love of God?' But it's clear that the Father has been doing so for years and years. Why can't Zacharia see him with my eyes? He won't for a moment allow himself to admire a man like that.

I believe the Father knows how much I love him. Otherwise, why does he indulge me so? Why is he really like a father to me?

This morning I got up really late. The Father was already giving tasks to the girls of the sixa. How he loves work! So long as he was at the mission, to the very last moment, he wouldn't leave anything to Father Le Guen, whose youth and inexperience must disquiet him. Father Drumont is really tireless, and because of that he's admired by everybody, even the pagans. People say that when he first came there was only the pretence of a mission at Bomba; a horrid church with mud walls and a mat roof; a tumbledown house left by his predecessor; and some distance away, half a dozen little huts – that was the school! Father Drumont set to work the moment he came. First he built the mission house for the Fathers; thirty metres long and more than twenty rooms, on a single floor! Then the church, one of the finest in the country, perhaps the very finest. And that was where he amazed everybody, for usually when the Superior of a mission wants to build a church, the first thing he does is to send to the bishop for an architect Brother. But Father Drumont didn't consult anyone; he directed the whole job himself. I wasn't even born then, but those who saw him never weary in his praise, even the unconverted. All the bricks and tiles were made by the sixa girls. Every week he called up some of the village Christians to help. But despite that there still wasn't enough manpower. So he put a girl from the sixa to work wherever a man was missing, and proved to our people that girls can do jobs that no one had ever dreamt of, like sawing wood into planks. And he himself worked with the masons, trowel in hand. Then, fearing that his works might still be deserted one day, he ordered that the girls should henceforth stay four months in the sixa, instead of three, before he would offer them the sacrament of marriage. The country people said that this stroke gave them the real measure of his intelligence. After that, many called him the Cunning One, especially the pagans. As for me, I hate that irreverent nickname. And the worst thing is, that the Father knows they call him that . . .

Yes, he came towards me while he was giving work to the girls of the sixa. He knew quite well that I hadn't been at Mass; he knows by now how lazy I am. He pretended not to see me while he was explaining to the catechist in charge of the sixa what quantities of sand and clay to use and whereabouts in the river or forest the girls must go to fetch them.

All the same, he saw me in the end:

'Denis,' he called, 'you and the cook should have left already. I'll follow you on the bicycle.'

He is always so indulgent to me, knowing that I love him like a father. Zacharia loves him too, I think. Otherwise the Father wouldn't be so soft with him. Yes, Zacharia must love him too – in his way.

When Zacharia and I got to Mombet we found the Father walking fretfully around the chapel with the local catechist. The chapel itself is in a frightful state. The walls are only held up by a ramshackle collection of wooden props. As if he could remedy this all by himself, the Father kept picking up handfuls of earth and stopping-up cracks here and there, while the catechist followed his example.

Zacharia stayed only a moment by the chapel, then vanished. I followed the Father and the catechist into the chapel, whose interior was in still worse condition. The mat roof, swinging from its nails, looked more like a fishing-net, and you could see the sky through it as if you stood in the open air. Naturally, the earth floor was pock-

16

marked all over by the rain and the walls are streaked with laterite. Logs lie scattered about the floor, and these are the seats! The catechist says that the men all refuse to come and repair the place. If he goes to summon one individually, the news spreads like wild fire and everyone else vanishes. He even says they rendezvous in the forest on these occasions and hold dances, all mixed up with the pagans. Finally, he discovered where they were meeting and surprised them there. He began by telling them how horribly they had sinned in joining pagan plays. Then he spoke to them of the chapel, which was all collapsing into lumps of earth and tatters of raphia. No one replied to him on either point, except a bunch of pagans who began baiting him. Everyone just went on dancing without a care. Once they start, he added, there's no hope of stopping them.

'And didn't you also want to join them?' demanded the Father.

'Oh no, no, Father! Besides, I'm not a Tala and I don't feel at ease among these people.'

At four o'clock, the Father began to hear confessions. There was a pitiful handful of people: a few young women, some older ones, three or four young men, and a fair number of children who had taken their first communion. I recognized the young men as the ones who had carried our luggage this morning at Bomba.

At about six the Father came gloomily out of the chapel and called to me: 'Denis, let us go and visit the people.'

The village stretches for a radius of about three kilometres around the chapel. It's not like my own country, where the hamlets just grow gradually in narrow clearings in the midst of the forest. Here the houses range off in long lines on either side of the pathways which sometimes twist, sometimes run straight or suddenly strike off obliquely.

Their houses are spacious and well-made, for they have plenty of materials from the nearby forest. They don't use oil-lamps like the people along the road, but everyone has hurricane-lamps or even pressure-lamps. All along the way we heard women singing or calling to each other, and men laughing and slapping their thighs. We saw clearly enough how they were. Often we saw a bicycle or a sowing machine standing in a corner. Cocoa has made them rich here . . . In short, they live careless lives, quite unlike the people in towns, or along the main roads. As the Father says, they don't strain themselves. And he adds that if they don't often remember God, it's because they're too happy. According to him only the miserable or the oppressed can have faith in God. And why are they better Christians along the roads, unless it's because they are constantly exposed to the exactions of soldiers and chiefs, or the demands of forced labour? Here they know nothing of all these woes. If God would only send them a little warning!

It was quite dark outside and the catechist had to lead us. We visited an old lady, a real Christian, who was too ill to get up any more. The catechist was full of her praises; she had paid all her cult dues and the Father could take her confession without scruple. So he began to hear her, while the rest of us, the catechist and I and all the people in the house, waited outside.

Next we visited another woman who had many young children and whose polygamist husband had never been baptized. The children were sitting around the fire and seemed frightened of the Father, who patted them on the head and asked if they went to catechism. We'd been there about twenty minutes when we heard a strong male voice thundering from the other side of the road. From the veranda of his house, which was perched up on a mound, the man called the catechist and shouted: 'Tell your boss' (what a name for the Father!), 'that I won't have any man, white man or priest though he be, spending so long in my wife's quarters. Do you get it? I won't tolerate . . .'

He was silhouetted by the beam of light which poured from the door of his fine house. He spoke so authoritatively that I was scared he might come down and tackle the Father himself. The Father understood his words well enough, but he continued calmly speaking to the young woman, a good Christian who had been to confession that very afternoon. At last we came outside. The man was still leaning over the parapet of his house and the Father, seeing him, cried out:

'Ah, so there you are! You'll catch it one day, you'll see! You will burn in Hell! Then come and tell me if it's so funny.'

But the man replied: 'Sorry, Fada, no be certain I go burn in Hell. No certain at all . . .'

Such insolence! He must have been drunk. We visited several houses and altogether we were presented with half a dozen chickens, with which the catechist and I returned to the presbytery.

I went to the kitchen to tell Zacharia that the Father wanted his dinner. To tell the truth, there wasn't much for Zacharia himself to do. All he had to do was point out the tasks to the catechist's sons, who were all busy about the fire and our pots. Zacharia was lying on a bamboo bed and one of his feet was resting on the ground. With this foot he beat out a gentle measure while his lips were rounded with a song. Hearing me say that the Father wanted his chop, Zacharia sat up as nonchalantly as a hero in a slow-motion film, or a snake that's been stuffing itself and, believing itself hidden from human eyes, is in no hurry to move. Finally, he raised his eyes and asked me: 'So, little one, how went the tour of inspection?'

I replied loyally and told him about the impious folk hereabouts. But this didn't seem to please him and he cut in angrily: 'So what? Isn't that normal enough? What is it to them, all your confession and Communion and God knows what? I ask you, what is it to them? They are busy with something else, my little father. Money, money . . . that's the great thing in life, man! Just open your eyes and look around you. You're still wet behind the ears. But since you love religion so much, perhaps you'll grow up to be a Father yourself one day. Then you'll know what money is. Then you'll know why we all run after it, the priests just as fast as everyone else, maybe faster. You think everyone is as thick as the people on the main road? Oh no, my lad! Here, they are smart enough. Count yourself lucky that they've dashed us six chickens!'

Something was rolling about at the foot of Zacharia's bed. At last I spotted a calabash. So! I should have known as soon as I came in. That smell, and the way those boys were smirking at me. Zacharia has found nothing better to do, on the very first day of our tour, than to get stinking on palm-wine. Anyway, drunk or not, he got more and more arrogant.

Whatever time can it be? My God! Perhaps I shall never lose this stupid habit of going over everything again, instead of just examining my own conscience for the day and going to sleep, as I used to. Wow! I hope the Father won't really give up this place, so fine and rich and populous as it is! Will he really abandon it? It would certainly be the first time. And perhaps tomorrow's journey will be more encouraging . . .

Timbo

The village of Timbo begins scarcely five kilometres from Mombet. Which means the people here are just the same as those we left behind. And it also means that the Father hasn't had time to lose his angry mood of yesterday. Now he is working, as he does every evening, going through the parish registers of Timbo with the local catechist and closely questioning him. I listened as much as I could, and I certainly gathered that there's no hope of things taking a better turn here. If I hadn't cherished any hopes of Timbo last night, perhaps I shouldn't feel so bitterly let down now.

Some of the Timbo catechist's remarks are really frightening. When the Father asked him: 'How do the people think in general, what do they say of religion?'

He replied, after much hesitation: 'Father, they say that a priest is no better than a Greek trader or any other colonialist. They say that all any of you are after is money. You are not sincere with them, you hide things from them and teach them nothing.'

'I? Hide things from them?' fumed the Father.

'That's what they say, Father.'

'My God, what do they mean?'

'They say that you must be hiding things from them. What about all the whites who live in concubinage with loose women in the town, do you ever rage against them? Far from it, you shake hands with them, go to their parties and ride in their cars back to Bomba. Nevertheless you preach that, after baptism, the blacks should cease to visit their own relatives who are not Christians. You are really a very dangerous man, for if everyone listened to you, the wives would all leave their husbands, the children would no longer obey their fathers, brothers would not know another and everything would be upside down. That's what they say, Father.'

At that, the Father was silent. He pinched his lips and tugged at his beard. His cheeks drooped and his eyes swelled out just as they did this morning during the palaver at Mombet. Ah yes, that famous palaver!

When I think how easily everything goes along the main road. There are so few serious matters that most of our time is spent on things of very minor importance. The importance of the palaver is that it's meant to put the Christian village completely in order before the priest departs for a whole year's absence. On the road everyone, having heard Mass and the sermon, attends the palaver in a state of excitement and enthusiasm; for having already judged all the issues at the rumour of our approach, they come in the hope of hearing their own verdicts confirmed. Hence they murmur, clap or burst into wild laughter to express themselves during the proceedings. How I loved to hear them! I didn't fully realize it at the time, but looking back I see our tours of the roads as a paradise.

But hereabouts, good Lord! It's not so much a palaver as a law court, so grave are the cases brought before us. Yet most of those mentioned never even bother to turn up. For them, the Father's court is not a real one, though it represents the one authority truly worthy of respect. If they were summoned by the Administrator's court in town they'd come creeping in like slippery snakes, like guilty dogs expecting punishment. Yes, with his flock of soldiers and policemen to bring them in, he's lucky enough. But at the Last Judgement we'll see who will win, who will prove the stronger . . .

And even if they do come to palaver they seem passive and sluggish, as if the whole business were of no interest to them. These Tala people are real bushmen.

Anyway, our palaver was certainly quite a show at Mombet this morning! The unmarried mothers didn't trouble to show up. The Father called out their names, everybody turned round, but not a soul! But it's just as well, really. What could the Father have said to them, and what good would it do? We'll see them sooner or later at the mission when the fancy takes them to get their wretched infants baptized.

Then, a woman came up to the bar, mother of a family and married to a polygamist. She spoke of her son, who had contented himself with a civil marriage. He'd refused to send his bride to the sixa to be prepared for a true marriage and, though a Christian, had been living with the girl in this state of sin for six months.

'What shall I do, Father?' she demanded. 'My son is big now and doesn't obey me. It's his father that he listens to, but his father isn't a Christian and laughs at our marriages. So what can I do?'

When he questioned her about her relations with the sons, she replied: 'But, Father, I have five boys apart from my eldest. Two of them are at school with you, in Bomba. I have to visit them every week and carry their food. Nearly fifty kilometres every week, and so heavily loaded! Think of it, Father. Here are the other three' (the frightened children were clinging to her gown), 'too young for school yet, as you see. But I have to dress and feed them, which keeps me in the fields until sunset every day, Father. So I scarcely have time to know if the eldest is even alive, especially since he's married.'

She waved her arms as she talked but didn't seem vexed with anyone, indeed she sounded rather amused. Her cotton gown, very soberly decorated, fell to mid-calf, according to the Father's orders about the length of dresses. Her big arms, strong as a man's, made me think of the fury with which she worked on the farm to bring up her children.

'And your husband,' demanded the Father, 'what does your husband do all this time?'

'Oh Father, you know well enough how it is, after all the years you've lived amongst us. I am his first wife, true enough; otherwise I shouldn't have been baptized. But that doesn't mean that my husband has only my children to worry about. We are four wives and over a dozen children! How can he keep all those by his own efforts? We have to help him all we can!'

Even the Father was subdued by this frankness. He was about to speak, but I saw a flicker of resignation cross his face.

'But your husband?' he said after a pause. 'Have you tried to show him God's will in this?'

'Oh Father, I speak to him every moment I can of his soul, of Heaven and Hell, but he answers me with sarcasm, saying, "This white man, this priest, can't you see that he's duping you? There's not a word of truth in it. He lies all day long, like the rest of the whites. How can you believe a word they say, poor woman?" After that, I didn't say another thing.'

Then, shrugging her shoulders, she added: 'How do you expect a poor woman like me to talk back to a man?'

Although she didn't look sorry for herself, this woman filled me with pity.

The next to come to the bar was a young man whose wife was in the sixa at Bomba. She'd been waiting there vainly for months for him to fulfil the conditions of Christian marriage. He didn't wait to be interrogated by the Father but pitched right in: 'I've only come here, Fada, to ask what you intend to do with my wife.'

The Father started and I felt a storm brewing in the air.

The young man continued: 'It seems I have to tell you again, though you know it well enough already. My wife and I were properly and legally married. But one day she took a strange fancy in her head and ran away to your mission. Instead of sending her back to me like a sensible man, you took her in. I have sent word through the catechist that I wish her sent back to me. But it seems he hasn't done anything, so . . .'

'Are you a Christian or not?' thundered the Father, who could stand no more.

'That is beside the point,' he replied in a cool, sarcastic tone. 'Certainly I was baptized, if you want to know. But does that give you a right to confiscate my wife? Do you know that I have paid seven thousand francs to have her? Seven thousand . . .'

The Father soon saw that it was no use to bully this firebrand, so he adopted a softer manner: 'Don't you know that a civil marriage counts for nothing, if it is not completed by the sacrament?'

'Fada, I could reply that only the Administrator has authority over me and that only a civil marriage counts with him. But what's more, your marriage will cost me far too much. Oh, I know all about it! All the arrears of the cult dues to pay, both mine and hers, and at the current rate! No, really, I haven't the money for it. In any case, my wife has spent over four months in your sixa and worked for you free all that time. Fada, I think we understand each other. You've had her labour for four months already; send her back to me and we're quits.'

I saw the Father rise slowly to his feet, walk round the table and give the insolent puppy two resounding slaps on the cheeks. And he had earned them! Such arrogance! He held his hands to his cheeks and glared at the Father with the most concentrated hatred and rage.

'Clear off! Get out of here!' bellowed the Father.

But he didn't budge. The Father, who had just sat down again, jumped up and bore down on him once more. Only then did he decide to move. At the threshold of the chapel he turned and began hurling insults at the Father, who instantly ran after him. They burst out into the courtyard, the young man running half-turned and still shouting abuse. Then the Father gave up the chase and returned, quite puffed out, to the chapel. The audience watched impassively. What a people! If it had been on the road, everyone would have fallen upon that rascal.

At last a name was read out and a very old woman, almost toothless, came forward. She had to answer the charge of failing in her Easter offering for the last four years. She replied that she lived only for the sacraments, but being now too old to work she had no money to pay her cult dues.

You could see she was poor. Her dress was ragged and filthy. And for some reason her mouth kept trembling, perhaps because she had so few teeth.

'Haven't you a single relative left?' the Father asked her.

'Oh yes, Father. But they say they won't pay my dues any longer, they've done it long enough. They aren't Christians themselves, you see, and I want so much to confess and take Communion. If only my poor daughter were still alive, I'd have plenty of money and could pay everything. But since she died, my son-in-law pays no regard to me. "When the daughter dies, the son-in-law dies"; don't they have that saying in your country also? I'm so longing to take the sacraments, but yesterday the catechist refused to let me near the confessional, because my dues aren't paid. Can't you give me a dispensation, Father, when you see how miserable I am?'

Then all at once she burst into tears. I was sure the Father would finally yield, but he didn't. He simply advised the old woman to pester her relatives until they paid up. He explained that he couldn't relieve a single soul, for fear that hordes of people would then come before him to play comedies of poverty and helplessness.

The Father was right there. At all costs he must keep off those clowns who long to act the beggar, or soon no one will pay at all. Heavens, what a palaver!

It was nearly noon when we left Mombet, the three of us together. The Father didn't mount his bicycle this time, but walked beside us all the way to Timbo.

We walked along the path, while the eldest son of the Mombet catechist pushed the bicycle in front of us, surrounded by the porters sent for our loads by the catechist of Timbo. We gazed at the forest, and often we saw a fine monkey high on the branches, playing with his long tail and filling his great eyes with false candour and astonishment. If we made a slight menacing gesture, he would leap instantly into still higher cover, as if to say: 'This is where I normally stay and I only came lower to greet you, thinking you unarmed. But now I'm not so sure, especially since you have a white man with you.' I love the instant freshness of the forest, so sudden after the fierce heat of the clearings hard by.

As soon as they glimpsed us from Timbo, they burst forth into the 'Marseillaise', in the high innocent voices of little children. The path was strewn with flowers for a couple of hundred yards before the chapel and the walls of this were festively decked with palm-fronds. This little ovation reminded me of the way we are always received along the roads. It was a gay welcome which, unhappily, meant nothing; for the catechist had spared nothing to give us a false impression.

As soon as we arrived, the Father patted the singers on the head and made a little speech, saying that he was their good shepherd and they were his lambs. If he had deserted them for three years, it was only for their good. They must certainly have missed him, but now he was returned to them. They must rejoice in regaining their good shepherd who came only to feed them.

It was really touching and the Father kept lowering his eyes to hide his feelings. Once, his voice even trembled.

Zacharia has just given a cruel parody of this speech, spiritedly enough, since we are alone. He claims that such sentiments are utterly ridiculous. To begin with, he says, no one understands what's meant by a good shepherd, since we have no shepherds in this country. When a man has only three or four goats, he doesn't trouble with them, confident that they will feed well enough in his neighbour's field. Secondly, people here like to feel pity for a stranger, but they certainly don't relish being pitied in their turn, as the Father pitied them in saying: 'How you must have missed me; your good, kind shepherd!'

Zacharia always manages to be sarcastic at the Father's expense. He does it with diabolical joy if the Father has especially laid himself open to attack. But even when it is not so, Zacharia always manages to find something to ridicule. He is a disturbing and rather dangerous man, and I'm keeping my eye on him. But what good will it do? Plenty of people have tried to warn the Father about his cook. Ugh, this Zacharia!

The chapel here is not yet in ruins. The roof has even been re-done and doesn't let in water. The altar is decorated with flowers and green branches and is crowned with a big image of the Sacred Heart, bought by subscription among the local Christians.

As at Mombet, there were very few at confession, though perhaps a few more men.

At about four in the afternoon someone came urgently demanding the Father, who had just finished confessing the faithful. A man working in the fields had had an accident. He had attacked a tree with his axe, but it was impeded by creepers from falling properly and had fallen upon him instead, pinning him to the ground and crushing and piercing him below the belly. His brothers and neighbours had not succeeded in extricating him when we arrived, the Father, the catechist and I. Since it was difficult to get him out, the Father said they should leave him quiet while he made confession. The man spoke with terrible difficulty. He had been baptized, but since that time had been living an irregular life. The Father made him swear that if he survived he would give up his 'outside woman' and pay up all his arrears to the cult. The Father then prepared to hear his confession and we all moved away. The villagers seemed much impressed by the scene. The Father was crouching at the ear of the prostrate man. The branch was buried right in the ground and had mutilated him horribly; he was no longer even kicking about as he was on our arrival.

I am happy to think that this event might have shown them the right path again. And perhaps, if they mend their ways, the Father will not feel obliged to renounce this country.

The man died as the Father was giving his absolution. What a lucky chance! This man who never dreamt of confession, who would have died without the sacraments, whose soul would have appeared before God in the worst possible state if the Father hadn't been present at the scene, behold him now already among the blessed! But how many people get a chance like that? And the tree had chosen to pierce him just below the belly, so he was punished exactly where he had sinned! In tomorrow's sermon the Father is sure to dwell on all these coincidences and draw them out before the faithful.

The Father helped them to free the body, which wasn't easy. Some villagers wanted to hack the tree into sections, which would have risked a still worse accident. The Father ordered them to set fire to the bush. As the bush burnt the creepers snapped and released the tree, which fell at full length to the ground and so freed the body of the unhappy Garba – Joseph Garba, as I later learnt he was called. Poor man! His wife, or rather his concubine, who had been forbidden to approach the body, uttered cry after cry from the village, which pierced us with all their despair, far away as we were in the forest.

Because of this tragedy, the whole village was in mourning this evening when we paid our visits. While we were walking the path, which here, as at Mombet, turns into a street, the Father explained to us that men often have need of misfortunes like this afternoon's to bring home to them the instability and unreality of the things of this world.

We called first upon the chief, who has a good brick house with a pan roof. There were an impressive number of long arm-chairs ranged on his veranda. Like most chiefs, this one seems to prefer a quiet life and time to enjoy it. He's an old friend of the Father's, having known him ever since he arrived in Bomba. Indeed, long ago they seem to have been closer than now. But this evening the chief was out. Instead of waiting to welcome his friend, he had vanished, leaving a present of a large buck tied to one of the trees before his house. One of his people attended us, and I saw the Father's face fall as he listened to him. Perhaps the Father wanted to pick a bone with the chief, drawing on the parallels between this afternoon's accident and the case of the chief himself. For I gather that the latter was once a very good Christian, coming all the way to Bomba for Mass every

Sunday and consulting the Father in everything. Unhappily, his first wife did not bear him a son. He must have discussed it with the Father and been counselled to put trust in patience and prayer. But before long the inevitable happened; the chief took a second wife, and this was the first time since his baptism that he had taken a decision without consulting the Father. He came no more to Bomba. Then, having got the taste for polygamy, the chief began taking wife after wife, even though his second deprived him of the original excuse by bearing him children every other year. But despite all this he continued to profess his fidelity as a good Catholic, lamenting his exclusion from the sacraments and sending his wives to present their babies to the Father for baptism. And in this he behaved like plenty of others around here, who prostrate themselves with gratitude and celebrate for a whole week if they are told that they are still good Christians despite their polygamous practices. The Father, however, who seems to possess a special sense in these things, never lost faith that one day he would be able to lead the chief back, like an ever-beloved prodigal son, to the cradle of his forgiveness. But this evening, as on every occasion in the past seven years that he has visited Timbo, the chief has outwitted him and slipped through his fingers.

The catechist untied the buck and led it away. What a shame! With the arguments he could have drawn this evening from that horrible accident, I'm sure the Father would have won him over. And what a weight it would have thrown in the balance here in this village, where everyone is constantly weighing God against Satan; the Eternal against the Fleeting; the rough, thorny but straight path which leads to true happiness against the broad road, filled with flowers and perfume, which runs easily downwards to pleasure – what a weight it would have been, to hear that this great chief had at last acknowledged his errors, set at liberty his fifteen wives like one who throws open the door of a hen-house and fallen on his knees to the Father, demanding absolution! We moved among the dark houses, followed by the sharp cries of babies who seemed to know what was amiss.

The Father said: 'I shall not despair of winning him back one day. Who knows? I have succeeded with others.'

So he will not abandon this country! I'm sure he won't, so tenacious as he has always been. All the same, it's strange, this idea he has suddenly taken to give it all up, this discouragement. Where did it spring from, in one who was never discouraged?

> *Work with a will,*
> *Then strive harder still.*
> *And never give up,*
> *But work till you drop.*

'I shall not despair . . . I have succeeded with others . . .' Zacharia, when I told him this, claimed that the Father had indeed succeeded a few times, but so long ago that it's scarcely remembered! We called at a few more houses before returning to the presbytery. Apart from the chief's buck, we were given some chickens and several kilos of cocoa and groundnuts. Not much, but, as Zacharia says, we aren't on the main road here.

The Father scarcely ate anything. Zacharia, who was serving, looked vexed and demanded: 'Father, don't you like my cooking any more?'

Naturally, the Father denied it. What a frightful hypocrite that cook is! It certainly wasn't he who cooked the chop, but the local boys; not the catechist's sons this time, but some others who appeared from nowhere. Goodness knows what germs they have brought with them. How miserable it makes me to see the hypocrisies of Zacharia every day and be unable to say a word about them to the Father. And I daren't speak to Zacharia either. He would only ask me, as always: 'Who do you take yourself for? The son of the Father? Oh, I'm sure he has some somewhere, but they wouldn't be your colour, you little creep!'

After dinner the Father set to work with the catechist. I followed the interrogation as long as I could, then went to bed. Zacharia exasperated me again with his uninvited interventions. For instance, the Father asked the catechist this question: 'Why is it, do you think, that so many backslide from the true religion? Why did they come to Mass in the first place?'

The catechist answered: 'My Father, at that time we were poor. Well, doesn't the Kingdom of Heaven belong to the poor? So there's nothing surprising in many of them running then to the true God. But nowadays, as you know yourself, Father, they are making pots of money by selling their cocoa to the Greeks; they are all rich. Now, isn't it easier for a camel to pass through a needle's eye than for a rich man to enter the Kingdom of . . . ?'

But just then Zacharia blurted out, interrupting the wise words of the catechist: 'Get away with you! That's not the truth of the matter at all. I'll tell you just how it is, Father. The first of us who ran to religion, to your religion, came to it as a sort of . . . revelation. Yes, that's it, a revelation; a school where they could learn your secret, the secret of your power, of your aeroplanes and railways . . . in a word, the secret of your mystery. Instead of that, you began talking to them of God, of the soul, of eternal life, and so forth. Do you really suppose they didn't know those things already, long before you came? So of course, they decided that you were hiding something. Later, they saw that if they had money they could get plenty of things for themselves – gramophones and cars, and perhaps even aeroplanes one day. Well, then! They are turning from religion and running elsewhere, after money, no less. That's the truth of it, Father. As for the rest, it's all make-believe. . . .'

And speaking in this fashion, he put on an important air. I was boiling with indignation when I heard this illiterate gabble, this 'bla-bla-bla', as Father Le Guen calls it. I felt the sweat bursting from my forehead, running down my nose and cheeks, and gathering in great drops on my chin, I was that hot with anger. I would gladly have slapped his silly face. But the funny thing is, the Father listened to him with great attention.

Kota

What a bush place this is! I wonder if I shall ever get used to the
devil-may-care manners of these Talas. These palavers after Mass, in
front of a bored and sneering audience: Timbo was just the same as
Mombet. There again the unmarried mothers didn't bother to show
up, poor old women came to beg dispensation from their dues, and
so forth. And the people along the path who gaze at us passing as
indifferently as if the Reverend Father Superior was some vulgar
Greek merchant from the town. Nay, a Greek merchant would get
more attention, so long as they had some cocoa to dispose of. And my
God, the forest! The endless forest, with its howling chimpanzees,
its owls who screech even in daylight, its deep river that we have to
cross on flimsy rope-bridges, its sudden clearings blinding the eye
after the dark tunnels of the bush – oh, I shall never get used to all
this! And then my hope that every new stage will bring us an agree-
able surprise and the bitterness of being let down, two days back at
Mombet, yesterday at Timbo and today again at Kota. But the important thing is that the Father shouldn't give up this country, and
it's strange how calm, even cheerful, he is tonight after his jumpiness
these last few days. Just now, he's working with the catechist. He
seems pensive and relaxed, even amused at what the catechist tells
him. He was like that just now with the Administrator, whose jokes
always make him laugh.

This young white man reached here at about four o'clock. He was
riding a motor-bike with a side-car, like the one the mission has, and
had a soldier with him. The Father had just finished confession and
was standing in the courtyard of the chapel, reading his breviary.
When the young man saw the Father, he jumped off his bike and
came up to greet him, doffing his topee. *That* was a lesson for these
Talas, to see a white man, an Administrator, greeting a priest with

such respect, almost with veneration. If a priest were of no account, would he have done so?

'Jesus be praised, Father Drumont!' said the young man, smiling.

'Good day, my dear Vidal!' the Father replied, shaking his hand warmly.

I began to recognize the Administrator.

'Enthusiastic as ever?' joked the Father.

The Administrator laughed and said: 'Father, you've no idea what a nice surprise it is to find you here, at the end of such a pathway, like a divine apparition in your immaculate white soutane. Soon I shall begin to believe in guardian angels. But I forbid you formally, yes, formally' (and here he put on a grave manner and made big gestures with his right hand), 'to describe as enthusiasm the cheerful brightness I owe to a vocation so sublime, so unique even – along with yours, of course. However, I continue to maintain that our two activities are really one and the same.'

The Father was also laughing.

'What about you, Father Drumont, as always full of decision, spirit and apostolic zeal? Eh?'

The Father looked sulky and pouted his thin lips, but Monsieur Vidal laughed again. He offered the Father a cigarette, stuck one in his own mouth, and kept talking all the while he was lighting it: 'Oh, Father, I know how it is! A touch of choler when the weather turns hotter, or down in the dumps because of something you've heard? Pooh! You'll soon get over it. Excuse a greenhorn like me saying it to a veteran like you, but it seems to me the great thing is to love this country in spite of everything, all the disappointments and all the homesickness. Look at that sun, so strong, high and enormous! Look at that majestic forest, so immovable and indestructible! To me, it's worth a bit of malaria to gaze for only an hour at that swarming savagery, that prehistoric universe which has no match in our feeble Europe, all those unforgettable terrors.'

'A poet as well,' muttered the Father giving him a dirty look.

'Now don't sneer at me, Father Drumont. I always dreamt of an Africa filled with monsters, but the truth is far stranger than the fiction. And you, Father?'

'Assuredly, our pleasures in this country are not of the same nature, my lad. You are always the poet, the lover of beauty, the dilettante, not really down to earth. Whereas I am completely down to earth, for I am an apostle. But I dare say all that is beyond you.'

The young man's face was alive with curiosity, but the Father looked grave and sent a vague sorrowful look over the distant canopy of the forest as if he had suddenly seen the answer there.

'You are sad today, Father? Is something amiss? But before you tell me, just offer me a drink. Then I shall hear you better.'

They went into the catechist's house, which had been prepared for the Father's reception. They sat on either side of the table, comfortably installed in cane chairs. I offered them lemonade, but M. Vidal said he would like something stronger, so I brought the bottle of rum from our loads. It was still full, for the Father rarely takes any.

The young Administrator drank quickly and pulled nervously on his cigarette. Then he asked: 'What has happened, then, Father? Surely you can tell your young Vidal? Hmm? What has gone wrong?'

'A little poser for you, Vidal. What sort of drama is likely to befall an old apostle like me, at one time or another?'

'Well, Father Drumont, evangelizing is itself a kind of drama: gathering a flock, guiding them towards a good end without losing a single one . . . but you have known that drama for many a day.'

'Quite true, my boy, quite true. But don't you see anything else?'

'Anything more than that? Ah, ah, ah! How I love you, Father! Why, beyond that, you must join company with the artist, as I have always said. You must join company with me, and your problems will become purely aesthetic: to model a race, exactly as one might a vase; to impose upon it the form that you desire . . .'

'Exactly,' interrupted the Father, laughing, 'that's just where you go wrong, my dear young fellow. You who are an amateur of art, just go and get a vase already fired and try to impose the form you want upon it – then see how you'll get on!'

M. Vidal hesitated a little: 'If I understand you, Father, evangelizing the blacks is like taking an old water jug and trying to turn it into an amphora? But what is there among them that corresponds to Christianity?'

'I don't know of a damned thing, but I suppose there must be something.'

'Animism!'

'Call it what you like.'

'And can that lead them to Heaven?'

The Father burst out laughing and exclaimed: 'Don't mix things up. The important thing is not whether it leads to Heaven, but whether it exists. For if it does, we shall find ourselves in the same situation as in the Islamic countries.'

'But look here . . . I'm trying to get on the same wavelength as you, but theology isn't my strong point. From my angle, it's enough to explain to the Bantu that our civilization, which they're so keen on having, isn't just a question of bicycles and sewing-machines; above everything, it's our Christianity.'

'In Islam, however . . .'

'Oh, Islam! Ha! Spare me your Islam, your Egypt, with the democracy of a king in the harem! No, Father, I beg you . . .'

'Never mind the king in the harem. But what about Japan, or the Celestial Empire?'

'You're surely not comparing animists with Buddhists!'

'But, my dear Vidal, a religion, even if it hasn't a Bible or a Koran, even if it hasn't inspired a policy of conquest, can be none the less real for its adherents.'

After a long pause, the Administrator replied: 'Father, if the Bantu sincerely cleave to Christianity, of their own free will, doesn't that resolve the problem? Why torment yourself like this? What good can it do? And anyway, I believe you have a big following here, don't you?'

'At last we are at the heart of the problem! Don't deceive yourself, my dear Vidal, my following is not so good. The problem that really torments me is this: those blacks who have chosen Christianity, did they do so of their own free will?'

'What do you mean? Surely no one could constrain them to accept a religion?'

'Ah, there speaks M. Vidal, the col-on-ial ad-mi-nis-trator! No, let's not quarrel today, I beg you. I'll tell you a secret. It's only the people on the main roads who make good Christians. The ones hereabouts are extremely refractory.'

'And so?'

'Don't you see the connection?'

'Certainly not!'

34

M. Vidal had drained his fourth glass of rum and was devouring the Father with his eyes while puffing rapidly at his cigarette.

'Then I'll explain it to you. The people on the roads live in constant terror – I must use that expression, even though it usually exasperates you – they live in perpetual fear of requisitions, forced labour, floggings, soldiers. Do they sincerely believe, or do they turn to me as the one consolation, even though I can't really protect them? That is the question which ravages me now.'

They looked silently into each other's eyes. Suddenly the young man cried out: 'Father, did you really say that only those on the main roads make good Christians? Were those your words?'

'Yes, why?'

'Then rejoice, Father, rejoice and cast your cares away! Soon you will have both your road and your flock. Good news, eh?'

'Are you off your head?'

'Listen, Father. The tour I'm making now is just the curtain-raiser for a really big project. We are going to drive a road right through the Tala country. We've been authorized to start work whenever we think fit, so it's only a question of weeks now. We can't leave a fine country like this without any means of communication, can we? My boss and I have already sketched the route on the map; now I'm trying to see how much this ideal route would cost, bearing in mind the actual lie of the land. So there you are, Father? Isn't that interesting news?'

'Yes, interesting indeed.'

They looked carefully at one another. Then the Father asked: 'Will you have machines?'

'Machines, pah! What do we want machines for? Good heavens, would that be worth our while?'

'In other words, you propose to employ the methods of the Congo rubber companies?'

'In God's name, is that any skin off your nose? Your palmy days have come again; you'll have hordes of faithful converts! Isn't that enough for you?'

'It is also my duty to protect them.'

'Absolutely! You will protect them, spiritually. You will tell them: "My dear children, you must accept the sufferings of this vale of tears. In death, you will find your reward." Oh, these priests! And you want to invoke the Congo rubber scandals! Do you suppose we should blush for them?'

'My dear Vidal, I assure you I haven't the heart to quarrel today.'

'But while I think of it, just tell me what wages you pay at Bomba. Can you tell me that? Your mission didn't burst up out of the ground at one wave of Jesus Christ's wand?'

'At least, we made no use of forced labour.'

'So you say, Father, so you say. You say to them: "Go and work at the mission, or you'll all go to Hell." Is that not a worse constraint than any earthly one?'

'How you go on, Vidal!'

They both laughed again.

After taking another glass of rum, the Administrator rose and took his topee, saying that he must go. As if waking from a bad dream, the Father sighed briskly and rose also.

'Father,' said M. Vidal from the porch, 'when a man begins to doubt his mission, is he not finished, or at least on the way to being so?'

'It is possible. Why?'

'You'd better think it over, Father.'

They both laughed aloud. Then the Father said: 'Monsieur Vidal, do you know what a greenhorn is?'

'Say on.'

'Someone who never doubts his mission.'

The Administrator laughed louder than ever and moved towards the path. He started his engine and gave a parting salute to the Father, who returned it from the courtyard.

I think it was a really merry evening. Since then, the Father has seemed more gay and confident, more calm.

We made our visits very late, because the Father had to say his breviary and took a long time about it. The Father asked the catechist to take us to some of the former Christians. And to each of them he said: 'Beware, God is not mocked! He is gentle and patient, but all the same, He will not permit anyone to mock Him, and you have pushed Him to the limit. You were part of the great family of God. You asked for baptism and we gave it; you were one of us and now you have abandoned us. Do you suppose you can get away with it? Come and go as you please? Ah no, my child, that is mockery of our

Lord; and God does not endure mockery. And if, one of these fine mornings, He should send you a little punishment, just remember that you drew it on yourself and be glad that He has warned you against the wrong path. For He could well have refrained from the warning and waited until you died in mortal sin. He could well have waited, for what would He lose by it? So, if you get a little punishment one of these mornings, a little misfortune, just be glad that He has taken the trouble to warn you.'

As soon as he had spoken these words, we left their houses . . .

My God, how tired I am! I went to bed as soon as the Father had taken his chop and I'm still not asleep, still thinking of that young white man, that Administrator . . . A chimpanzee howling! Whatever makes them howl like that? . . . If only I could sleep! I keep thinking of that young man and everything he said. Surely it was a joke? Yes, it must all have been a joke; but he said some things that I'd dearly like to understand. Why did he mention Egypt, for instance? What had that to do with the matter? Egypt . . . the Ten Plagues of Egypt . . . the Pharaohs . . . the Flight of the young Jesus . . . the Massacre of the Innocents? Oh, I'll never understand, and I'm so tired! If only the Father wouldn't be like that, so sad and discouraged. How he's changed! He never used to be like that, when he forged ahead with drums beating, looking neither to right nor left. Then they flocked to him. Oh, it's true that hereabouts they were always difficult. Boy, that story about the road! I think I understood that they would drag them from their houses and make them work all day in the hot sun, digging and carrying earth from morn to night. I'm sure that was it! I knew God would give them a rap one day. Ah, now I understand! A misfortune had to come to them sooner or later. I saw them making the road from Manding to Zomba; it was horrible! Men working all roped together and with soldiers watching them. If one fell, they flogged him where he lay until he staggered up again. That road, my God! If only they will make it! If only they begin work soon! We shall see the Talas weeping with humiliation and weakness and despair, like the people on the Manding–Zomba road. It's astonishing how men thirst for God when the whip is cutting their backs. Don't give up, Father! They will come back to you. Hullo, I think I'm going to sleep! It's astonishing how happy I feel all of a sudden. After all, it's not so bad to make a tour; better than going to school every day! It's true the food changes too much, except the Father's, which is always special. For Zacharia and me, who are always fed by the catechist's wife at each stop, these changes are really a strain on the digestion. One day groundnuts, and before we're used to them, it's maize! But it's always like that on tour. Anyway, Zacharia gets out of it by pinching the Father's food. Perhaps that's why he had diarrhoea last night; you can't mix African and European chop without risking diarrhoea. I'm glad he's got it, anyway. Every half-hour, he ran behind the house. And of course, the arrogant ass wants to conceal it! He thinks a lot of himself, just because the girls fall for him. I could pretend to be tough too, because plenty of girls turn to look at me. And when I dress up they call: 'Oh, look at the little choir-boy!' But I despise girls. At last, I'm going to sleep . . . Got a bit of a tummy ache – perhaps I'm getting diarrhoea too . . . Ah, if only they'll build that road, if they'll beat and persecute these people, then perhaps they'll all return to God . . .

Bitie

Our stay at Bitie is almost over. Tomorrow afternoon we must be on our way, as usual. Bitie will have proved by far the most hospitable village we have visited in this wretched Tala. I doubt whether we shall find another like it. Here the people were really friendly, and they offered us such presents! Three sheep, plenty of eggs and chickens, a hundred kilos of cocoa and almost as much in groundnuts. The Father must be happy about that, at least. Just before this tour, he got from Europe a machine for expressing groundnut oil and he was counting on returning with enough nuts to feed it. But up to now we'd got hardly any. The catechist has promised to find porters tomorrow to carry all this stuff to Bomba mission.

Although everything isn't perfect here, the chapel is like new. Whitewashed all over and really looking smart. The catechist is a little skinny fellow who stutters. He has seven children, two of them grown-up. They have taken some trouble for us, and prepared a really nice surprise with real dahlias and balsam flowers. I was able to decorate the altar with these, instead of the big wild flowers of the forest which I've been using since Christmas. The Father was astonished at these fine flowers, but the children explained they had grown them in beds among the fields. The best of them is Michael, the eldest, who was at school in Bomba. He says he is now engaged and will soon come to enrol his fiancée in the sixa. Apparently he has never slept in the same house with her, which must be unique around here, where most men sleep with their girls for years before bringing them to the mission. But there's still something funny about Tala, even Bitie. The catechist says people here are the readiest to accept Christian marriage and to send their fiancées to the sixa for three months beforehand. But the strange thing is that they always take a second wife soon after the ceremony. It isn't this fact which surprises the catechist so much, for with all the money they're making from cocoa a second wife is almost inevitable; but what puzzles him is that at the very altar and in the midst of the service, they are already thinking about their next choice, have already negotiated with the parents and paid part of the bride-price. That's what is upsetting, he stammers.

And the Father asked him: 'Perhaps they make church marriages for the sake of the ceremony? The custom here was to celebrate a marriage with seven whole days of festivity. Don't you think their love of ceremony might be the attraction?'

'That may be part of it, Father, certainly. But I don't think it's the whole answer. For I can think of men who hate festivals and can't stand the sound of drums, who still run to the church for marriage, without for a moment being good Christians.'

But it's not altogether so bad if they do take second wives, after at least getting properly married to the first one. At least the teaching of Christ has not left them quite indifferent. And they do usually send their extra children for baptism, paying a higher fee than the good Christians. The Father always writes on the baptismal records of such children *'Ex fornicatione ortus'*. This must mean that their fathers are polygamous and that's why they must pay a higher fee. *'Ex fornicatione ortus'*; I've never dared to ask the Father what it means. It must mean he's dissatisfied, especially if *fornicatione* in Latin means the same thing as in French. I must remember to ask Jean-Martin, the new Vicar, when I get back to Bomba. Jean-Martin, oh, the lucky devil! I wonder what he's doing at this moment?

If the Christians of Bitie are so keen on taking second wives, that must be why there were so many women and children at confession, and so few men. But they'll come back when God's anger smites them. Wow! Just wait till they begin that road! I didn't misunderstand the Administrator yesterday, they are certainly going to make it. For this morning the Father confirmed my happy idea about it. When we had come a certain distance from Kota, the Father pushing his bicycle and walking with us, he suddenly said to Zacharia: 'You know that they're probably going to cut a road this way?' He said this with a sort of wink in Zacharia's direction.

'Oh, yes?' said the cook.

'Yes, the Administrator told me yesterday.'

40

At first, Zacharia said nothing. He had seen the Father's wink but hadn't understood it. He thought for a bit and then said: 'It's a good thing, Father. This country certainly deserves a road. So many people and so much cocoa.'

That's all he could find to say!

'But,' pressed the Father, 'it's a great misfortune.'

'A misfortune? How come? Are you afraid they'll get still richer, Father? Because, once there's a road, they certainly will.'

There was a sort of challenge in his eyes. The Father walked between us, pushing his bicycle, with Zacharia on his right. I was eager to discover whether the Father was as happy as I about the new road.

'Don't you understand?' continued the Father, 'they will drive them from their houses, tie them together like beasts and drag them to the site. Then they'll work from morning to night, bent under the hot sun. Is that not a misfortune?'

'True, Father, I hadn't considered it like that. You're right, what a price they'll pay for their road before they get it! Why didn't I think of that?' He thought for a moment then added: 'I saw them working on the Manding–Zomba road. It was really terrible, Father. They died in heaps. But you must remember it yourself, for you went many times a day by motor-cycle to confess the dying. Surely you remember?'

'Yes, yes, Zacharia. We shall see . . .'

They walked side by side in silence. Their leather sandals beat the path with an irregular rhythm, like an apprentice drummer practising. Their eyes were lowered, and the chain of the bicycle purred as they went. Suddenly Zacharia spoke again, without raising his eyes.

'But, Father, you must be very happy about this, no? Isn't it just what you longed for? They'll be treated like beasts and in their misery they'll run to you, saying: "Father, you alone are kind. You are truly our Father. Forgive us for not having heard you before." Why not admit it? Isn't it true they will return to you now?'

Oh, this Zacharia! To think that he dared say that to the Father! And then he burst out laughing.

The Father said nothing, he only went: 'Hmmm. . . .'

Then he jumped on his bike and went ahead pedalling slowly and looking around him, as if admiring the forest. His patience with

Zacharia is astounding. He wasn't even angry. No, he is certainly not the man he was. How strange!

But Zacharia! What a swine he is . . .

It's nearly five kilometres from Kota to Bitie. While we were passing a small village, I saw a girl making signs to Zacharia from a veranda. When we got level, she greeted him openly and Zacharia went towards her. He took her hand and they talked gaily together like old friends who have met by chance. Meanwhile, I waited on the path for Zacharia. But he followed her into the house and soon I heard him calling: 'What the hell are you doing out there? Come on in! This little funk! How will you ever be a man? Come on!'

I didn't dare refuse. I'm really beginning to dislike this Zacharia. As soon as I came in, he said: 'What are you scared of, eh? Of me? Of her? Speak up, what's the matter?'

'But I'm not scared,' I said angrily.

'Then why did you stay out there on the path?'

I didn't answer him; I was looking at the girl and thinking I had seen her before. I'm sure I have. But where? Never mind. She was certainly looking nice. She was wearing a short dress, only just below the knees, all decorated with bright flowers. She must be a lawless hussy to ignore the Father's rules about the length of dresses. But she is certainly pretty. She laughed a lot at Zacharia's jokes and showed her white teeth, which were filed in the middle to make a little gap. She took off her scarf and showed part of her fine black hair, which was trained in long ringlets towards the neck, where they all were gathered together. She is really a beauty, and I keep wondering where I've seen her. She was very familiar with Zacharia and kept looking at me with the corner of her eye. Once she said: 'Look at the Father's child!'

They both laughed and I tried to join them, just to please Zacharia. We stayed nearly an hour in that house, before Zacharia said we must be on our way. Then they whispered in each other's ears. I couldn't hear what they said, but the whole thing looked fishy to me. The two of us started off again and Zacharia whistled all the way, very pleased with himself.

But goodness, how comforting it is to find a village like Bitie. Of course, it's not like a roadside village, but things would be well enough if we had a few more places as good as this. And then the

Father wouldn't have taken this strange fancy to give everything up . . .

Zacharia must be ill again. His door hasn't stopped creaking since we went to bed. What is all this coming-and-going? Funny. I thought he'd got over his diarrhoea. Another noise from his quarters! As though he were talking to someone – all sorts of whisperings and murmurs. If the Father heard that, he'd think that I was involved. Thank God, his house is some way off!

How lazy I feel tonight! Luckily, I met a boy here from the school in Bomba and he will serve Mass tomorrow morning in my stead. He came here to convalesce with his family, so giving me a chance to sleep late for once.

And this morning I asked a local boy to do it. But this one had never been to our school and he must have made a hash of it, for the Father didn't look very pleased when he came from church. He never likes my playing that trick, for he complains that the village boys can't speak Latin properly, that they muck up the ceremony, ring the bell all wrong and generally get everything muddled. But this time I can sleep late, as I did this morning at Kota . . .

But what on earth is happening in Zacharia's room? A creaking noise now, so he must be really ill. And who was he talking to just then? Perhaps the catechist was offering him a remedy. All the same, he did nothing but spruce himself up while the Father and I were making our visits. This village is like one huge cocoa farm divided by straight paths, with the chapel at the centre, for every house is built in the shadow of a cocoa tree.

Yes, at Kota this morning I slept really late, thanks to that local lad, and I didn't get to the chapel till the palaver had already started. There was one really disturbing case, a numerous family whose head was a pagan polygamist, with three wives after the first. That first wife was a Christian with many children, the eldest being a man already. Because of his bad relations with one of his uncles, this son was tried at the time of the latter's death. For hereabouts no one is ever supposed to die from natural causes. So they always manage to try someone for witchcraft, although the Father has told them many times that people often die of disease or dirt or because God so wills it. But the Talas will have none of it.

So the young man was declared guilty of his uncle's death, simply because they had once been rivals in love. To prove his innocence, he went to consult a well-known sorcerer. For here even the best Christians make use of sorcerers in an affair of this kind.

The Father summoned this young man to the palaver, but he didn't appear, although a Christian, and only his mother was there to answer for him.

'Why did you let your son consult this witch-doctor?' the Father demanded. 'Don't you know that I have forbidden it?'

'Father, I didn't give him leave to go. In fact, I forbade him to go to that man's house, being a Christian as he is. It was his father who ordered him to go and consult that rogue Boto, Father. . . .'

'Who is this Boto?' asked the Father impatiently.

'Boto is Boto, Father. You must know him by now, after all the years you've lived among us.'

'Around here, everyone seems to be called Boto! Do I really know this man, this Boto?'

'Yes, Father, you must know him. Why he's the famous man-with-the-mirror, against whom you are always preaching. You know him right enough!'

At this point someone stood up in the audience and said: 'It's Sanga Boto they are discussing, Father. Yes, Sanga Boto, everyone knows him. You're sure to meet him tomorrow, or the day after. He's always somewhere about the country.'

The Father said it would suit him well enough to meet this fellow. Personally, I've often heard of Sanga Boto. In fact, I believe he's had lots of scraps with the Father before. I wonder what will happen when they meet this time?

While the Father and I were making our rounds, I had such a curious feeling. Bitie is not simply full of the usual carefree atmosphere of this country, but adds to it a kind of pure, unmixed tranquillity. I don't know how to explain the joyful sensation which filled me. Was it that round, brilliant moon, as luminous as the Blessed Virgin in one of our illustrated texts? Was it the soft, mysterious light which floated over the forest, the cocoa farms and the houses? Many gramophones were playing here also, filling the evening with their strange and empty cries; but even this didn't annoy me. Many boys were still playing in the dusty compounds before the houses, despite the late hour. And when they saw us passing, they cried with such touching sincerity: 'Jesus Christ be praised!'

Bitie reminded me of my village before the road got to it, and these boys were like myself in those days. Then my village too enjoyed this mysterious calm. Mother told me, before her death, of all the evils that road had brought amongst us. And my father only escaped forced labour because he was the catechist, for he was rounded up and driven to work like all the other fit men of the place. But the Father came and explained that this was his man, so the white overseer let him go. My mother nearly died of joy, when she saw him led back to the house by the Reverend Father . . .

Gosh! Still all that row from Zacharia's place . . . a rhythmic creaking mingled with whispers and little moans. It's been going on for hours. I'd give a lot to know what's going on in there!

Ah, Bitie will have been a good stop, when all's said and done. Just because of this place, perhaps the Father won't give up Tala after all. Sodom and Gomorrah would have been saved by a single just man. And the Father won't abandon this country while there's a single village in it that's more or less just . . .

Sanga Boto, the man-with-the-mirror! I've been hearing about him for ages. Perhaps he's the one spoiling this country? What has this witch-doctor been doing to turn so many people from God? If the Father catches him, he'll surely get him locked up. Then we shall be free of this charlatan.

Evindi

Well, this morning I let that young boy serve the Mass, as planned, and the Father didn't seem to mind much. So perhaps he served it quite well, having been at school with us in Bomba. Anyway, the Father seems careless of such details now. He speaks seldom, far less than usual, and is always saying his breviary to himself by day, whereas formerly he did it only at night.

So I left it to this boy and didn't turn up myself either at Mass or at the palaver afterwards. I don't suppose I missed much – the usual unmarried mothers, the Christians flirting with witchcraft or polygamy, or simply living with loose women – I know it all.

We left Bitie late, because there was so much to arrange. And we received many more presents, for which we had to fix porterage to Bomba. We also asked the porters to get some Communion wine for us at the mission and to meet us with it here this evening. We are just beginning to run short, though we still have plenty of wafers, for the communicants are even fewer than the Father expected.

This time, he jumped on his bicycle as soon as we left Bitie. He was so gloomy and dejected that it pained me. This is the strangest thing about our tour, for I certainly never pitied him before. I always admired him as one might Christ himself or one of His Apostles, or at least John the Baptist. And now here I am, feeling sorry for him. But it's when we pity someone that we feel closest to them, and just now I certainly love him much more than my own father.

How wretched he must feel! He came among us to bring us the Good Tidings, caring nothing for himself. He thought only of us, in the example of Christ himself. And this is how we reward him! It's true that Bitie was not too bad, but for every true Christian in Bitie, how many godless ones! And now, as we go along, people look at him as if he were no one at all. How cheap they hold my poor beloved Father!

Perhaps he thinks now of his own country, which is known to be so beautiful; of his father and brothers and sisters. Perhaps he lost his mother when a boy, just like me. And perhaps his father remarried, like mine. I do wish he would sometimes talk of his family and his country, but he talks so little! All he has told us is that the cold falls in large lumps from December to March and that everyone is a Christian and goes to Mass on Sundays. How grand it must be there! Provence! Yes, that's the name of his region – Provence. And there every man takes one wife only, and girls don't sleep with their boys until they are married in church. It's been like that for centuries and centuries! According to the Father, there are no forests in Provence. You can look out for more than five kilometres on every side and see the land all scattered with stone churches and tall belfries. How splendid! And it seems that in summer-time, from June to September, the sun rises at four in the morning and doesn't set till ten at night. Cars, trains and aeroplanes without number. Ah, Provence what a place! I can see it now . . .

Anyway, as I said, the Father left Bitie on his bicycle and ran ahead of us. Zacharia and I were walking some distance behind the porters, when suddenly that same girl came bursting out of a house. She looked even prettier than yesterday. She touched my hand and laughed with all her teeth as she began teasing me again: 'Behold the Father's son!' she cried.

She walked a long way with us, joking all the while, and just before we reached Evindi she left us, making little signs at Zacharia.

Everything is rotten here at Evindi. There isn't even a catechist any more: the presbytery is empty and all sunk in grass. A young lad who recently left the Bomba school has agreed to act as catechist for us.

When we arrived, he had already summoned all the Christian women and children and set them to sweeping out the presbytery. Some of them cut palm-fronds and laid these along the walls of the church, inside and out, and around the altar as well. Others started weeding the courtyard, while the rest were sweeping. It was all quite gay and they were happy that the Father had decided to stop here despite the neglected state of everything. It seems that the catechist

47

went back to his village, saying that the Father didn't pay him enough. Also, that the men of the village had forbidden their wives and children to go and help him with his farm, which made it impossible for him to go on. He hasn't even come to see us, though we waited all afternoon. How shameful for a catechist to demand money, when he's supposed to labour for the love of God! Can Zacharia be right after all? Is everyone simply running after money? It looks like it, when a catechist starts wanting a rise. Perhaps he'll show up at Mass tomorrow?

It's difficult, because this fellow is the only one in the village who can read; hence, the only one who can be catechist. The young man who's helping us now has to go soon to the town and can't do it for long. He wants to get married and so must go to town for a few months to make some money. But he's really done well today and found everything we need. A few hours after our arrival he had bunches of bananas hanging from our veranda and rows of pineapples ripening beside the Father's house. He also found us some eggs and a chicken, but the Father ate that. Zacharia and I made do with eggs and groundnuts at first, until he swiped what was left of the chicken.

What a headache this place is! Perhaps they're trying to punish us for our good reception in Bitie.

Only a handful of children and old women came to confession. The Father advised Matthew, our young helper, not to demand the receipts for their cult dues, so they all came straight into the church. Meanwhile, the Father went into the courtyard to prepare himself for hearing confession. Just then came a sound of drumming far away, accompanied by a chorus of women singing. The Father paused on the threshold of the church, listening. So did Zacharia and I, on the veranda of his house. All three of us stood rooted, listening.

At the other end of the courtyard, Matthew and his helpers were finishing the clearing of the place. The Father called him and began questioning him, but instantly fell silent again when the drums gave way to xylophones. Now it seemed that the dance was less than three kilometres off and you could hear everything distinctly. The xylophones had fallen into a deep-toned, rapid melody where the theme constantly returned with an effect that was obsessive, neither gay nor sad. And suddenly another xylophone, with a high clear pitch like a woman's voice, launched into a solo whose strong, provocative line marked the entry of a young girl into the dance. Zacharia couldn't help whistling the air of this solo. The Father glared at him but Zacharia just whistled on, so he turned away with a shrug. And, for myself, I saw that young girl leaping into the ring. I saw her naked breasts trembling and her whole torso moving in the most disgusting way. I saw the ring of women clapping to mark the frenzied rhythm of the xylophones. I saw the menfolk, young and old, sitting aside and commenting on her skill with appreciation – all exactly as if I had been there myself. I remembered that this was just what the Father had been fighting against for twenty years, and saw how everything that he detested was suddenly flung in his face.

Zacharia went on whistling and stamping the rhythm with his feet. The Father turned to Matthew and said: 'Go and tell them to stop the dance.'

'But, Father, those are not our people dancing, those are the pagans.'

'That's not the point,' said the Father, 'go and tell them that I won't put up with it. I must have peace now. They can start up again tomorrow after I leave, if they must. But I won't have it while I'm here, above all on the first Friday of the month.'

'Father, they are far off and don't intend to bother you.'

'I'm not concerned with that. Go and tell them to stop at once. Say that I insist!'

Matthew looked miserable and kept twisting his hands about. With a trembling lip, he blurted: 'Father, I don't think they will agree to stop.'

'Then tell them that they'll have me to deal with if they don't.'

Matthew set off doubtfully in the direction of the dance, looking like one with no hope of success. The Father swept into the church for confession while Zacharia and I went into the house allotted to us and began arranging it for cooking.

Zacharia called four of the boys among the sweepers and set them to fetching water, lighting the fire, peeling the potatoes, and killing and plucking the fowl. In other words, they did everything for us. It's like this in every place; Zacharia always manages to avoid doing a stroke of work.

While they were racing around, Zacharia said: 'How can he stop them dancing, when they aren't even Christians? The first Friday of the month indeed! They'll all laugh at him.'

Then, after a moment: 'What? Why does he want to stop them anyway, I'd like to know?'

And a little later: 'I thought your priest had learnt a bit of sense. But he's always so jumpy.'

It's me he's getting at, I know. When he gets at me like this, sometimes I shut up and sometimes I answer back, especially if I can avoid sounding spiteful. This time I spoke up: 'You should tell him that yourself – that he's too jumpy and that he needs to learn sense.'

Zacharia has no idea how I hate him. He couldn't possibly have taken my remark amiss. I wish he had really spoken to the Father in that fashion. Then perhaps he'd have got a slap for his pains. He really goes too far, this Zacharia!

After an hour, Matthew returned. The dancers, of course, had told him to buzz off. He looked really furious, like me. I really like this boy. He came and sat down in our house and said: 'Zacharia, what do you think we should do?'

'Oh, just take it easy, man!'

Matthew was sitting on an empty packing-case while he and Zacharia talked. They know each other well, because Matthew spent over six years at Bomba mission. I didn't quite grasp what they were discussing. It seemed that Zacharia was asking news of someone. He knows everybody around here; this is his ninth tour of Tala.

It was nearly six when the Father finished confession and came out of the church. He came over to us but Zacharia, who was lounging on a bamboo bed, didn't even stir. The Father recognized all the boys who were helping and asked about their parents. They all came from polygamous households, but had Christian mothers. He gazed hard at them, I don't know why. Then he turned the same gaze on me, as if he had only just got to know me, or were looking right through me to the soul.

Matthew told the Father that the people at the dance had told him brutally to clear off.

'Don't go far away,' the Father advised him, 'just wait for me in the compound.'

The Father prowled up and down the courtyard, reciting his

breviary. The drums were really warmed up now, alternating with frantic bursts from the xylophones.

The light was fading and the Father had to hold the breviary close to his eyes. From time to time he stopped, raised his head and stroked his beard. Finally, he shut the book and came back to our house, telling Matthew and me to follow him. Zacharia could come too, if he wanted.

'Where are you going, then?' asked Zacharia.

'I can't put up with this dancing on the first Friday of the month. If I hadn't arrived it might be another thing. But to dance like this, so close to a priest of God, and on the first Friday! No, it's beyond bearing!'

'But,' exclaimed Zacharia, 'they've already told you that it's pagans who are involved, not Christians!'

'What difference does that make?' shouted the Father, rushing off. He was really wild, just as if they had insulted him.

We all set off, leaving Zacharia behind, for he didn't hide his opinion that we couldn't behave here as though we were on the main road. But the Father wouldn't listen. I was delighted to see him back to his old self. I had been quite ashamed of the change in him. If he once lets up, if he resumes his doubtful manner of the last few days, everything will be done for.

We strode along in the moonlight, drawing nearer to the dancing-ground, where the sound of drums and xylophones rolled forth unceasingly. As we passed through the homesteads we saw those who hadn't gone to the festival, mostly old people, squatting on their verandas and talking and laughing at the tops of their voices. But as soon as we drew near they all fell silent. Only the little children playing in the dust greeted us and this they did in the most charming fashion. Their first reaction on seeing a white man was to stand stock still, for the Father had tucked up the skirt and sleeves of his soutane so that he looked at a glance like any common-or-garden white. But the moment they recognized him, they all cried one after the other: 'Jesus Christ be praised! Jesus Christ be praised!'

In one homestead two boys accosted me with shouts of: 'Give us a medal, choir-boy, give us a medal!'

I had to disappoint them. But in another house near the road someone was playing a Christian tune on a guitar. The Father strode up to that house, and we all followed him. It was quite dark inside, but by the flicker of firelight we saw a young man lying on a bamboo bed. His chest was bare and a lappa hung low over his loins. He stopped playing the moment we entered, but finally he stammered: 'Jesus Christ be praised!'

The Father and I shook his hand, the Father asking him why he played that tune on a guitar. Did it signify that he thought often of God? The man replied that he spent days on end playing tunes like that; he was a Christian named Gaston and had been to confession that very afternoon.

'So, Gaston,' asked the Father cheerfully, 'are you married yet?'

'Not yet, Father, but I hope to be if I manage to make a little money in the next cocoa season.'

'And how do you live?'

'As you see, Father . . .'

'Who cooks your food?'

'My old mother, who is away for a few days. She is also a Christian.'

'And where does she sleep as a rule?'

'Naturally, Father, she sleeps here, in the same house with me.'

'Aren't you ashamed?'

'How do you mean, Father?'

'I mean that you ought to be ashamed, a good Christian like you! How can you share one house with your mother? You must build another for yourself alone.'

'I know, Father, but I have so many things to do just now.'

'You have a concubine, perhaps?'

'No, no, Father! Truly I haven't.'

'Are you sure?' pressed the Father, laughing softly.

'But, Father, I am a good Christian!'

'And you haven't even a single concubine?'

'No, Father, not a one.'

'Hmmm . . . and you expect me to believe that you live like that? Come now, Gaston!'

Then we all laughed and the Father said: 'Do you tell lies sometimes?'

'Sometimes, perhaps. But I'm not lying now. Matthew can confirm everything I told you.'

'Very well, Gaston. One man like you was enough to have saved Sodom and Gomorrah from total destruction. Have you heard of Sodom and Gomorrah?'

'Yes, Father. I often read the Holy Bible.'

'Very good, Gaston. Stay as you are, for who knows, perhaps it's because of you that a great misfortune has not already befallen this country?'

We left, and as we went Matthew sang the praises of Gaston, who is a relative of his. It's odd: why should there be men like Gaston who both believe in God and sincerely practise their religion, and others who think only of vice, like those who are dancing now in defiance of the Father's prohibition? By this time, we were right by the market-place and the ground shook with the heavy thunder of the drums. A patch of bush still hid us from the dancers, but the noise was stupefying: drums of all sizes, hand-clapping, the singing of the women and the cries of the men.

Suddenly we burst out into the vast clearing. They were dancing before the chief's house, whose pan roof shone brilliantly in the moonlight. The women formed a huge circle around the drums, while in their midst two young girls danced almost naked. The other women clapped to mark the rhythm of the dance, and every now and then one of them uttered a piercing ululation to excite the contortions of the dancers. The men were watching everything keenly, ranged on the long veranda of the chief's house, a dark mass against the pale walls. They didn't recognize us at first, because of the bizarre way the Father was wearing his soutane.

Then suddenly they saw who we were. The women and children shrieked like a lot of frightened chickens. The men up on the veranda just gazed down on us without moving.

Without a moment's hesitation, the Father fell on the xylophones and scattered them in pieces. Then he turned to the drums, but they were more difficult to break. He lifted a great drum in his arms and threw it down with a terrible sound. He still hadn't managed to break a single drum when the chief came rushing from his house like a wild beast. He was wearing nothing but a pair of drawers. It seemed he was asleep when we arrived and someone had just woken him up. This man was tall and powerfully built, roaring like a thunderclap: 'What's happening here, eh? What's happening here?

What man has dared to carry war right into my village? Who dares to smash my xylophones? What shall I do to him now, tell me? What shall I do to this man who comes smashing my xylophones and breaking the peace of my household? I believe I shall kill him. Yes, kill him I must, indeed I must!'

While shouting these words he was all the time bearing down on the Father, whom he had already recognized. And he came on as if he really meant to strike him. He was only a few centimetres off and already shaking his fist. At that moment his people threw themselves between. Wow! I was really scared for the Father then! My God, what a country! He would really have struck the Father if he hadn't been prevented. They surrounded him and pinioned his arms to stop him, but the man was devilishly strong and fought like a lion. There were moments when he almost escaped them and all the while he was yelling: 'Just let me get at him, brothers! Let me kill him, I beg you! Let me rid you of this plague of a priest, this cursed white! Brothers, let me crush this verminous dog with my left foot and you will hear of him no more. What the devil is he doing here in our country, I ask you? He was starving in his own land; he ran to us and we fed him; we gave him land and with our money he built fine houses upon it; we even gave him our girls for three months at a stretch. But that isn't enough for him; now he even wants to stop us dancing! It'd be no surprise if he came to take our houses from us and pretty soon he will, I warn you. No, look here, just let me kill off this shit of a priest! I'll tear his beard off! His hour has come! Now at last he'll pay for all the plagues he's brought us since he dragged his eunuch's dress over our land . . .'

But his people still held him and did their best to calm him down, saying: 'Let it be, chief, let it be. It's just a provocation, so let it be . . .'

At last they mastered him. He stood there panting while the Father, calm as Jesus himself, stood there with his hands on his hips and taunted him: 'Come on, then,' he laughed, 'come on and strike me.'

There was a low menacing murmur all around us, for the men had all come down from the veranda and ringed us about. The women who fled at our arrival had also flocked back. Hearing himself taunted thus, the chief began to struggle afresh and yelled out:

'Listen to him, brothers, just listen to him! ... me in my own compound, this scalded swin ... he defies me? The shame smears on to you also ... let me tear at his ears and make them a bit less re ...

But his fellows refused to let him go. Finally an ... came from the house, coughing and tottering, who said ... ...r: 'Listen, my son, listen to me. Have you forgotten you're de ... with a white man? What are you thinking of? Do you suppose he'd dare to defy us like this unless he was sure of the support of all his people? They always hang together like that. Go and rest, my son. Let him go his way and don't offend him. You can never be sure, with them. Go and rest, my boy.'

Then the old one went off, stooped and still coughing. I'm sure this was the chief's father.

The chief himself was still glaring murderously at the Father, but they gripped him tight. The Father looked back at the chief with a sort of amused pity, quite free of dislike. The women and children now crowded round us, like chimpanzees, who always retrace their tracks once they know what it is that has frightened them, however dangerous it may be.

'I am not a white man, to you. I don't wish to be a white man to you. I simply want to make you understand that you can't dance like this on the first Friday of the month, because Jesus Christ . . .'

The chief burst in: 'Go and stuff yourself with your first Fridays and all the other Fridays! Jesus Christ, Jesus Christ . . . another damned white! Another that I'd like to crush with my left foot. What? Jesus Christ? Do I know this fellow? Do I come and tell you about my ancestors, huh? Jesus Christ? I scorn him, if you only knew how I scorn him, your Jesus Christ. Just let me pull your ears a moment to make them a bit less red . . . Jesus Christ! Vermin!'

I'm sure he must have been drunk. He couldn't have spoken like that otherwise. Then he went back to his house, still muttering blasphemies between his teeth and insulting Jesus.

Then a man who stood close by said: 'I'm not a Christian, Father. I've never been baptized and I don't suppose I ever will be. Nevertheless, I believe that God exists. I just want to ask you one question: suppose the whites were dancing here tonight instead of us and you

by, would you rush in and break their trumpets and
guitars? Answer me sincerely, Father.'

The Father hesitated a moment before he said: 'But I didn't come
to this country for the whites. I came for you, for the blacks. I'm not
concerned with the whites. They are bad men and will go to Hell like
all bad men.'

'And what about us, Father?'

'Why, you could so easily go to Heaven. You are so near to it
already. That's why I get so angry – because it needs so little more
for you to enter Heaven.'

'What sort of thing, Father?'

'To give up dancing, for example.'

'But how should we live without our dancing? You whites have
your cars, your aeroplanes, your trains. . . . But we have nothing but
our dancing. And now you want to take that from us. What could
we do instead?'

'You could pray to God, and worship him.'

They were silent for a moment, looking at us musingly. The moonlight poured down the sloping roof like heavy oil. Soon, our ques-
tioner spoke again: 'Father, it seems to me that if Jesus Christ had
really thought of us, he would have come himself to discuss the
matter with us. Then perhaps he would have consented to let us
dance. That's how it looks to me: what do you think?'

'Exactly so. Jesus Christ has ordered me to tell you . . .'

'Told you? But you are a white man, Father!'

Hearing these words, the Father looked disturbed. I don't know
why he's taken this fancy for listening to all this foolishness. Until
recently, he would just have sent this fellow packing, whereas today
he seemed really to be discussing seriously with him, listening to all
his illiterate nonsense. I'm sure it's a mistake to explain things carefully to them. Quite enough to tell them that they'll roast in Hell,
that's all. Oh, what hopeless people! This country is really the worst
you could think of.

The Father was so depressed by their replies that he couldn't continue the discussion, so we started back to the presbytery. It was only
then that I saw Matthew again: he must have lain low during all
that fracas – scared stiff, no doubt. The Father soon put it all behind
him and began eagerly questioning Matthew. . .

Hullo! there goes Zacharia's bed again. Will he never get rid of
his diarrhoea? He's certainly got his due, anyway. Now he'll learn
that one can't mock God or one of his ministers, which is just what
he's done to the Father all these years, and especially on this trip . . .
Ah, yes, I remember. It was about Sanga Boto, the famous man-with-
the-mirror, that the Father was questioning Matthew. According to
this boy, Sanga Boto is certainly in these parts and we're sure to run
into him farther on. The Father said: 'So long as . . .'

My God! Who can Zacharia be talking to at this hour? There! A
little stifled cry, like a child, or perhaps a woman. Yes, that's it perhaps, a woman's cry! Heavens, is it possible? Has Zacharia really
got a woman with him? I'm going to listen carefully. At present,
everything is still. There goes his bed, creaking again! Whatever can
he be doing? Lord, there's no mistake now! A woman's cry. And
the bed creaking ceaselessly. My, just think of Zacharia with a
woman, here, in this house! Only a few metres from the Father,
who's probably still talking to Matthew! What can they be doing
together to make the bed creak like that? What shall I do now? I'll
go and tell the Father everything . . . No, better keep quiet; keep out
of the whole dirty business. Just as long as the Father knows nothing
– otherwise he'll imagine I'm in league with Zacharia. I'm sure
Zacharia will land us all in trouble. You can't behave like that without provoking some calamity. Better not to think of it. . . .

Ah yes! after listening to Matthew's tales of Sanga Boto, the
Father said: 'Just so long as I catch up with him!'

I think just the same; if we can only meet him! The chief of
Evindi had to give up his dance after all. As for Sanga Boto, we'll
teach him to operate in our area! . . .

More creaking from Zacharia . . . and now, those little moans
again. . . . Oh, my God, what a devil this Zacharia is! What a Lucifer! Must try to ignore all these dirty goings-on. If only I could sleep,
it would be easier. . . .

The Father ate almost nothing this evening. . . .

But what woman can it be? Perhaps the one who's been following
us since yesterday? And where have I seen that one before? I'm sure
I know her from somewhere . . . Another stifled cry! I'm sure it's
her. Why does she cry out like that? Can't she just lie peacefully? I
mustn't think of it any more . . . must get to sleep now . . .

After supper this evening, I took a huge jigger out of the Father's right foot, a real monster. He doesn't get many as a rule, because he wears shoes and stockings. But when one of those blighters sneaks into his shoe, he doesn't feel it, till it's big as a nut, like tonight . . .

It must be really late and I still haven't slept at all. And still that racket next door! Will it never finish? I mustn't think about it; I've just been to confession . . .

Ekokot

This is one of our most important stops, an extensive village with a big population. But the presbytery is set a little apart, as if in flight from all the tumult of the village. There's a small road nearby which is said to have quite a bit of traffic, timber lorries for the most part. I've already seen two pass since our arrival, the first motors I've seen for a week.

We're now over thirty kilometres from Bomba mission. Thirty kilometres from home! It's far.

They say that Ekokot is going to be made into a big mission, like Bomba, and that the task is being given to a black priest who is now expected. I pity him in advance. It will be no joke trying to found a mission in this country, among these people. I really feel sorry for this black priest. Not having the same experience of the place as the Reverend Father, how will he take it? Perhaps they're going to send Abbé Jean Bita. He'll know how to look after himself; probably the only man, apart from the Father, who could succeed here. His impact on the people he works among, Christian or pagan, is already a legend. And he also has quite a reputation for working miracles. But I've never heard the Father mention any of these miracles of Jean Bita's, even though the black Christians talk of nothing else. At one time the Abbé was Vicar at the Mission of N—, where he served under a white Father Superior. Thanks to him, hordes of people were converted in an area which was very slack before. This was the work that made him famous in the country, especially on account of two miracles he worked there.

One day he was violently rebuking a young man for his neglect of the virtue of chastity. When the young man answered him insolently, the Abbé said: 'As a punishment for that, you will sleep in the forest tonight.'

Naturally, the young man covered him with sarcasm. Nevertheless, he got lost in the forest on the way back to his village and wasn't found till the next morning.

On another occasion, when the Abbé was crossing a river on tour, he saw a crowd of girls bathing in the nude. This was something he had many times forbidden and he said to them: 'All the priests have strained their lungs telling you girls not to bathe naked near the pathways, but it's all a waste of breath. This time I'm going to punish you and you've certainly deserved it. Whether you are Christians or pagans, I command you to stay for two days in that river exactly as you are now, naked and upright.'

The girls thought it was a joke at first but there they had to stay, naked and upright, for the whole two days.

It's surely Abbé Jean Bita who will be coming to take over Ekokot, though it's only a rumour at the moment. If he does come, it will mean that the Father has given up at least an important piece of the Tala country. And this is something I don't want, despite the fiendish ingratitude of these people, their impiety and their horrible iniquities. But I begin to fear he will renounce them. He's been so queer lately. Like last night at Evindi, when he condescended to discuss things with those idiots! And he's made no reference to it since, although one word to his good friend the Administrator would be enough to get that awful chief dismissed. I really begin to fear that he'll give up . . .

What's this? Is it raining on my bed now? Yes, it is! Not really surprising, since the houses in this Ekokot presbytery are so badly kept, like everywhere else in Tala. My God, what rain! And it's been raining like this since before we left Evindi!

Ah, Evindi! I'll never forget that place. At the palaver this morning we had fresh evidence of how vice has gripped the whole country.

A woman appeared before the Father, accused of doing nothing when a young man, who wanted to marry her daughter, was forced to pay out five thousand francs. Five thousand, what a price!

'How could you agree to sell your daughter at such a rate?' demanded the Father. 'Five thousand francs! Aren't you ashamed? A Christian selling her daughter for five thousand francs!'

'But, Father, you know how it is. You know very well how it is.

You know that our children only belong to us women while we carry them in our bellies. After that, it's not our affair and we can say nothing. You know all that, Father. What could I do? This young man came along and asked to marry my daughter; so I suppose, for it was all discussed in the men's house. They always discuss serious matters there, where there's no smoke and the walls are cleaner. They talked a long time there and disputed about the bride-price. Finally they agreed on five thousand. My daughter and I knew nothing about it though it was her they were discussing. When they'd already reached agreement, they sent for her, my husband crying out: "Kaba!" When she heard her name, she went running to them from the women's house. She was really scared going in among them like that, but her father pointed out a young man and said: "Look at that man. He will be your husband, won't he?" "Certainly, father," she replied. And when she came back to us, she cried her poor heart out! You must have known all this ever since you came to live here. What could I do? If it was my affair, I would surely give up my daughter without demanding money, as you've always told us to do. Oh, perhaps I would have asked for a few household things. Our forefathers always did so, and they must have had a reason. But, as I told you, it's not my business.'

The Father sat looking at her and stroking his beard. Suddenly his face twitched and he said: 'You could have spoken to your husband. You could have threatened to report him to the Administrator. Don't you know it's forbidden for a father to demand five thousand francs for his daughter? Five hundred francs is the most your husband can demand of his son-in-law; not more than five hundred. And that's a law, made by the Administrator. Surely you know all this?'

'Oh, Father, he beats me so much! And if I threatened to have him sent to prison, I really believe he would cast me off. He hates anyone to contradict him. If he hears that you have spoken ill of him, then next time you come on tour he'll forbid me to see you.'

The Father turned to Matthew, who was standing beside him: 'Is it true that her husband beats her?'

'Yes,' said Matthew, 'all the time.'

There was a general murmur of assent from those present, women for the most part. The Father agreed to readmit this woman to the sacraments and before taking her seat, she declared: 'I thank you too much, Father, I thank you too much! If you could just read my heart, you would see there the whole spread of my gratitude. I am a good Christian, Father; I believe in God and I've always paid my cult dues – I can even show you the receipts.'

'Don't bother. Just sit down,' said Matthew, with a trace of nervousness in his tone.

Then another woman came up to the bar, crying pitifully and trembling all over. Matthew leant over and explained her case into the Father's ear. Her daughter had been married to a polygamist, but it wasn't this she was reproached with, since she also was in the power of a tyrannous husband. Her real sin was to make frequent visits to this daughter, even though she was now the wife of a polygamist.

The woman wept still and covered her face with her hands.

'Listen,' said the Father, 'take care. Give up these visits to your daughter!'

Through her tears the woman managed to stammer:

'Father, she's my child, my own child, and I love her. . . . Punish me in any way you like, Father, but don't forbid me to see my daughter. I would die! Have pity on me . . .'

The Father said he could change nothing: it was his rule that a Christian mother must make up her mind to cease such visits.

We left Evindi as soon as we could. There had been rain in the night and the path was wet, so my canvas shoes were smothered in mud. I must remember to wash them tomorrow. . . . The Father walked some distance with us and then went ahead on his bicycle.

We met the same girl just before reaching Ekokot. As usual, she hailed us from a veranda and we went in to join her. She is such a beauty, I'm certain it was she who was with Zacharia the night before. She was wearing a dress of banana green with a pattern of flowers printed on it, a dress which fell only to her knees and which had a triangular opening in front, with its point falling just between the breasts. These fine breasts stretched the material in two great swellings on either side of the opening. When she laughed, the skin of her cheeks fell into tiny dimples and her eyes blazed with a strange brilliance. Her skin was so fine that she looked like someone who spends her whole life bathing: not a single scab, not even a tattoo-scar! And her hands were so soft and small that obviously she seldom worked with them. Today she was wearing very white canvas shoes and she smelt nice – but then she always smells nice.

She knew everything that had happened at Evindi last night, for she made fun of the Father about the whole affair. 'He'll have to tangle with Sanga Boto soon,' she laughed; 'Sanga Boto is around here somewhere.'

Of course! She was with Zacharia last night and he must have told her everything!

So Sanga Boto is hereabouts. Another account the Father will have to settle! I don't know exactly what will happen to him, but something certainly will. If only the Father could work miracles, like Abbé Jean Bita, he could say to Sanga Boto: 'You'll stay rooted to that spot until I say you can move.' Then we'd see Sanga Boto, the pillar of Satan, the enemy of God Almighty, planted in the ground, unable to move an inch. That would be a real miracle! The Father must really try to work one this time. . . .

Just before we left her, she and Zacharia were whispering together. I think she said she was coming tonight. I wonder how long they've been getting away with their filthy tricks? . . . I'd give a lot to know how long it's been going on. Perhaps since that time when I thought Zacharia had caught diarrhoea again? Yes, that must be it. Wow! And to think I suspected nothing! What a fool I was! Just think, I never dreamt of it and it's been going on for days, perhaps for a whole week. Now I understand why Zacharia was so bucked about going on tour. My God, what a rascal! . . .

Plenty of women and children came to confession, but very few men. It was pretty poor for a big centre like Ekokot, with all its villages.

There is a little school here which teaches children up to the second preparatory year, after which they come to us at Bomba. The place is run by two monitors who were trained at the Bomba mission. They had done their best to ensure that the Mass will be sung tomorrow and I'm sure they prepared a good welcome for the Father, but I didn't see it because I arrived long after. However, when Zacharia and I did arrive we found the courtyard of the presbytery strewn with flowers.

We ate really well this evening – better than at Evindi. Plenty of meat and eggs. I've certainly had more than my fill of groundnuts these last few days. The Father did give us a big piece of bread but Zacharia coolly took it all himself. He didn't deign to reply when I asked for my bit. Such pride! And when I think that he's certainly keeping it for that girl . . . the Communion wine has arrived, and a little choir-boy of Ekokot will help me serve the Mass tomorrow. I haven't decided yet whether to stand to left or right: I ought to serve on the right, because of the bell. In the bush, no one knows how to ring it in the elegant way we practise at Bomba. Yes, I shall serve on the right. Anyway, it's always the acolyte on the right who is most noticed . . . but that's pride, and perhaps my pride has influenced my decision? Ah well, I shall let him serve on the right after all; I don't want to be proud like Zacharia. That's settled, then. After all, my work is certainly more noble than Zacharia's and I'm sure the people, the girls especially, admire me more than they do him. Only, I don't want to boast about it, like Zacharia. . . .

When we made our visits this evening there were a whole heap of us and I wonder what sort of impression we made. The Father went in the centre, surrounded by the two monitors, the local catechist and myself. I've heard that there is a Protestant community here in Ekokot but apparently it has very few converts as yet. Funny, though, that it should have any, after all that the Father has told us about that evil religion.

We visited several Christian mothers and we found them all hard at work. These mothers of families work prodigiously, for even at that late hour they were shelling groundnuts or chopping meat, or bathing their children. Never tired, they were always glad to see the Father and lamented that he had neglected them for so long. They told him everything that had befallen them: births and deaths, happy events and family misfortunes; and they prayed to God for their husbands, but without much result. But with all that cocoa and money, is it likely that men will think of God? They drink and take new wives and acquire all sorts of new wealth. But the curious thing is that they never think of dressing their children decently, or those who are their wives in the eyes of God.

We didn't stay long in these houses because of the smoke, which is suffocating for those unaccustomed to it, or who have lost their immunity to it like myself.

Several natives of Ekokot have their wives in the sixa at Bomba and it was these men who came to confession this afternoon. We visited them to see whether they were properly preparing themselves for marriage, but really we had already been informed about all of them by the catechist and the two monitors, who don't miss a thing. Nevertheless, we visited them to encourage them all to make a virtuous preparation.

At last we went to see the chief, who invited us to sit down and offered us drinks. The Father said that he wouldn't take an aperitif, but the chief looked quite happy about it and I wondered why. Perhaps he was glad that the Father hadn't depleted his store of liquor. Also, the Father's visit alone was evidence enough that he hadn't forgotten the chief. No one drank anything and the bottle just stood there on the table.

The chief's house was really fine, with big cane chairs, long wooden tables, a hissing Aida pressure-lamp and a high bamboo ceiling. Quite a place. There were two weird photographs on the wall. The first showed a naked man holding his hernia in both hands, a hernia so vast that it fell like a heavy sack down to his knees; he was skinny and had a very bad colour. In the second photograph stood the same man, with no hernia, a good colour and plenty of flesh on his bones. He was still naked, but this time he held between his fingers his long, slim penis. Very strange photos, but ones you couldn't help gazing at. The Father also looked at them, though he didn't make any comment. He seemed quite relaxed, however, and he said to his host: 'So, chief, when will you be converted?'

The chief thought for some time before replying: 'Oh, Father . . . Mmm, well, when I've had enough children!'

'Indeed!' the Father exclaimed.

'Certainly, Father; you know what I mean. You know my first wife, eh? The one I married in church? Well, she's sterile. Yes, Father, she's sterile! So, you understand me when I say I was forced to take other wives in order to have children. But when I have enough children I shall perhaps let my other wives go. Yes, perhaps . . .'

'Oh, of course,' said the Father, without enthusiasm, 'but I scarcely believe you will ever let them go.'

'Oh yes I shall, Father. Anyway, as long as they are willing to go.

As long as they are willing to leave their children. If not, what can I do?'

The Father laughed sardonically between his teeth and said: 'You think yourself very smart, chief, but I think I know my polygamists by now. They're all like you; they all say it's only for the sake of children and that they'll let their wives go as soon as they have borne enough. But they never do, even when the household is brimming with children. Don't think yourself smarter than the others, chief.'

And they laughed together a long time. There was a sort of resignation in the Father's laughter, as if he'd given up hope of converting the chief and was obliged to accept his polygamy.

A man entered, one of the chief's people, I think. He was thoroughly drunk, staggering along and singing in a whining voice. On seeing the Father there he shut up, then suddenly burst out laughing and said with difficulty: 'Fada, fada, what ting you go do? You wan' take 'way de people goods? What kin' of 'ting is dat?'

The Father laughed and we all joined in, even the chief. The drunkard seized the bottle from the table, filled a glass and poured it down his throat. Then he began staggering about the place and mumbling incoherently, so that it was painful to watch him.

We rose to leave, but the chief detained us a moment, saying he had some presents for us. He gave orders to his people and they came with twenty kilos of cocoa, a goat and some chickens. We set off, with the catechist carrying the cocoa, one of the monitors leading the goat and the rest of us clutching the chickens. One of the Father's chickens kept flapping its wings and screeching out, so that the dogs ran barking from the houses, thinking we were robbers.

As we reached the presbytery, we were joined by the junior catechist, who had been out collecting news. He reported to the Father as we marched along, saying that Sanga Boto was in one of the nearby villages, vaunting his skill to the people. He would return very late to his 'headquarters' in Ekokot and the Father might catch him easily.

So the Father has decided to catch Sanga Boto! One of the monitors remarked that if he did so there would be no difficulties, because the chief seemed well-disposed. But the catechist said: 'Oh, I know the chief by now! I know him pretty well. He seems well-disposed all right, but then he's scared of the young Administrator Vidal, who's on tour hereabouts. The chief knows that a word from the Father would get him destooled at once. But he's even better disposed to Sanga Boto, that much I do know.'

We reached the presbytery, with the Father's chicken still squawking and flapping like mad. Then one of the monitors said to him in French: 'Give it me, Father. Let me hold it for you.'

'Take it then!' cried the Father, laughing, 'I give it you with all my heart.'

'Thank you, Father,' said the lad. . . .

Oh, my God, how weary I am! . . .

I keep wondering what the Father will do to Sanga Boto, if he really catches him. I must keep my wits about me, because I certainly want to be there.

How dreadfully humid it is here!

There are lots of houses in the presbytery here and Zacharia has one to himself. At least I shan't be kept awake by his creakings and whisperings. All the better, as I've just confessed myself to the Father. I never like to serve the Mass without taking Holy Communion, even when we're on tour.

Perhaps I'd better keep awake. I have a feeling there's going to be an expedition and I'm determined not to be left out. The Father was asking mainly about this famous Sanga Boto when he questioned the catechist and the monitors after dinner: 'Do many people go to consult him?' he asked.

'Father,' said the catechist, 'they look on him as on a god.'

'And what does he tell them?'

The elder monitor replied: 'It's really very odd, Father. It's like this. He sits before a big mirror, with his back turned to the door. It's usually quite dark where he is, and by his side he has a large pot full of rainwater. So, when a client comes in, he advances until Sanga Boto, who can only see him in the mirror, tells him to stop. The client stops, looking guilty, terrified and yet hopeful, like a schoolboy expecting punishment. Then Sanga Boto might say, for example: "One of your parents has died quite recently, not so?" "Oh, yes, yes! That's true," stammers the visitor. "And you too have recently been ill?" asks the sorcerer. "Oh, yes, that too is true. Absolutely true," says the other. And he keeps on asking questions of that sort until the client says: "Why do you ask me all this? Since you know everything already, it's useless. Ask me no more, but look into my secrets and advise me." Then suddenly the sorcerer will say in an astonished voice: "What? That's strange! That really is strange! . . . I see an old, stout man with a fly-whisk in his hand. He is naked to the waist and has a lappa round his loins. This is very odd! Have you, perhaps, many enemies?" "Yes, certainly," blurts the client, "and the one that you describe is the worst of the lot. That's Dumga, I recognize him at once. He's got it in for me, because he can't get a baby with any woman at all, no matter who she is. Whereas, with me, it's quite the opposite!" And so he blethers on, telling Sanga Boto everything about his life and receiving only a little petty advice in return. That's one of his devices. Above all, Father, don't try to put him in a difficulty: he'll extricate himself brilliantly and contrive to make you look foolish in the process.'

The Father was shaking his head in admiration. I wondered if he'd suddenly taken it into that head to admire Sanga Boto, whom he ought to look on as his worst enemy. No, fortunately, it was only the monitor that he admired, for after listening to him, the Father said: 'You're a smart lad! Yes, much more intelligent than anyone would expect in this country. You can't imagine how pleased it makes me to meet a smart lad like you. Men like Sanga Boto are really dangerous. They descend on a population full of superstition and naïvety, and then bamboozle them with a lot of trickery and mystification. Then they are ready to start exploiting them. Is it true that people give him lots of presents?'

'Oh, fantastic presents,' said the monitor. 'They really heap them on him. Why, I know a chief, some ten kilometres from here, who was so delighted with Sanga Boto's services that he gave him his daughter as a recompense.'

'He can no longer count his money, Father,' cried the catechist. 'He can't count all the money he's piled up. While we catechists, servants of the true God, live on in misery. And it's a wonder we don't perish of hunger . . .'

'He keeps a regular court,' added the younger monitor, 'to say nothing of his wives, more than a score of them. But he keeps a court also, quite apart from his wives.'

Then the catechist said: 'Oh! We've seen others before who were popular and favoured like this Sanga Boto. But in the end people discover the emptiness hidden by their trickery and mumbo-jumbo. Then they abandon them, or even abuse them and make songs up about them. Sanga Boto will get the same, one day.'

The Father winced and scratched his leg with a sigh. Then he opened the presbytery record where all the Christians were listed. The catechist and the monitors sat beside him and he gave them cigarettes. I would have liked to try one, but I didn't dare to ask.

I went out and began washing my canvas shoes, which were smothered in mud. I wanted to wear them tomorrow, but I doubt if they'll dry in this humid air. Never mind, I'll put on the khaki ones, even though they're not so nice. And I must also wear white, to look decent.

It must be late now. Amazing how cold it gets here; I'm cold even under my big blanket. But I'm beginning to get sleepy . . .

They are still talking down there and I'm beginning to doubt if they'll go out tonight. Oh, how sleepy I am! . . .

I wonder what Zacharia is doing now with his girl? . . .

He barely appeared for the Father's dinner tonight, leaving all the cooking to the local boys, as usual. Now and then he came out to supervise; but the moment it was finished, he vanished and hasn't been seen since. Straight back to his house, thinking of nothing but that girl. And he pinched my piece of bread for her too! I'm still wondering where I've seen her before. How lovely she is! Her name is Catherine. Yes, that's what Zacharia calls her: Catherine . . .

Ekokot

Oh my God, what a day of calamities! This tour is really beginning to take a bad turn, and I wonder if we can stave off a real disaster. Dear God, help us to avoid it! Don't abandon us! We are on a slippery slope . . .

The Father is very ill . . . a temperature of 104° . . . he may even die . . . he has eaten nothing and is delirious. Zacharia is at his bedside and is giving him quinine tablets to swallow.

I couldn't sleep in my old room because of the heat, so I've taken a room in Zacharia's house. I can hear that girl bouncing about next door, bouncing without rest. Zacharia isn't in there, because he's looking after the Father, so I expect she's bored all by herself. Catherine . . .

The Father is really bad. He must have swallowed a ton of water, for he was wearing a soutane and rubber-soled shoes, and those must have pulled him down. He fell straight into the water and wasn't rescued for a long time. They pressed his chest and the water spurted from his mouth and nostrils. Oh dear! How will it all end? And to think how we boasted this morning, how our Christians exulted while Sanga Boto's people wanted the earth to hide them, they were so miserable and ashamed! What will the unbelievers think now? What will Sanga Boto himself think? Is he beginning to rejoice in his turn?

It was late in the afternoon when some people came here asking the Father to go with them and administer Extreme Unction to an old woman on the point of death. We followed them, accompanied by the catechist and headed for a village about four kilometres from Ekokot. It's part of the parish, but we missed it out yesterday on our visits because it's so far off the route. But the Father was pleased with this opportunity to call on the Christian families of the place after all. We had to cross a river by canoe and we passed without trouble, although it was in flood. The ferryman knew his business and didn't attempt to go straight across. He headed upstream, against the current. But the waves of dark water came right up by the stern and spun us about in a way that terrified me, for I'm not used to rivers or to canoes. Then suddenly the ferryman swung us sharply towards the opposite bank. I was still scared, because we appeared to have gone past the landing-place, but the current brought us in and we finally tied up alongside the canoes already there.

The Father gave the final sacraments to the dying woman, who was in her last agonies. He tried to talk to her, but her jaws seemed locked and she couldn't shape her words. Afterwards we visited the other families with Christian members, before returning to the landing-place where the ferryman was waiting with the canoe. The catechist went in first and advanced to the bows before seating himself, with a firm grip on the two sides of the boat. I followed him and did likewise, being careful also to keep my weight low. Then came the Father, but he made no attempt to crouch down; he stood bolt upright in the middle of the canoe. He had an abstracted air, perhaps because he was thinking of how easily he had worsted Sanga Boto, and he flicked at the water with a thin stick he was holding. The ferryman sat on the flat stern of the boat with his legs hanging right in the water on either side. He seemed perfectly at home, but then he's used to it.

The river was swollen with recent storms and it must have been raining again upriver, for the water was angry and black with mud. The ferryman set off again at the same sharp angle, so as to avoid catching the flood water on his beam. I kept turning round to look at him, perched right out there on the stern. His shorts were ragged and filthy, like an antelope skin stretched out to dry out but which has caught more rain than sunshine. His torso was naked and water kept splashing in his face. I really admired the fearless way he sat out there, leaning dangerously over the water at every stroke of the paddle. He had very long arms and a long torso, with short, strong legs; really a born canoer. He kept grimacing, although he seemed to be paddling us effortlessly along.

The Father was upright in the middle of the boat, looking out over the wild water. He said to the ferryman: 'Well, my man, how are you?'

'Very well, Father. More or less.

'My man,' said the Father, 'my man, I'm glad to hear you are more or less well. Are you a Christian?'

'Oh no, Father, no! I'm simply studying for it. I've already failed twice in the catechist's examination, but I shan't give up . . .'

Meanwhile the canoe had completed its oblique passage across the river and was very close to the bank. But in talking to the Father, the ferryman had let himself be carried by the current. Seeing the situation, he began frantically paddling, but he couldn't avoid the collision. The bows of our boat crashed into the side of one of those tied up at the landing. The shock was tremendous, and both the ferryman and I were hurled into the bottom of the canoe, while the Father and the catechist shot into the water. When we struggled up we couldn't at first see the Father, though the catechist had surfaced between the two boats and was holding them together to prevent our being swept away.

The ferryman leapt into the water in the general direction of the Father's fall and for some time we saw nothing but the heaving back of the torrent. Then the ferryman reappeared, towing the Father at arm's length. He dragged him to the bank and began massaging his chest. The water spurted from him but he lay inert and unmoving on the sand. We called for help and a number of men came running up, pagans for the most part. They carried the Father to the presbytery, where he recovered consciousness and sent them away. Then he got up and changed his clothing, but he soon lay down again, looking quite exhausted. Soon he began shaking with fever. He sent Zacharia to heat water and took a bath in a tin basin, after which he lay down and took some quinine tablets. By now his temperature was 104° . . . I only pray, dear God, that it isn't serious . . . What will Sanga Boto think? What will he say? And his followers, who were all crushed this morning? And what about our own Christians? Just so long as they don't say that Sanga Boto put a spell on him! That would be a real calamity . . .

And how we triumphed this morning! How well everything seemed to go!

Between the Low Mass and the High Mass the Father called

together the catechist, his assistant, the two monitors, Zacharia and me, telling us all to follow him. He stalked along silently with his face screwed up. Zacharia was willing enough to come along, but I think he came only to jeer. He was very smartly dressed and kept chuckling to himself. Our little posse swept through the village, with many people coming to their doors to watch us pass. They all gazed curiously and a few boys followed us at a distance.

Then the Father asked the assistant catechist: 'Which is his house? Don't point at it, whatever you do! Just walk in front of me. Walk in front!'

The young man began leading him, while I marched at his shoulder, along with the catechist and the monitors. Zacharia trailed along behind, looking self-important and unhurried.

We surprised Sanga Boto in his very nest of devilries and lusts. He was a big man, slim and very black, sitting at a table piled with pieces of money and banknotes, which he was counting. He was wearing a cotton singlet and a lappa, tied very loosely around his haunches. When we swept into his large room he looked up with an expression of astonishment, if not fear, eyes staring, mouth hanging open and face crumpled up. His bare feet were resting on his slippers.

The Father demanded of the assistant catechist: 'Is this Sanga Boto?'

The assistant nodded, and without a moment's hesitation the Father seized this limb of Satan by the arm and dragged him clean out of the house. Sanga Boto made no resistance, but had difficulty in following the Father's breakneck pace and kept stumbling over his slippers. He was terrified and began whining: 'Father, Father, what have I done? Why treat me like this? What have I done? . . .'

But the Father pursed his lips and ignored him, pulling him by the hand. He was leaping along with great strides and Sanga Boto came skipping after him. And soon I saw that he had lost his slippers and was finding the path painful to his feet, but the Father just kept blasting along. His lappa began to slip and he grasped it with his free hand, striving to pull the other from the Father's grasp so that he could re-tie it, but the Father hung on like a vice. The lappa fell off and Sanga Boto was dragged shamefully through the village in short cotton drawers. He cried out that he was naked and couldn't enter the village like that, but the Father kept striding on and a crowd of women and children gathered laughing behind us. Some men also began laughing, but these were all young ones. The older men came from their houses and watched us from their courtyards or verandas, with a surly expression.

In this fashion we regained the presbytery. The Father told them to beat the drum for High Mass, although it was early. He rushed into the church, threw Sanga Boto on his knees before the Communion-table and went to put on his vestments.

Sanga Boto knelt there weeping. He wept silently, but I could see the tears running down his cheeks. The two monitors stood behind, guarding him. I also watched him closely. One of his wives came to give him clothes: a blue shirt, a pair of khaki shorts and leather sandals. She was also crying, but she wept too loudly and the catechist told her: 'Get out! You're making too much row!'

She hurried away fearfully. The Father sent for me, but I had been so busy looking at Sanga Boto that I'd forgotten I was to serve the Mass. When I came into the sacristy, the Father said crossly: 'Get ready, then! What are you waiting for?'

The friend who was assisting me was already dressed, like the Father himself. I rushed into my choir-boy's vestments under the Father's eye. We paraded before the altar as if about to begin Mass, but I wondered whether we really would begin at once. After a moment's prayer the Father rose, imitated by my assistant and me, and turned towards the large congregation. I believe many pagans had come also, and all were gazing at us expectantly, as if awaiting a wrestling-match or an unfamiliar play. I glanced quickly at Sanga Boto, who lowered his head. Then the Father bellowed at him: 'Get up!'

He did so, still keeping his head down, and the Father bellowed again: 'Come here!'

He came fearfully towards us, looking much smarter in his new clothes. He's such a funny fellow that I can't be certain he was really scared; perhaps he was just ashamed, or perhaps he was just playing the fool. As we came out of church I heard some of his familiars talking about the incident and they were sure he was simply playing the fool, having no intention of mending his ways or keeping a single one of the promises he had made to the Father.

Sanga Boto stood before the Father like a schoolboy expecting punishment. The Father read some Latin prayers and then made a big sign of the Cross with his right hand, just in front of the penitent. It looked like a benediction, but I suspect it was more of an exorcism. I told Zacharia later that it was an exorcism, a sign for chasing out the devil who had lived so long in Sanga Boto's body; but Zacharia just roared with laughter, saying it was impossible for devils to live in men; men do as they please and the devil has nothing to do with it. He added:

'I myself am the proof of it. They could exorcize me for ten years, and I'd still do just as I please.'

I said nothing in reply. What good would it do? . . .

Yes . . . the Father made that sign before Sanga Boto's face and said to him in a loud voice: 'Sanga Boto! . . . So there you are, Sanga Boto! I've been looking for you a long time and now, here you are, the incarnation of Satan! You came here to deceive my Christians, the children of God. The Apocalypse tells us that many prophets shall come, but they will be false prophets. Now the prophecy has come true. Now look here, Sanga Boto, the God who made us all and is the Father of us all, God whom you never cease to injure, is merciful and just even to the worst of His children, even to you. Because of His mercy, He asks nothing but to forgive you your sins. But His mercy also demands that first of all you reveal to these Christians, to these His children, all the lies and chicaneries you have used to deceive them. Then only will He be ready to forgive you all your sins. He forgets all our faults when we repent. So, speak up! Admit all your villainies. Turn towards them and speak!'

Golly! Then Sanga Boto told them everything. At first he was mumbling and the Father told him to speak up. Immediately he did so, like a child.

He admitted everything: his mirror that was just like any other; the tricks he used to impress people and the stupid questions he asked them: 'You have lost a close relative recently, I believe?' 'You have many enemies, don't you?' As if everyone has not lost a relative 'recently'? And who doesn't have, or suppose himself to have, lots of enemies? I'm amazed they could be taken in by such rubbish, such childishness.

Sanga Boto explained many things. He admitted that he or one of his assistants would hide an evil fetish under someone's threshold or between two thatches of his roof, so that the sorcerer could later find it with a great display of triumph. He would know everyone by name, not by magic means, but because his informants spent weeks in each village before his arrival, discreetly collecting this kind of information.

What a scoundrel!

The audience listened to him in complete silence, without a murmur of disapproval, even a cough. The same people who always coughed throughout the Mass now listened as if to the Messiah himself. It was impossible to judge how they were reacting to him.

When Sanga Boto finally fell silent, the Father began to question him about his supposed cures. Sanga Boto replied: 'I'm not responsible for the reputation of healer that has grown up around me. Sick people came to consult me and after going home they would suddenly imagine they had been cured. Perhaps they really were, I can't tell. But in any case, it wasn't by my means. It isn't my business to heal people, but to try to explain to them why they are unhappy, why they aren't successful and what are the secret causes of their misfortunes. How they will set about avoiding these causes in future is not my affair. And I certainly don't aim to cure their diseases. Once you set out to do that, you are likely to lose your reputation quickly enough, unless you really know the trees and herbs that will help people. But I haven't that knowledge and I don't aim to care for the sick, still less to cure them.'

The Father smiled and made another sign of the Cross before Sanga Boto before asking him: 'Have you been baptized?'

'Yes, Father,' he replied.

'What is your baptismal name?'

'Ferdinand, Father.'

'Well, Ferdinand, God has pardoned you. Go now. But if you really wish to be at peace with Him, if you want Him to be pleased with you as a good father is with his son, let all your wives go, save the one that you love most, and come and see me again when I'm back at the mission. I shall help you, you'll see. But, first of all, you must release your wives and abandon your sorceries.'

The Father fell silent a moment, as if reflecting; then he asked Sanga Boto: 'Do you still remember a prayer?'

'Yes, Father.'

'Which one?'

'Our Father which art in Heaven . . .'

'Very good, my son. You have not altogether forgotten God. Neither has He forgotten you, for you see how He has sent us towards one another. "Our Father which art in Heaven . . ." Do you know who taught that prayer to mankind, Ferdinand?'

'No, Father.'

'Well, it was Jesus Himself! Jesus, the Son of God, and that is the prayer which God loves best. Speak it! Speak it aloud, and let everyone in the church hear you.'

And Sanga Boto recited the Lord's Prayer in a loud voice. Then the people began murmuring together, but I have no idea what they said.

After this we began the Mass, which Sanga Boto heard on his knees beside me. The schoolboys sang execrably and the Father gave many signs of exasperation in speaking the service. My young friend also made many blunders, perhaps because he was scared of the Father.

There were few communicants and some of the crowd began sliding away just before the sermon. The Father spotted them and cried out loudly that the doors should be closed. The catechist ran to close them, but I didn't wait for the sermon because I had to go and prepare the Father's table. As I was taking off my vestments in the sacristy, however, I gathered that he was discussing the church, which has only one brick wall at present. He pointed out that it was likely to remain in this state, unless all the Christians came to work on the building. I listened a moment longer, in case he might mention the black priest who was coming to establish the mission at Ekokot, but perhaps he discussed it later. I'd really like to know what he said about it and whether he repeated his intention of abandoning the country to another. Perhaps he'll change his resolution after all, following his grand success this morning. Isn't it something to be able to say: 'I have brought even the infidels of Tala back to God'? He must also have commented on Sanga Boto's conversion. A real triumph . . . so long as it isn't all spoilt by today's accident.

I found Zacharia in the kitchen when I came from Mass. He was quite cool and kept whistling the tunes they played on the xylophones the other day . . .

I wonder whether we'll leave tomorrow? It all depends how ill the Father is.

There! She's still bouncing about in the other room! Poor thing, she must be bored without her Zacharia. It spoils everything . . .

Well! So Sanga Boto confessed everything, and was really scared! He was even converted. One devil less in the countryside. But what will he make of the accident? . . . The Father was really magnificent this morning. The best part was when Sanga Boto lost his slippers and his lappa, but the Father still dragged him mercilessly along by the arm. And the people laughed so much that the sorcerer turned quite black with shame. I'm sure it was shame that made him cry later, too. Poor fellow! Anyway, everything came right in the end and he'll come to see us soon at Bomba, unless he was just making a play of the whole thing. Personally, I think there's only one way of dealing with infidels and limbs of Satan; with a strong arm, and perhaps the Father has learnt it this morning. He was really his old self, the one I love, the one I know. All the same, it's funny how he has behaved since we started this tour – almost as if he was afraid of people. He lets them talk a lot of rubbish about God and religion, and he actually listens to them. And sometimes, instead of shouting them down, he tries to give them long and careful explanations, almost beseeching them.

If only he isn't too sick. At one time I thought he was actually dead. He was lying inert on the sand with the water pouring out of him and his eyes quite shut. I wept to see him like that. Indeed, I wept so loudly that most of the crowd thought him dead too.

How she moves about, that girl! Yes, Catherine, that's her name. Well, Zacharia was really frightened at first when he saw the state the Father was in. Perhaps he really loves him and has simply taken up this bad habit of poking fun at him. But when he demands a rise, he adopts such a tone that I can scarcely think he's joking. Why does he want so much money anyway? He lives like a prince at the mission, plied with meat, eggs, rice, bread, coffee and milk. And whenever the mission fields are harvested he never takes less than a hundred kilos of groundnuts. The mission has built him a fine brick house too, so why does he want money so much? The Father has even promised him his old bicycle at the end of the year, if he behaves himself. He's really fallen into things! And after each tour he gets a large part of the Father's presents, so he's already got a flock of goats and sheep in his native village. During our last tour, I noticed a really shameful arrangement. The new Vicar, who is an innocent, refused all the presents he was offered. But Zacharia had arranged for the assistant cook, who was in the touring party, to accept all the presents without the Vicar's knowledge and send them off to him at Bomba. When we got back, they divided the booty between them, but naturally Zacharia took the lion's share. When I told my father about it he was angry, because Zacharia hadn't given me any. But I wouldn't lend myself to that sort of deal for anything: it's nothing better than robbery.

But that isn't enough for Zacharia. He has to lug girls about with him on tour too. Ah, if only the Father knew! But I don't intend to get mixed up in it . . .

Oh, the little one is opening her door . . . Is she really going to retrieve Zacharia from the Father's bedside? My God! Where can she be going at this hour? Better not to think of it . . .

This evening the Father was so ill that he took nothing but a hot soup. Just so long as he's well enough for us to leave tomorrow.

Who's knocking at my door? . . . Who can it be? . . . What does she want? What on earth can she want with me now? . . . Ah, that girl . . .

SECOND PART

But, my dear child, a pretty young girl smells just like an apple. And what's so disgusting about that?

Dostoievsky

Ndimi

Monday, 9 February

Oh mother, dear, dear mother! . . . Poor lost mother . . . I feel so alone . . . Why haven't I got a mother like all the other boys my age? Perhaps if I had a mother I wouldn't be so unhappy. Perhaps I would tell her everything. And what would she say? Oh, she wouldn't be severe with me. More likely she would console me. That's what a mother is for, to console her child. How wretched I am! . . .

Oh mother . . . I would so much like to tell the Reverend Father. I want so much to confess myself. But I daren't, I'm too frightened. How frightened I am! . . . I've already served Mass this morning at Ekokot without taking it. What would the Father think? And what would he say if I now confessed myself to him? I looked all through the village to find a boy to serve Mass instead of me; but I couldn't find anyone.

Oh God, what shall I do? I'm so unhappy. And all because of that cursed girl, that Catherine. Ah! She is Satan herself, worse than Sanga Boto! I should have watched out, indeed I should. But how could I have done? How could I suspect that she wanted to make me do that?

It was last night, and I suspected nothing. I was simply lying on my bed and I was worried about the Reverend Father who was down with fever on account of that accident on the river. I thought with terror of all the water he had vomited on the river bank. I suspected nothing. I couldn't know. And she knocked at my door. Before I could get up to see who it was, she was inside, because I'd forgotten to push the bolt. Oh, I should have suspected then! She was in my room. Before I could say anything she struck a match and said: 'Aren't you asleep? Ah, I've caught you thinking about girls, you little wretch!'

I said nothing, I was too surprised. By the brief flare of the match

I saw her white combinations, her naked throat, her breasts which swelled out her garment just where the shoulder-straps began. Already she was sitting on my bed. The match had gone out and it was once again quite dark in my room. I was propped up on my left elbow. In the angle of my stomach and my legs I felt the pressure of her almost naked back. Then she lightly rubbed herself against my thighs, moving her bottom to and fro. And I stayed there, resting on my elbow, saying nothing because I was too astonished. I had never been so close to a girl. And I began to be afraid. My heart was beating with terrible violence and with each beat the blood mounted into my head like a river in spate and made me shake. A devilish tom-tom was pounding in my ears, sirens were screaming in my skull. It sounded as if an aeroplane was loose in there. That girl had unloosed all the cacophony of hell in my head. Why didn't I take warning in time, my God? Oh, that girl . . . I should have watched out. It would have been better to run out of the room. I still wonder what kept me there.

And all this time the bottom of her naked back was there in the pit of my stomach. The bottom of her back which she kept moving to and fro. Once, I moved towards the wall to get away from her touch, but she moved too and I felt her there again more acutely than before. She said: 'I don't know what's wrong with me, I can't get to sleep. And neither can you, it seems?'

I said nothing and she gave a deep laugh. I heard her laughing in little chuckles. She said again: 'Go on, you priest, you! Aren't you ashamed of yourself? A fine little man like you playing at priests. What an idea!'

Still I said nothing. I stayed resting there on my left elbow. She pushed still harder against me, wriggling her hips.

I was helpless with all that racket in my head: bells which clanged away wildly as if it were a day of consecration for a new church; the aeroplane engine which was revving up for take-off; the sirens singing in chorus for some unknown festival, and that accursed tom-tom. Now there were xylophones as well. And that machine which made my whole chest tremble as if I were in a train or riding a lorry on a road torn by the rains.

My throat was dry. She said again: 'Why don't you say something? What's wrong with you?'

Three times I wetted my lips and I managed to say: 'This is my room, not Zacharia's. I came here because it was too stuffy in the other house, but it's my room. . . .'

I noticed that my voice was doing tremolos like the new Vicar when he's singing the Mass.

She laughed and said: 'Do you think I'm going to eat you?' She turned her back to me again.

I felt sweat pouring all over me, on my brow, my hair, my arms, my stomach, my back. I was shivering with fright . . . No, I wasn't afraid; I must have been hot, because I was sweating . . . Agh! I can't say now whether I was cold or hot. I was sweating great drops and at the same time I was shivering as if I'd slept out in the rains. My chest was bursting.

My sex was worrying me, because it wanted to stand up, like it does at dawn when the doves are singing. But there wasn't room for it to stand up; that girl Catherine was pressing against me so hard.

Suddenly I wanted to piss! I felt certain that if my sex, struggling to stand up, went on butting against that girl's naked back, I would finish by wetting my bed. However, I had taken a piss just before going to bed.

She lighted a match and looked at me. Then she asked: 'Why are you so scared?'

I was ashamed.

'Who told you I was scared?' I stammered.

'Who told me! Why anyone can see you're dying of fear!'

'Please go back to your room, I beg you! For the love of God, leave me alone.'

'Be quiet, you little fool. Your Father might hear you. Suppose he finds you here with a girl; what will you say then, eh?'

And I kept quiet. Later, I said: 'Zacharia will be back soon. What will he think? Please go away . . .'

'Listen, you fool, Zacharia isn't coming. He's sleeping somewhere else tonight. And if he does come, I'll say we were talking together. You see, I was right when I said you were scared? Aren't you ashamed of yourself?'

I could do no more and I gave up.

I lay down on my back and she lay close beside me. She turned

83

her back to me. Then suddenly she turned towards me and I stayed still. The need to piss, which had left me for a moment, came rushing back. My sex stood up again, but this time it stood under my night-shirt and was quite free. These jolts were shaking me like a lorry again. For a moment my desire to piss diminished and I said to her: 'What are you doing? What is it you want?'

I didn't really want her to go away any more, I was curious. I pre-ferred her strange and perhaps sinful movements to anything she might say to me. But at the same time it seemed to me proper to speak to her roughly and adopt a high tone.

And all at once I burst into sobs, I really don't know why. I wept in little stifled sobs. My God, You are witness that I cried, that I didn't want to do it. It's all her fault. You know it, I didn't mean any harm. It was she who came into my room when I was thinking of nothing but the poor Father. I wasn't thinking about girls, it isn't true. My God, it was all her fault. You are witness.

I wept and she passed her arm under my head and said: 'Don't cry, my fine little man. A fine little man like you doesn't cry.'

She stroked my cheek and said: 'I'm your sweetheart, you know that. So then . . .'

'I'm going to cry,' I sputtered.

I heard her give her deep laugh again. She said it wouldn't be good for her or for me if I cried. I kept quiet and soon stopped crying. I wanted to ask her questions: how long she had been going with Zacharia, and where she came from, and why I had this feeling that I'd seen her before somewhere. But some kind of shame stopped me from asking those things.

I wiped my tears with my right hand and I found her own hand on my cheek. Our hands mingled finger to finger. She said to me: 'You aren't crying now, are you?'

I said nothing.

She said it was a good thing I had stopped, because a fine young man like me should never cry. What was I thinking of? Had I ever in my life seen a fine young man crying? I hated her talking to me like that but I didn't tell her so.

I didn't feel her hand sliding under my nightshirt, but I trembled when she touched me. I wondered what she was after, but I didn't really suspect anything because it had never happened to me before.

Oh, if only I'd known what she was doing I would certainly have taken care. But I didn't know and that's what has ruined me . . .

How sweetly she smelt, Catherine! She smelt so sweet and her firm breast was pushing against my left arm. For a moment I thought of turning against the wall, but I didn't know what she was doing and so I stayed where I was. And her hand went gliding and caressing down my side and it was cool like a snake. I trembled all over and she laughed at it. I had almost stopped breathing and there was no more noise in my head. Only I felt again a crazy desire to piss . . .

She tickled me; I laughed despite myself. Oh God, You are witness that if I laughed it was despite myself! I laughed when she tickled me and she told me not to make such a noise or someone might hear us. I believe she was really glad to hear me laugh, because up to then I had done nothing but tell her to go away.

She began to tickle me without stopping and I had to hold myself in, in all senses, so as not to laugh. But she kept on and I said: 'Catherine, stop it, please!'

She stopped abruptly, got up quickly and lighted a match, and then bent over me where I was lying on my back. She had a strange look. Everything I admired in her face was there, a few millimetres from me: her pretty teeth which showed when she laughed; her cheeks which went into little curls when she smiled; her small forehead which made one think of a rectangle, her wide eyes . . . And she smelt so sweet!

She said: 'How do you know that my name is Catherine?'

'Easy!' I said, 'I have heard Zacharia.'

She gave a stifled laugh and said: 'I never thought you were listening. You always looked as if you hadn't heard us.'

She gave me a little tap on the cheek. The match went out.

'Guess what my name is,' I challenged her.

'Oh, I know! It's Denis.'

As our hands were now parted, I took hers again and once more we mingled them finger to finger. Oh, that time it was my fault! But I did it without thinking any harm. I don't even know why I did it now.

She gently squeezed my fingers. She was once more stretched out on the bed.

She said to me: 'Turn towards me and lie on your side.'

But I didn't, and she said: 'Don't be afraid, little idiot, I won't do you any harm. I won't tickle you again. You'll see, this will be very nice.'

I turned towards her, not knowing what she was about. Ah, if I had known what she was about, my God, You are witness that I wouldn't have turned. If only I had known!

I turned towards her. I felt her hand glide gently like a snake towards my belly, then on my thigh, then on my leg, down to the sole of my foot. She moved it on to the other leg, climbing slowly up, then on to the thigh, then . . . but she didn't get back to my belly. I felt her hand squeeze between my thighs and she grabbed hold of my sex! I trembled all over and Catherine hissed: 'Don't play the fool! Keep still.'

I didn't stir: I didn't know where I was. I let her do as she wished. My sex was standing right up now and Catherine pressed it and I felt queer. Catherine squeezed me up against her and I could hardly breathe. I felt her hard breast against my chest and my mouth was against her cheek. We were both puffing like mad. I was beside myself and she went on squeezing my sex, which had swollen unbelievably and was now as hard as a piece of wood. There was no more noise in my head, but the need to piss had come back, it flooded me, it rushed upon me most terribly and I said to Catherine: 'Let go! Let me go, I'm going to piss . . .'

She took me in her arms; I thought she was going to pass me over her, but she rolled over on to her back and pushed me against her. She opened her legs and once more grabbed hold of my sex.

And all at once my sex disappeared! And Catherine was moving herself on the bed, to and fro, to and fro, without stopping . . . I was plunged in a swamp and at the same time a fire was raging in my belly. Catherine took my buttocks in her hands and jerked herself about on the bed. She bit my cheek and her firm breasts were thrusting into me. And always that terrible desire to piss . . . Now I couldn't hold it any longer. I said as much to Catherine.

'Piss then! What the hell are you waiting for?'

At that moment I saw that my sex was not cut off, but that it alone was plunged in the swamp, like a foot, while all the rest of me was outside. But it was an odd swamp, which sometimes tightened and sometimes relaxed, and the need to piss came and went in rhythm with it.

'Good God! Piss, come on and piss! What are you waiting for?' said Catherine.

'In a minute, in a minute!' I said.

And I was terribly ashamed. I even said to her at one moment: 'Perhaps it would be better if I went and pissed outside. I don't like doing it in the bed.'

Catherine was cross and said:

'Idiot!'

Then I felt the need to piss passing away quickly like when one frightens a child. Catherine again took my buttocks in her hands and began to move herself about. I was beginning to get tired. She whispered: 'Move! Move like this!'

And I moved. Now I did everything she told me, I was so tired. All the same I moved a certain number of times.

A little snake, a very tiny snake uncurled itself from my spine; without haste, it detached itself and moved its coils through my loins; it thrust itself gently, it glided timidly and furtively into my belly. What I felt now was not the need to piss, but to die. I was going to die! . . . It was a terrible feeling. I wanted to cry out; I believe I did cry out a little. I felt Catherine's hand on my mouth.

Catherine was heaving about wildly . . . I felt myself contracted in a spasm of ultimate agony. . . .

I cannot say what happened afterwards. I think I must have slept, but I'm not certain. And perhaps I had really died and been revived by a miracle. Before her death, my mother often told me of people who had died and come to life again a few moments later. She said it was important they didn't stay dead too long, otherwise they could never get back again. Perhaps that's what happened to me. I really died, and I came to life again a moment later. By a miracle!

And when I awoke Catherine had disappeared. The bed was wet beneath me as if I had pissed in it and I had an itchy feeling all round my sex. It was all scaley, soft and sad. I felt it for a long time. I wondered what had happened, and then I fell asleep again.

It was only this morning that I realized!

It was Zacharia who came to wake me. I couldn't have woken up in time by myself. Zacharia asked me: 'Hey! What's up with you today?'

I got up and Zacharia said I was very late and he would prepare the altar while I washed.

It still wasn't quite light. Catherine brought me water in a basin off her own bat and told me to wash myself and hurry. Zacharia said to Catherine as he went out: 'Get yourself out of here before the Father comes this way. He's in the chapel at the moment, but you never know.'

Zacharia went out, but Catherine didn't go at once. She watched me while I pulled on my drawers under my shirt, because I didn't want to wash myself naked in front of her.

I had pulled up my drawers and was getting ready to wash. I was tired and a bit clumsy, like a drunkard. Catherine came up to me. She took me by the shoulders as my mother used to and then took off my drawers. I was stunned, but I let her do as she wished. She washed me carefully, especially between my thighs. Then she dried me very thoroughly. She put my clothes on. Then she washed my left foot, dried it and put my shoe on. She did the same thing with my right foot. She tied the laces of my shoes as if I had been her child. She buttoned me up from top to toe. She sniffed me for a long time, as if I had let off a bad smell. I was going to serve Mass, but just as I was going out Catherine kissed me on the cheek and said: 'Don't worry about your old Father, he's getting on fine.'

I was clumsy in serving the Mass; I was so sleepy. However, I couldn't afford to make a mistake, and I don't think I did. I thought about what Catherine had done to me the night before and I looked at the Reverend Father; he was as white as a sheet. His face was strangely pale in the wan light of the candles which burned on the altar. He had shaved off his beard and I scarcely recognized him.

I did not take Communion.

In the sacristy I watched the Father take off his ornaments and I saw he was wearing a black soutane. Ever since I became a boy at the mission I had never seen him wear a black soutane.

He must have recovered from yesterday's accident, but he was terribly white. He had never frightened me so much and I began to wonder why. It must have been because of his colour and of Catherine! Every moment I expected him to reproach me for what I had done with Catherine the night before. It seemed to me sometimes that he must know about it, that he couldn't not know it. And I had to try very hard to stop believing this. I came out of the chapel without helping at the usual palaver with the communicants.

At lunch I had the feeling that it wasn't him I was serving, that it was some new priest just arrived from goodness knows where, someone I didn't know. I was expecting him to ask me questions to find out if I was stupid or clever, good or bad, honest or thievish. I expected him to ask me dirty questions, as many white priests passing through the mission at Bomba had already done. I asked myself why he had put on that funereal black soutane, why he had shaved off his beard, why he suddenly wanted to look younger. However, he wasn't as pale as formerly. His colour gradually returned, but I didn't recognize him any the better for it.

The two monitors came in and spoke of Sanga Boto. He had suddenly disappeared during the night. He had taken everything with him; his wives, his court, all his riches, forgetting nothing. And he had put it about that it was he who had engineered the Father's ducking in the river, to give him a little sample of his powers. He said that he could have drowned the Father if he had wanted to. But he had stopped short of that because he was kind-hearted and there was nothing vengeful about him. He had let himself be pushed about and humiliated simply because the Father was a white man and because his brother Vidal, the Administrator, was a terror to the country. He was far more frightened of Vidal, who might throw all of them in prison, than of the Father, who was just another sorcerer like himself. According to the monitors, no one was talking of anything else but Sanga Boto and what he now said about the Reverend Father. Many people believed him hereabouts.

When I came out after giving the Father his lunch, they were still talking. It seemed to me that all that business of the Father and Sanga Boto had happened long, long ago. It seemed to have nothing to do with me, as if I were outside that particular family. And I couldn't re-enter it until I had confessed, which I hadn't the courage for.

I was terrified of telling him all that, I who had always been so

89

pure! The Father would forgive me anything in the world but that. I was sure he couldn't tolerate the idea that I had acted like a little pig with that girl, without even knowing where she came from.

And yesterday I hadn't yet done it! I was still at peace then. Oh, my God! Why, why must I confess it? Must I really? You know quite well that I meant no harm – or only a little – because I let it happen. Dear God, why must I confess it all to the Father? Why did You invent confession? You who see everything, know everything, foresee everything anyway? Can't You pardon me, God, without making me confess?

But it's no good. I know I must confess everything right away, otherwise the Father will begin to suspect. And we still have to do, let's see, Tuesday, Wednesday, Thursday, Friday, Saturday, Sunday – six days of our tour to complete! Six Masses which I shall have to serve without taking Communion! I can't get away with it. The Father is bound to suspect something. My God, how miserable I am! If only it was Jean-Martin, the new Vicar, I'm sure I could tell him everything without hesitation. That one wouldn't be shocked. . . .

But the Father! I, whom he calls his little angel! More of a little Beelzebub than a little angel! What shall I do? Right! I'll get up now, go and find him and tell him everything, from A to Z. That's what I'll do.

No, I haven't the courage, after all.

Two days ago, everything was so nice. I was tranquil and happy. As soon as the doves called at dawn, I got up and served the Mass. As I came out the sunlight was pouring down over the trees and birds were singing in the bush.

Well, everyone is turning away from Christ here now, as if it didn't matter any more. But if the people here are worthless, at least there are good Christians in the rest of the parish. If these reject the religion of Christ, the others have welcomed it and thanks to them Bomba will finish up as a big fine mission. We'll have an organ in the church, a tractor to work our fields and all the rest of it. What does it matter if these people want to wallow in paganism? But I didn't understand. I didn't know how happy I was. When I saw the Father's difficulties here I almost wept, not remembering that everything would be better in the rest of the parish.

And I hate Zacharia! I hated him anyway, but now I'm frightened of him because of Catherine. This morning, the Father went ahead again on his bicycle. Zacharia and I walked along together, and just before we reached Ndimi we caught up with Catherine. Catherine, as always, was waiting on a veranda, and she called out to us. But it wasn't necessary, because we'd already seen her.

We went in. She was prettier than ever and gayer than all the previous days. She had changed her dress and was now wearing a blue poplin one and sandals. She laughed aloud at everything and nothing. She was so much at ease and I was shy, even a little frightened.

She had bought us a calabash of palm-wine. She poured a glass for Zacharia and he drained it straight off. Then she poured one for me, but I said I didn't want to drink. But she put the glass to my lips and obliged me to drink it. She did that three times altogether.

I was drunk and went out several times to piss. Catherine laughed a lot and looked at me knowingly. Zacharia laughed too, but I could see he didn't know anything. I was miserable; I kept thinking how in the coming night he would do that thing with Catherine and I would be all alone in my bed. And I wanted some accident to happen so that somehow I could be alone with Catherine and we could do that again together. I wouldn't be frightened this time.

I looked at her a lot and she kept looking at me and laughing. I wanted terribly to do that thing again, not in the night this time, but by day, so that I could see her naked body, see her breasts, her buttocks, and her sex with its little bush of hair. And my own sex stood up again at the thought and pushed hard against my shorts. Oh, I would have given anything to lift up Catherine's dress!

But all this happened when I was drunk. Forgive me, God, it's just that I was drunk! I wouldn't have dreamt that the Devil could get hold of anyone as he has got hold of me since last night. And I let him do it, wretch that I am! I didn't resist for an instant!

I don't know how things are at Ndimi, but probably no better than elsewhere.

Ndimi is a no-account little village anyway. There is a catechist here, but he beats his wife and she has run away to her parents in her own village. But she turned up again as soon as the Father arrived and accused her husband. This affair took ages to settle.

Several people came to confess, but half of them hadn't paid their fees and the Father chased them off, shouting: Go and confess to the Devil!'

For a moment I thought I could go and confess with the few people remaining in the chapel. Perhaps in this way the Father wouldn't know who I was. But in the end I didn't dare; the Father would certainly have recognized me when he began asking questions.

We visited the village and the neighbouring compounds, but we went into very few houses. And we didn't get many presents; a few chickens and some measley kilos of cocoa. The catechist promised to bring them himself to Bomba if he couldn't find a porter. Anyway, Bomba is not far. For several days now we've been moving in a big circle. Although we were moving away from Bomba for the first six or seven days, now we are approaching it again.

Everyone here knows about Sanga Boto and the Father's accident. Some old women came to weep over Father's miraculous escape from death. They said that Sanga Boto was very strong, an incarnation of Satan in fact. The Father was foolish to attack a man as powerful as that. Better leave it to God Himself to deal with Sanga Boto, when it pleases Him to do so – that's what they said. But the Father looked vacant and didn't seem to listen to them. He said nothing in reply.

And Zacharia's bed has begun creaking!

He disappeared as soon as the Reverend Father had taken his dinner. No sooner had he come than I thought I heard other footsteps after his . . . Catherine! I'm sure it was Catherine! Ah, my Catherine!

But what am I doing? I mustn't think about that girl. After all, it's all her fault that I'm in such a state. She's like an unfaithful wife who's been playing around in her husband's absence and who's frightened to tell him when he returns. All the same, she'll have to tell him sooner or later. Yes, that's what must mark out an unfaithful wife, that boundless shame.

And I, haven't I shame also? Yes, I'm deluding myself. What I'm feeling isn't fear at all, it's shame. All the same, I am a bit scared. And tomorrow again I must serve the Mass without communicating. I looked everywhere to see if I could find a boy who knew how to do it and wanted to, but I couldn't find anyone. The catechist hasn't any children. Apparently his wife is barren and that's why he beats her.

Sometimes, when I serve the Mass without communicating, the Father calls me later and says: 'Don't you want to confess yourself?'

What shall I do now if he calls me like that again? Perhaps I shall tell him then . . .

Zacharia and Catherine are bouncing in their bed and whispering together. I can hear them whispering, but I can't hear what they are saying. I wish I could. Perhaps she's telling him everything . . . Perhaps . . . No, it's impossible, no! She was so sweet with me this morning. She washed me! It's so long since anyone has washed me. It made me think of my mother.

Ziba

What an escape! The Father has really been lucky this time. Another fanatic like this afternoon's and I wouldn't give much for his chances. What a business! Zacharia is right when he says that there's something weird about this country and the Father must watch out. Perhaps it's the forest that makes everyone so wild?

No one suspected a thing. The Father, who hadn't yet started confession, was talking to the catechist in his house and Zacharia was in the kitchen. I was behind the chapel with the catechist's young son, looking for flowers in the bush.

Suddenly we heard many wild and hurried footsteps, then some cries of pursuit, and we rushed out of the bush to see what was happening. I saw this man come running, waving a spear with an immensely long handle. He was wearing a pair of ragged khaki trousers, bare-breasted, and with a tall, lean figure. The veins stood out in his arms, which were as long and thin as his spear. He ran through the glaring sunlight on his long black legs, shaking his spear and panting heavily. His mouth hung open and his eyes were turned up beneath his sweating brows. A crying and shouting mob was chasing after him, calling out: 'Stop, stop! It's me, Bimbo, telling you to stop!'

'It's Abo calling you! Stop at once!'

'Don't you hear Gono calling you to stop?'

'You'll ruin yourself if you do that! ...'

So they kept yelling as they ran after the furious man. And many crying women ran with them.

I was standing in the courtyard of the chapel, which formed an angle with the Father's house. The Father must have heard all the noise, for he came out into the courtyard too. Hands on hips, he stood waiting for the man who careered towards him along the footpath. Now the cries of the people redoubled, all of them calling 'Stop, stop!' or 'Get into the house!' I also wanted to tell the Father to go inside but there was no time, for by now the catechist had also emerged and, seizing the Father by the hand with a loud cry, had jerked him into the house.

The man was now loping slowly along with suspicious glances around him. This enabled his pursuers to catch up and hurl themselves upon him, both men and women together. There was a huge confusion of cries, oaths and tears. They broke the man's spear in pieces and, tearing each of these from his grasp, threw them far into the bush. I realized that what they most resented was the danger of bloody reprisals he would have brought upon them by killing a white.

The Father had come out again and, despite the catechist's entreaties, insisted on remaining. Zacharia was poised in the kitchen doorway, watching everything nonchalantly. The courtyard was a mass of shouting and weeping people which the Father, hands on hips, stood watching silently. The man was still furiously disputing every fragment of his spear with the crowd, until at last they tore the last fragment from him and threw it far off. He got up, his face distorted with anger, his eyes bloodshot and his mouth dribbling. Everyone was now quiet and we heard him panting as if at his last gasp. He began yelling: 'I'm going to kill someone . . . I've got to . . . I feel that I'm going to kill!'

I don't believe he had yet seen the Father. He raved to himself, spinning round in circles, and the crowd made a space around him instead of controlling the lunatic. Only the Father stayed where he was, until the man saw him and cried out: 'Ah, there you are!'

He hurled himself at the Father like a boar, butting his great head against the priest's brow with a sharp crack and sending him crashing into the dust. I burst into tears and ran into the Father's house to find something, a knife, a club, anything with which to kill that wretch. But I found nothing and came out again, still weeping.

Outside, everyone was shouting and crying. I saw the Father sitting up, blood pouring from his nose and a big lump on his forehead. The catechist led him into the house, while the men threw themselves upon the lunatic and stretched him on the ground, swarming over him like bees. I saw Zacharia cleaving indignantly through the crowd, making straight for the swarm in which the man was buried. He kicked three or four times at the swarm and it was scattered. Zacharia seated himself on the man's back and began beating him, especially about the head. The fellow's face was in the dust and he struggling to get up, but Zacharia bore him down with his weight and sought out his eyes, nose and mouth with his blows. Once he picked up the man's head and turned it towards him, giving him several punches in the mouth, while the women raised a fearful din. The man's face was white with dust, which filled his ears, eyes and nostrils and hair. He was trembling and groaning with agony. Zacharia kept hitting him in the most sensitive spots and gradually his face crumpled up, with blood pouring from his nose and mouth. The women wept and the men said: 'Just what he's deserved! We shan't try to defend him.'

Zacharia is a strong boy. How I loved him at that moment! Watching him bash that man, I suddenly lost all desire to cry. He beat the prostrate man until he was almost lifeless, then got up and brushed the dust from his limbs. The villagers picked up their man, who could no longer walk unaided, and carried him away.

We went into the Father's house and I helped Zacharia to beat the dust from himself. The Father was stretched on his back, fully dressed. After a while he sat up and his nose bled no longer. We brought him a basin of water to wash his head in and I brushed all the dust from his soutane while he dried himself. He said he felt fine, apart from a slight headache, but he didn't mention the great bump that still stood on his forehead. He took some aspirin and, at about three o'clock, began to read his breviary, while Zacharia and I went out.

Zacharia was in a rough mood and so was the catechist, who came to control the candidates for confession. He dismissed brutally all those who hadn't paid their cult dues and shouted at them, old women included: 'There's only one person who can confess you: Satan! Yes, Satan!'

I went to help Zacharia in the kitchen and for once he was preparing the food himself. He was still in a foul temper.

When the catechist had finished at the chapel he came to join us. He brought a small calabash of palm-wine for Zacharia, who gave me one glass of it. This wine was sweet, just how I like it, and I drank it, for since Catherine made me drink all that wine yesterday I've had a constant thirst.

The catechist said: 'It's fantastic!'

We sat in silence.

Zacharia looked thoughtful, most unusual for him, and he said to the catechist: 'Where's the Father? Do you know where he is?'

'Yes, he's in the confessional.'

Zacharia drummed pensively on the empty case he was sitting on and said: 'I'm always telling the Father to take care, but he's always too trustful. Nevertheless, I've said to him often enough that things here are different from on the main road. Here they don't give a damn, for life is good – plenty of cocoa, palm-wine, peace and so forth. No forced labour on the roads, no tax-collectors, no soldiers and policemen. So, naturally, they mock at him. On the roads they hope he may be able to protect them, but here they have no need of him. They laugh at religion here . . .'

He fell silent a moment and continued tapping on the box. Then he drank a glass of wine and said: 'All the same, I keep telling the Father to take more care. But he can't see that he exasperates them. He still happily babbles to them about Jesus Christ and a lot of other guff like that . . . How he talks! He gives them the whole lot. But the people are changing. Ten years ago, even in a bush place like this, people took things quietly. They let themselves be baptized and what-have-you, just to see what it was like. But now, it doesn't interest them . . .'

Once again he was silent. Really, I wonder if he isn't right. When he talks like this, without boasting, I can't help wondering if he isn't right.

The catechist said: 'It's really terrible. No one is interested any more, except the women. Only the women have religion in their blood; the men are completely indifferent. They claim that there's no difference between a Greek trader and a priest, even one like Father Drumont. And for evidence, they point to the wealth of the Catholic missions, all the presents which the Father collects and all the cult dues. They say the Father is as greedy a tax-collector as the Administrator. And as for the cult dues, what is the point of them? But they love him all the same. So long, at least, as he doesn't hide their fugitive wives in the sixa and doesn't humiliate people like Sanga

Boto. For here they all have faith in Sanga Boto, who says he has been charged by the ancestors to struggle against the whites. He claims that all whites are the same, whether they come as traders or as priests. All of them have the same ends, he says. Ah yes, it's really very difficult . . .'

They both drank another glass of wine and Zacharia replied:

'Our mission is really rich and big; it makes me very happy to work in such a place. But the Father doesn't seem to realize how rich and important it is. The people are still very faithful, especially along the roads. It's only here that everything's going to pot. With the roadside Christians alone, the Father could build up the mission as much as he likes; he could build a new brick schoolhouse, buy an organ, a tractor, some lorries and a groundnut-oil machine. He could have everything he wants just from their pockets alone. Already our church and our Fathers' house are among the finest in the whole country. But he must take it into his head to win the people of Tala at all costs. This is what obstinacy leads to . . .'

The catechist got up and Zacharia said: 'Well, how about doing me the favour I asked of you just before that stupid business happened? There's a village near here whose name I forget, but it's on the path we came by. You'll find her there, and her name's Catherine. A smashing girl, splendid legs and eyes . . . and what tits! You'll find her there; off you go! Tell her you're coming on my behalf and say that I'll come myself this evening to find her at my friend Mbo's place.'

The catechist laughed aloud and said: 'For a man who spends his days beside the Father, a saint, almost a martyr, you are very close to Hell, my dear Zacharia. It's like one of the bad angels . . .'

But Zacharia laughed himself and replied: 'Oh, as for that, you know I'm not a man of God . . . not even a catechist. I work for my master and that's the end of it.'

'But all the same . . .' murmured the catechist, and off he went.

We didn't see Catherine this morning. She was supposed to be waiting in that village and must have seen us pass, but she didn't dare hail us because we were walking with the Father. Yes, that must be it. She didn't dare, because the Father didn't go ahead of us today, the road being too rough for his bicycle.

This road is really bad, all grown up with bushes which no one bothers to clear and all the footbridges swept away by the rains. So the Father pushed his bicycle and we walked with him as far as Ndimi. Catherine must have been waiting there for us but hadn't the courage to call out.

What a road! Nothing but a trail in places. And as we came along we met some women. We heard them singing in the distance, the usual songs about the man they love, and how fine he looks, and how he must buy them dresses and head-ties. When they came round the corner of the path and saw us, they all fell silent, scared of the Father. And as they came abreast they all chanted in chorus: 'Jesus Christ be praised!'

The Father greeted them, all the same. I didn't think he would. They were all carrying baskets of cocoa on their backs to sell in the town. They'll reach there tomorrow morning and that's why they were so gay.

We also crossed some fields and saw women working bent in the sunlight, hoeing the soil and planting groundnuts. There were many fields lying side by side on either hand in the vast clearing. Where the women had finished planting, the fields were all scattered with little breasts of earth. The Father looked around contentedly as we walked through the fields, and every time we came level with a group of women they stood up and called: 'Jesus Christ be praised!'

The Father answered them tirelessly. Whenever he recognized one of these women, he stopped to talk to her and ask her questions. How was she? . . . And how about her children? . . . And her husband? . . . And how many children had she now?

Now and then the pathway plumped into a great puddle of water. How on earth does the Administrator manage to pass this way on his motor-bike?

Ah, yes! After the Father's accident we had a visit from M. Vidal. It was after four and the Father had finished confession; he was pacing about the courtyard reading his breviary.

Suddenly M. Vidal appeared, riding his motor-bike with the usual soldier in the side-car. He leapt off and ran towards the Father, who closed his breviary and stood awaiting him.

M. Vidal seemed nervous and disquieted, looking anxiously at the Father as he took off his helmet. Then he bowed slightly and said: 'Good day, Father! I've had that fellow locked up by the police of the nearest chief. Yes, he's in the sub-division prison right now. My goodness, what a swine!'

The Father smiled and said: 'What fellow are you talking about, Vidal?'

'What fellow? Why, the one who nearly killed you! Yes, that one . . . I was only about six kilometres away and someone came to warn me. I came dashing over to protect you. Oh, admittedly I am a bit late! But all the same, I've clapped him inside.'

'I'm devoted to you, my dear M. Vidal, but I have no need of your protection,' said the Father.

'Indeed, Father! . . . But, anyway, I'm not asking your advice. If a fellow makes a prick of himself, I lock him up, and there's an end of it. That's my job. If you want another martyr to this blasted climate – Strewth!'

'So! You seem to have changed your tune!'

'My tune, no. You exaggerate. But this sun is really beyond itself. And then, like you the other day, I've got the blues.'

'Impossible!'

'O.K. Laugh away if you like.'

'And what about the road?'

'Soon, Father, soon. We shall start work one of these days. Ah, that will change my mood all right! I can't wait.'

'And . . . do they know?'

'Who?'

'The natives, naturally; the most interested parties in every sense.'

'Oh, them! They'll know soon enough. Listen, Father. I have a proposal to make: all those who are Christians, I shall exempt from the work. Won't that be a help, eh?'

'You make me ashamed, my dear Vidal.'

'So, it's understood. But tell me, why did that nigger want to do you in?'

'To begin with, he's not a nigger. I detest that expression.'

'And what importance does that have, a mere expression? Did you understand me, or not?'

They went together into the Father's house and I gave them Cinzano. They drank and lighted up; then the Father said: 'Well, it was a very common sort of case. One night a woman came to the mission, demanding our protection.'

'Protection against what, Father?'

'Protection against her father and her husband.'

'How come?'

'It's a long story. Her husband, who was really only her fiancé, had paid half the sum that was asked of him. He had promised solemnly to pay the rest as soon as possible and had got his wife on the strength of that promise.'

'Ha, ha, ha! Only the Americans would make a half-sale like that. So?'

'He went off with his wife. But, when the time came, he proved to be a bad payer. As you can imagine, he wasted no time in getting the marriage registered at the sub-divisional office. But, to his mind, the price was too high. For his part, the father refused to lower it by a single cent. So they had a long series of palavers before the chief, which raised the young man's hopes.'

'And what did the chief say?'

'He put all the blame on the young man, because he hadn't kept his word.'

'Do you know roughly what the bride-dowry was?'

'Several thousand francs, as usual.'

'But the chief knows that the legal maximum is five hundred francs.'

'Don't be a donkey, my dear Vidal. You know that the natives always find ways of getting round that. The chief couldn't do a thing. Especially as the colonial authorities never give them much support in affairs of that kind.'

'Go on with your story, Father.'

'Well, one day the father decided that he'd been begging for his rights long enough. He went to the young man's house with a gang of men more or less related to him. They would have torn the girl away from him, if the young man hadn't managed to call up a gang of his own people, also more or less related to him, to drive them off. After an indecisive struggle, the attackers retired to their village, swearing to come back again in force.'

'And what of the girl; did she take sides in this affair?'

'At heart she was with her husband, all right. But, in justice, she wanted him to acquit himself with her people. But in any case her opinion counted for very little in the matter, I must remind you. In the end, she decided that the best solution was to seek refuge at the Catholic mission.'

'The Catholic mission? You're joking! Why there? Why not at the regional prison?'

'I've already told you that this happens often. Usually I call together the husband and the father and bring them to agreement. Then they ask to be baptized, as a token of gratitude, and everyone is happy.'

'Ah, ah, ah! . . . In fact, everything ends up to your advantage!'

'To the advantage of Christ, my dear Vidal.'

'No!'

'Yes, my friend, to the advantage of Christ.'

'Christ or no Christ, you're a rascal. So then . . .?'

'This time it wasn't so easy. I must admit that I've failed all along the line. Perhaps the times themselves are changing? Or is it just the Tala country that's so intractable? Anyway, despite all my summonses, this young man would not agree to come and talk with me at the mission. And, on the other hand, he seized every possible opportunity to demand the return of his wife.'

'And where did you stow this wife of his? In your sixa, no doubt?'

'Certainly, in the sixa. She lived there with fifty or sixty other girls, while I made every effort to get her man to come and meet me at Bomba. All this time, he was nagging the catechist here, laying siege to him for days at a time, demanding his wife and insisting that the catechist was my right-hand man. If you can believe it, he bombarded me with long letters stuffed with insults and threats. And he forced the catechist to carry these letters to me at Bomba, charging him: "Tell your boss that if you don't come back with my wife, you're a dead man." '

'What!'

'Yes, as I say. One day the catechist got frightened and didn't return to Ndimi, so I was obliged to send another catechist who had more courage.'

'Well, I can see you have a hard life. But let's look at it again. What was this affair to begin with? A simple civil case, wasn't it? And what right have you to meddle in the matter? It was no concern of yours. It was rather a matter for us. I have caught you in flagrant trespass upon the civil domain. Do you understand how serious that is, Father? It's very serious.'

'Perhaps it was really your affair, but you generally handle such things so clumsily . . .'

'Just a minute, Father. This young man very nearly finished you off. You seem to have forgotten that.'

'And what does that prove, my dear Vidal?'

'Listen to me: no one has ever come near to killing one of *us*. No one, do you hear me?'

'What do you know about it, Mon-sieur-the-Ad-min-is-trat-or? Anyway, you have your sharpshooters to look after you. Look at your motor-bike now. Do you observe that curious object in the side-car?'

'And you, Father; what about all your catechists, pray? I recall that this man had his face completely bashed in. Who was responsible for that little job, eh? One of my sharpshooters, perhaps? Or perhaps Christ Himself? It seems that He meddles a good deal.'

'My cook was a bit annoyed; one can hardly be severe with him for that.'

'Ah yes! A proper little rascal, your cook.'

'That may be your opinion.'

This Administrator is really an odd man: it's impossible to tell when he's joking and when he's in earnest.

After a long silence, the Father resumed: 'My dear Vidal, I don't wish to dispute your rights. But there's one aspect of the matter that interests me more than any other. This woman cannot go back to her home now without asking for a Christian marriage.'

'Really?'

'Yes, it always works out like that; it's like a regular epidemic. They are always coming to seek refuge with us, for one reason or another. And once they are in the mission, they are gradually persuaded, with the assistance of the catechism classes, that only the sacrament makes a union strong and respectable.'

'But it's only the Christians who think that way.'

'Oh, pagans too, Monsieur Vidal, I assure you. They are all impressed by a church wedding. You know how it is: the songs, the rituals, the bells and long white trains. For they all wear white trains here, even those who've had a string of babies before marrying.'

They both laughed heartily and the Father went on: 'Then the wives tell their husbands that they will indeed come home, but only on one condition – a church wedding. But you are aware, no doubt, that this ceremony also requires a single condition – baptism.'

'So, the trick is done. This is certainly no work for amateurs.'

'But it still didn't catch with this young man. He began nagging the new catechist as well. And he continued sending threats of death to me at Bomba. But I didn't take them too seriously; I thought he was just a loudmouth.'

The Father was calmly gazing out through the declining sunlight. I filled the Administrator's glass for the fourth or fifth time, and he quickly sank it again. He cracked a few jokes to make the Father laugh and got up to leave. He said, laughing: 'Have no fear, Father. I'll look after you. I've always told you we are both in the same boat. You still don't believe me, but one day you'll see . . . It's getting late, Father. I must move.'

'My dear Vidal, I'm asking you as a personal favour to let him go.'

'Let who go? That fellow? . . . Ah, no! So that he can come and polish you off? No, thank you.'

'But he can't, you know. You said yourself that he's all beaten up.'

'Ah, but you don't know these niggers; they just don't feel pain. If you could see him again now, you'd find he's forgotten it already. Ah, ah, ah!'

'Monsieur Vidal, I entreat you.'

'You must be a real masochist. But don't count on me to satisfy your masochistic tendencies.'

'Don't play the fool.'

'Very well; it's understood. Since you're so set on it, I give you my word as a *gentleman* that your little amateur assassin will be freed two days after your departure.'

He came close up to the Father and murmured: 'Listen, I don't want to be mucked about with. If this lout settles your hash for good and all, fine! You'll go straight to Heaven . . . yes, in the end, fine! As for me, in the meantime, I shall stay here on earth.'

'Is it a promise?'

'Yes, yes, certainly; it's a promise.'

Monsieur Vidal left at six o'clock, saying that perhaps he would encounter the Father again before his return to Bomba.

The Father returned to his breviary. I went to the kitchen and found his chop ready and set to warm near the fire, but there was no sign of Zacharia. Then I went to prepare the altar for the Mass tomorrow morning. The catechist's son had managed to find some very pretty flowers for it. A boy like this would have been my salvation at Zibi. He's at our school in Bomba and I didn't expect to find him here. He came home to see his parents and couldn't get back to Bomba for the beginning of the week. He will serve the Mass tomorrow in my place.

What a relief! But for him, I would again have had to serve the Mass without communicating. Please God, forgive me, even without confession, since all the same You see, hear and know everything. Just the idea of confessing that to the Father is torment. Will he want to know all the details? And he will know that I've done that thing with Catherine!

Perhaps he'll ask me who Catherine is and where she comes from. And that may bring other complications. Oh, I see it all!

Anyway, I can surely communicate without having confessed. What's to stop me? God, who sees all and knows my repentant heart, will forgive me. Crikey! What a business. Later, I shall confess myself to Jean-Martin. I'm sure he won't be shocked and wouldn't worm all the details out of me.

The Father came to table at eight o'clock. The catechist ate with him and I waited on them. During the meal, the Father told the catechist that he was probably making his last tour in Tala. The catechist exclaimed: 'Are you going back to your own country, Father? Have you had some bad news?'

'No, I'm not going home. At least, I hope I'm not going so soon. But it's possible they'll entrust Tala to another mission, unless they start a new mission at Ekokot. In either case, Tala will no longer be my concern.'

'But, Father, you know that if you abandon this country everything will be lost. You know it, Father. Everything will be lost.'

'Oh, I'm not so sure. Suppose they send a priest who can get on with the Talas, a black priest, for example? Or suppose that a great misfortune strikes the people, they'll return to God fast enough. And perhaps that misfortune is even now approaching, perhaps it is at hand. But I love them too much to wish to witness their suffering. So, I prefer to abandon them.'

I believe he was talking about the road. The catechist was struck dumb; perhaps he thought this was a phophecy.

After taking his chop, the Father went through the Zibi registers with the catechist. Just as I was leaving, the Father asked me if I was very tired. I said no.

'Poor angel!' said the Father. 'He wept so bitterly when that man tried to kill me.'

He smiled at me and I tried to smile back.

'Are you sure you're not too tired?'

'Yes, Father, quite sure.'

'Well, go and polish my shoes then. You're a good lad.'

While I was polishing his shoes, the Father began questioning the catechist. He asked why the number of practising Christians had fallen from two hundred to less than fifty. The catechist went into a long rigmarole, but I didn't follow all of it . . .

Ah! There's Zacharia coming back at last . . . There! Some more footsteps following his . . . Catherine, of course. Only just in, and already they're murmuring together.

I haven't seen Catherine since yesterday and I'm so longing to see her. Perhaps she's forgotten me already . . . perhaps she's forgotten that she washed me yesterday morning and rubbed so hard between my legs. I do so want to see her again. Catherine . . . My God, I mustn't think about her! . . .

Yes, I didn't catch just how the catechist explained that huge drop in numbers. I was looking at the Father, still wearing his black soutane, and thinking that one of these days I must surely confess to him. And I was wondering what expression his face would take, what gestures he would make and what reproaches he would heap on me for doing that with Catherine.

Perhaps he would be so disgusted that he'd set off straight away for France. My God, don't let him abandon us all . . .

Already Zacharia's bed is creaking and I'm falling asleep . . . I wonder where I've seen Catherine before . . . I remember there was a big grey stain on the sheet on Monday morning at Ekokot. I just hope the catechist didn't think things when he found it. But he'd have thought something, anyway, because stains like that are not made in so many different ways . . .

Akamba

I feel so tired and heavy-headed; perhaps I'm getting a touch of fever. I've eaten scarcely anything today. I have no interest in food while I feel so down.

Yet it needs so little to put everything right; all I have to do is find the Father and tell him all about it. Perhaps he won't even fly into a rage and demand all the details. All the same, it will pain him; oh, I'm sure it will pain him and make him feel deceived! Perhaps he'll feel quite ill with disgust. How bitterly ashamed I am!

And this is what I've been brooding on all day. No wonder I have no appetite.

My head really feels quite heavy, almost feverish. And perhaps a bout of fever is the best thing that could happen to me. But I don't believe I've really got fever yet.

I was obliged to serve the Mass at Zibi this morning. The catechist's boy overslept and I didn't know which house he lay in, otherwise I'd certainly have woken him. I waited till the very last minute, then I was forced to serve it myself...

How rotten I feel! . . . This morning I lowered my head with shame when the Father left the altar and came level with me at the Communion table. If only the tour were over, I could unburden myself of all this torment with Jean-Martin. . . .

I followed him at the Communion table, distributing Communion to the worshippers. These were mostly old women, plus a few children. I didn't feel so bad while I held the napkin under their chins. While he distributed Communion, the Father was reciting: *Domine non sum dignus ut intres sub tectum meum, sed tantum dic verbum et sanabitur anima mea* . . . And it seemed to me that he raised his voice unusually in reciting this prayer. Sometimes he raised his eyes to mine; then I would look away until his gaze was distracted again.

But the fear of his glance was with me all the time . . . *Domine non sum dignus* . . . To tell the truth, I spent the whole service in a frenzy of apprehension that he would look at me again. Yet he only did so two or three times.

I felt too ill to attend the palaver afterwards. I went straight out of the church and we left Zibi a little later. The path improved a lot after leaving Zibi, but it passed at first through a stretch of thick forest, dark, moist and silent.

A turning of the path brought us to a river which was somewhat swollen. Rains farther upstream had carried away the bridge and blocked our passage. Zacharia took off his shoes, picked up the Father and carried him on his shoulders into the water. I too took off my shoes and pushed the Father's bicycle into the river. The water only rose to my knees, but the current pulled at the spokes of the bicycle. Zacharia and the Father watched my struggles with amusement from the farther bank. Nevertheless, I finally succeeded and the Father congratulated me. We put on our shoes and recommenced our march, with me still pushing the bicycle.

A bit later, while still deep in the forest, we saw the women who were carrying our loads. They were standing beside the path and we could see that they had waded the river like ourselves, for their legs were wet to above the knee. All three of them stood in line gazing up into a tree with expressions of mingled curiosity and fright. We also gazed up in the same direction . . .

At first I could see nothing but squirrels and birds leaping around and creating a frightful racket overhead. With their tails straight up, the squirrels shook rhythmically as they screamed in chorus, going off like so many guns in salvo. The birds too, of every size and kind, kept screeching as they fluttered from branch to branch, but all their gyrations were around a fixed point.

Zacharia and the Father saw the snake before I did. They began speaking of it but I didn't hear them, being quite absorbed in the antics of the birds and squirrels. It was a long black snake clinging to a big branch and following all the contortions of the wood with its body. It lay quite motionless, as if dead. But a ray of light falling on it through the foliage made its whole body flash and glisten, as though waves of brilliance were pulsing to and fro all along it. This was only an illusion, however, for in reality the snake didn't stir amid all the cacophony and fluster of the other creatures. It had a sort of swelling in its neck, just behind the head. The women said that was made by a bird it had just swallowed, and this was why it lay there quite still, digesting the meal. This was also why the birds and squirrels were pestering it so loudly.

The snake was right above our heads and the Father lamented having left his gun behind, for he usually brings it whenever he goes on tour.

Just after this we entered a new section of the path, where it ran wide and level between two strips of cleared land and everything was drenched with sunlight. Here the Father mounted his bicycle and ran on ahead of us. Once again, we found Catherine waiting in the last hamlet before our destination. How pretty she is! . . . I don't hate her any more, I'm sure of it. It's true that I'm still very upset about what she made me do, but I don't hate her any more . . . And sometimes I imagine being alone with her again and once more . . . Forgive me, my God! I only let my thoughts stray like that when I'm not concentrating properly. But now I'm quite certain I've seen Catherine before. Where was it? I still can't bring myself to ask. But I'm sure that any day now the whole thing will be clear as daylight. I'm sure something will happen soon that will make it all plain . . .

Catherine was looking so charming that we stayed a long time with her, drinking palm-wine. Once Zacharia went out to piss and Catherine came over to kiss my cheek. After that, every time he went to piss, I crossed over to Catherine and kissed her cheeks, her neck and her eyes. She smelt so nice. Once she took me in her arms and squeezed me against her firm breasts and I began panting because she smelt so sweet. When my sex stood upright and I felt that same strange desire to piss, I realized that this game with Catherine was turning into sin, but even so I didn't leave her at once. Now it isn't only a single sinful act I have to confess to the Father, but several, all of them committed with Catherine! . . . And it's almost certain that he'll ask all the details, where I've met Catherine before and how I met her again and so on. Oh, I'm sure there isn't another man in the world as miserable as I am! . . .

Akamba is quite a big place, but I didn't have time to find someone to serve the Mass instead of me. I went with the Father and the catechist to visit the country, which has become beautiful again after a dried-up stretch. Here the villages are large and populous, full of fine houses, and the paths are so lined with cocoa trees that you can see nothing else as you walk along.

We visited various Christian mothers and they gave us plenty of eggs and chickens. But whenever we stayed long with one of them, the husband would appear with a displeased air. Here they are very hard on their women and extremely jealous.

As we were returning to the presbytery, we passed a big house with a pan roof, before which a number of girls were dancing amidst a tumult of drums and xylophones. As soon as we appeared they stopped playing and the girls gave over dancing till we were some distance off; then they all started up again.

The Father said: 'They are always scared of me!'

The catechist outbid him with: 'Yes, Father, they are really terri-fied of you.'

He was carrying the chickens tied together by the feet and they made one great squeaking package in his hand.

'Why are they so scared of me?' asked the Father.

'Well look, Father, aren't you the representative of God on earth?'

'But they don't believe it. I am nothing to them now, so they have no reason to fear me.'

'One is still fearful of the Good Lord, Father, even when one doesn't obey him.'

'You don't think that they are more scared of me as a white man?'

The catechist thought hard for a moment and said: 'Perhaps so, Father. Perhaps it is rather the white man they fear. But even if you were a black priest, they would still fear you a little, and they'd stop dancing as you went by.'

The Father walked ahead of us with his steel-tipped leather soles beating on the hard earth. Then he turned and asked the catechist: 'Tell me, if the witch-doctor caught them breaking any of his com-mandments, would they also fear him?'

'What do you mean, Father? Of course they would be frightened . . .'

'But why? The witch-doctor doesn't represent God!'

'No, Father, but he represents the Devil, and the Devil strikes terror also.'

As for me, I believe the catechist was in the right of it. But the Father fell silent and said nothing more for a long time afterwards. Then he asked the catechist what the people were saying about Sanga Boto. According to this chap, everyone around here knows about the Father's dust-up with him, but most of them refused to take sides in the matter. Some of the old people championed Sanga Boto, and the Christians naturally supported the Father. But most people applauded the Father when he captured Sanga Boto and applauded the sorcerer when the Father was nearly drowned in the river by his bewitchment. For here everyone is unshakeably convinced that this was Sanga Boto's doing and the sorcerer himself has not been slow to confirm the fact. So much so, he continued, that if Sanga Boto and the Father were to hold a football match in the village square, everyone would expect an equal contest. At this point the Father laughed softly.

'Do you know whereabouts Sanga Boto is just now?' he asked.

'No, Father, I don't. But you can be certain of one thing; he's got his wits about him now. Anyway, he knows your itinerary quite well and he certainly isn't going to cross your path. Quite the opposite, in fact; he's keeping well clear of you.'

Zacharia and the catechist were both present while the Father was taking his chop, and he talked to them a lot. Zacharia was leaning against the wall of the room, the catechist sat beside the Father and I was standing in the shadows behind him.

The Father paused in his eating and said: 'Oh, what a business! . . .'

After a while, he continued: 'I have worked nearly twenty years in this country! . . .'

And a bit later: 'It's been a pure waste of time, believe me . . .'

A bit later: 'There are so many things I should have seen long ago, if I'd only had the sense to notice them . . .'

Another pause, then: 'My God, what it is to be oblivious! . . .'

He wasn't at all angry. His face was touched with sadness. How I pitied him! How painful it is to see him so!

I could hardly bear to hear him talking all alone like that. I think Zacharia felt the same, for he spoke up as if to break the Father's monologue: 'Father, what did that young Administrator tell you yesterday? Did he speak again about that road of his?'

'Yes,' said the Father, 'he told me they will start work soon; it's only a matter of weeks now.'

Everyone fell silent, the Father eating and the others watching him. Finally, Zacharia spoke again: 'Don't give up the country, Father. People are going to change, I'm sure of it. They are going to have need of you here. Didn't you always say that all they need is a test to make them take the better way? Now that the test is at hand, you talk about abandoning the country to others. That's really strange; it's you who should harvest the fruits of all your efforts. Perhaps it's true that your efforts here have been a pure waste, but surely you should all the more be ready to wait a little?'

The Father stopped eating altogether and raised his eyes with a look of stupefaction upon Zacharia, who stood before him. Then he asked: 'Are you serious or are you joking?'

'Why should I be joking?' asked Zacharia nervously.

Then the Father burst out laughing. He laughed so long and loud that I feared he would spit out a mouthful, but mercifully he clapped his napkin to his face and prevented it. By the time he stopped laughing he was bright red.

'And it's you who tell me that!' he exclaimed.

At the same time he searched Zacharia with the wide gaze he has been turning on everyone lately; it's as if he saw them all, even the most familiar, for the first time in his life. And he said to Zacharia: 'I know you, you are the Devil, ah, ah, ah! You want to tempt me, not so? You have already forgotten what you said to me the other day about this road, eh?'

He laughed, but his face looked sad all the same and I saw that this was not the Father of old, always jolly or in a rage, never sad – for sadness is only for weaklings – always active, always bustling people along, waking them up and driving them to work.

'Father, I have been thinking since then. I feel I was wrong to talk to you like that, because this road business is nothing to do with you. They want to drive a road through, round up the people and flog them, but it's certainly not your fault. You have always been on our side, Father . . .'

The Father said nothing at first. He began eating again, but suddenly he stopped, as if smitten by a new thought. He drank a glass of wine, wiped his face and signed to me to clear the table.

While I was doing so, he spoke again: 'Look, Zacharia, the whites come here to ill-treat the blacks, and when the blacks feel really miserable they will run to me and cry: "Father, Father, Father . . ." all those who didn't give a fig for me before. And I am supposed to baptize them, to confess them and bury them. And this happy turn of events I owe to the wickedness of the whites! . . . But I, also, am a white man.'

'But you have always been on our side, Father,' cried the catechist.

'That doesn't stop my being a white man. And the Apostles of Our Lord also addressed themselves first to white men, but they couldn't change them or turn them from wickedness. Now the same whites have come here to inflict their cruelties on you. I refuse to draw profit from their malice; I cannot. And Christ refuses also. Look, it would be like the people of Saba. You know the reputation of that tribe, how they always travel in pairs? The first one walks far ahead, days ahead, sowing evil spells on every side; everyone falls sick as if there's an epidemic. Days later, the second Saba arrives; he takes pity on all the sick and sets about curing them. Naturally he knows how to but he demands piles of money for every cure he makes. And every coin he collects depends on his brother, who went ahead sowing misfortunes right and left. I don't believe in these pagan superstitions myself, and I use it just as a comparison, as a parable. But I have no desire to imitate the little comedy of the Saba.'

The Father gazed questioningly at Zacharia, and he replied: 'Perhaps it isn't really the fault of the whites, that they treat us so badly. Perhaps it is simply the will of God. After all, think of the Flood. That rain didn't fall for nothing, Father.'

'Ah . . . ah . . . ah . . . ah . . . ah! Zacharia, what a terrible fellow you are,' the Father exclaimed. 'Are you trying to say that God created white men just for the affliction of the blacks, and for their salvation? It's a clever idea, and may even be true, but all the same I find it a sad one. Anyway, I don't know the answer. All I know is that I'm tired out and I need peace and calm to reflect on all these things.'

Everyone was silent. I looked searchingly at the Father. The great lump on his brow was rapidly subsiding, perhaps because it had been so localized before. I wondered why he had laughed so strangely when Zacharia suggested that the whites might be tormenting us by God's will. It wasn't at all his usual laugh.

At last, the Father spoke again: 'Anyway, misfortunes don't last for ever. When their sufferings pass, will the people remain good Christians? Will they not return to their faithless ways?'

Zacharia said nothing; he stood thinking with a hypocritical smirk.

The Father asked him: 'And you yourself, do you believe in God?'

'Of course I do, Father. Why should you ask?'

'Good. And are you a good Christian?'

'What do you mean, Father?'

He sounded quite peeved and I thought he must be put out to discover that the Father was no longer deceived completely by his little tricks.

'And will remain so always?'

'Certainly! Always . . . even till death.'

But he couldn't avoid answering the Father's questions and I was delighted to see him in a hole for once.

'Don't you sometimes long to take a second wife?'

In my heart I knew that I had little right to vaunt myself above Zacharia, seeing what my relations were with Catherine. For at first it was mainly on account of Catherine that I had disapproved of him so much.

'A second wife? Oh, no, Father! Certainly not.'

'Are you quite sure?'

'Yes, I am sure.'

'All right, I believe you. I ask nothing more than to believe you. And you, catechist?'

'Me, Father? I am certainly a good Christian and there's no reason for me to change. I hate all witch-doctors and I have no desire to take wives. In any case, I haven't the money.'

The Father laughed a lot at that. Then he got up, saying: 'Well, it looks as if catechists and mission cooks are the only good Christians among the men here. I have longed so much to see men sincerely practising their religion.'

'But what about the roadside people, Father?' protested Zacharia.

'Oh, they may not last so long. Just now, they are plagued by the administration and they know that, unlike the other missionaries, I am with them at heart. That's probably the only reason why they put on the appearance of true Christians – in simple gratitude! But one day, when they no longer have need of me . . .'

It was now late and the rest of us went off to sleep, leaving the Father alone in his house . . .

Catherine is in with Zacharia, I can hear them whispering and bouncing on the bed. When I think that Zacharia has just been assuring the Father that he has no wish for a second wife!

Tomorrow I shall again serve the Mass without communicating. What will the Father think of it?

He has turned so funny lately; he's always probing, explaining and listening. Until now, he never explained, never questioned and never listened to anyone. He just gave orders and everything went perfectly. Just so long as he doesn't renounce Tala!

Teba

Everything is turning out as I feared. The tour is now really heading for disaster and it's almost upon us! Oh my God, what a mess!

If only I knew what Clementine was planning to do. And where she is tonight, in all this rain.

I'm sure she's not far off. She must be somewhere in the presbytery, but where? If only I knew. Is she in the church, perhaps? Or out in the rain? Or behind our house, or even the Father's house?

Yes, if I only knew what she was planning to do. Will she go and tell the Father everything? Wow! I honestly think that's what she's up to. She'll go and tell him the lot, and he's already in such despair!

Oh, my God, my God! What a business! What a catastrophe!

My mother always said there are no limits to what a jealous woman will do. She will kill her own husband without a moment's hesitation. That's what my mother said. Yes, she'll kill her own husband!

Oh God, if she should kill Catherine! . . . Oh, no, dear God, no! . . . Anything except the death of Catherine. If Clementine should kill Catherine! Since my mother's death I've never loved anyone as I do Catherine. I cling to her as I might to my mother. Oh, God, please keep her safe!

Poor dear Catherine, if anything should happen to her!

I ought to have got up and gone to warn Zacharia and Catherine in the hamlet where they are meeting. That's what I should have done . . . But the Father might have come to look for me while I was away. And perhaps Clementine, who must be outside somewhere, would have seen me and suspected me of being in league with them.

Why did she have to turn up? . . . Who told her, anyway? Was she spying on us all day? And how did she know that Zacharia was out when she arrived? She came straight to my room and for a moment

I thought it was Catherine, my sweet Catherine . . . Oh, I musn't think like that . . . Forgive me, Lord.

Yes, Clementine came to my room, with her finger to her lips, and said: 'What, have you no shame? So that's how it is! Zacharia takes the six girls on tour with him and sleeps with them in the very house of the Father! You've seen it all and you haven't told the Father anything? Little devil, aren't you ashamed? Sin doesn't shock you; you look on, you admire and enjoy it, all that sin! Dirty little devil! I shall go and tell everything to the Father; how you've seen Zacharia bring that wench every night into his house; how you join her on the road whenever the Father goes ahead; how you are there with them, watching everything and saying nothing . . . Shut up, you little rat! Oh, I shall tell the Father every detail!'

'But . . . but I know nothing about it . . . nothing . . .'

'Get away with you, liar! Dog of a liar! Do you dare to lie at that rate?'

And suddenly she collapsed into sobs, weeping to break your heart. And I too felt like crying, not for her, but for myself.

It's all so complicated and I'm sick of it! I've really had enough. I'm tired of the whole thing.

Clementine sobbed through her tears: 'He leaves me with a little baby, and it's all for that! I wondered why he was so tickled about going on tour, when he's so well off at the mission, never doing a stroke of work and leaving everything to his assistant or the boys. He seemed so pleased to leave the mission and go off on tour for fifteen days. I should have guessed something then. What time will they be here, eh? Come on, what time will they arrive? I'm asking you, you little rat.'

'But I don't know. I assure you, I know nothing . . .'

'You're lying! You're fit for nothing but lying, scum!'

Suddenly she turned really nasty. She held up her finger and bared her teeth like a bitch, as if about to snap at me. Then she said: 'Listen to me, little Father, if you say one word, if you open that lying dog's snout of yours, you dirty-minded little hypocrite, you just see what I'll do to you! I shan't tell what'll happen if you open that foul trap of yours, but you'll see soon enough!'

She swept out and left me sitting on my bed, utterly stupefied and staring like an idiot. She rushed off into the darkness and the rain.

Heavens, there's Zacharia and Catherine coming in! They are coming in . . . my God! What can be happening? Listen, they are opening the door of their room, whispering together . . . perhaps they suspect nothing? Now, what's going to happen? Listen . . . still silent in there! What? Isn't anything going to happen?

Listen, all the same. No! Not a thing. Just the sound of the rain.

So where is Clementine?

Nothing . . . Just silence and rain. What a night of horrors! Let me think no more of it.

And the poor Father, already plunged in such despair. Here at Teba there isn't even a church any more; nothing but a shelter, a mat roof thrown over some wooden posts. The catechist and some women have hastily surrounded it with palm-fronds, and it's in this apology for a church that the Father will have to say Mass tomorrow. What a country!

As for me, I still haven't confessed. And I shake at the thought that I'll have to do it one of these days . . . perhaps even tomorrow! I can't go on serving the Mass like this, without ever taking Communion. And now everything is more complicated than ever.

Catherine . . . Catherine . . . Catherine! . . . No, I mustn't think of her. After all, it's her fault that I'm in this fix. Catherine . . . But how can I stop thinking of her? Catherine . . . she was so lovely again this morning, knowing nothing of Clementine's arrival. Probably didn't even know she was in these parts.

Really, Clementine may have been hiding in the same hamlet as Catherine, spying on all of us! . . . Seeing everything we did! . . . Obviously Catherine can't have the slightest suspicion that Clementine is hereabouts and plotting some mischief against her. Otherwise, she'd hardly have come back with Zarcharia.

Ah . . . ah . . . ah . . . what was it that Clementine said! Now I understand! Catherine comes from the sixa at Bomba! That's where I've seen her before. I must have seen her many times among the girls there, many times.

Every morning the girls form in two lines before the sacristy, ready to enter the church. It's true there are many of them, more than sixty altogether, and I couldn't take note of them all. But Catherine is too pretty to be missed by even the most indifferent spectator.

After Mass, they assemble again in front of the sacristy, still in two lines. By this time it is daylight and they can be clearly seen as they file off into the sixa. You can see them all lifting their feet as they cross the high threshold of the sixa entrance.

Later in the day, they all assemble again by the Father's office for the distribution of their tasks. Here again I must sometimes have seen her. However, Catherine's hands are so soft, she is so pretty and elegant, that it's difficult to think of her working like the other girls.

So! Catherine is a sixa girl taken off on tour without the Father's knowledge. Just wait till he finds out!

But what about Raphael, the catechist who directs the sixa? Raphael must know well enough what's going on, for he knows every girl there by name. Not even one could disappear without his notice. So perhaps, knowing everything, it was he who revealed it to Clementine? Oh, it's all too much for me to follow . . . I'm sick of it now. And still I can't get to sleep. I have lost all my peace and joy; now even my sleep is gone. Before this, I used to sleep as my head touched the pillow. Nowadays, I spend my time thinking over all these events, tormenting myself and unable to stop.

Then there's the Father's terrible despair. While he was eating tonight he looked so miserable that I thought he might weep. Once, he said to the catechist: 'This country rejects me, I who have loved it so much!'

When I think how Zacharia had the effrontery to tell him yesterday, 'I am a good Christian. I have no longing for a second wife!' No, it's enough to make you sick.

I've always feared that Zacharia would bring mischance upon us, with all his careless irony, mockery and irreverence . . . Now it's at hand.

Catherine a sixa girl! My God, what a scandal!

Suppose her fiancé finds out? And I'm quite sure he will, especially if Clementine kicks up a dust about it.

I've always heard it said that the sixa girls behave shockingly, but I've never believed it. It must be true, all the same. And Catherine and Zacharia must have known each other back at Bomba. They must have done, and I didn't notice a thing. What an ass I've been! It's always like that; things happen all around me and I notice nothing.

But the most upsetting thing is Raphael's part in it all. He must have noticed Catherine's disappearance, especially as he calls a roll every morning. Just so long as it wasn't he who permitted her to come!

All the same, it's possible. See what bad thoughts I have now! Having been duped so long, I'm beginning to suspect everyone and everything.

Still, Raphael must have known about it, because there hasn't been a single case of a girl running away from the sixa without his knowledge. Yes, Raphael must have let Catherine go, in league with Zacharia! Worse and worse, my God!

And there's the Father, knowing nothing of it. And about to know it all!

What can Clementine be planning? And where is she now? I can't rest without knowing. Perhaps she's hiding in one of the houses? That woman terrifies me . . . What is she cooking up? And in all this rain, an absolute deluge! . . .

Once again, I shall have to serve the Mass tomorrow without communicating; I couldn't find anyone here to do it for me. Whenever we distribute Communion now, the Father throws me a look which freezes my spine. *Domine non sum dignus ut intres sub tectum meum . . .*

At Akamba this morning the napkin fell from my hands, I was so nervous. After that, I dared not show my face at the palaver . . .

I keep wondering why the Father doesn't ask me: 'Don't you want to confess yourself?' I believe it's his own worries that prevent him.

Kondo

So it's happened!

Everything has come about as I feared. For some time I have felt certain that it would finish like this. And, whatever I feel now, it certainly isn't surprise. I even feel a bit happy, as if relieved; for I realize now how just all my apprehensions were.

I'm only sorry about Catherine. She will suffer more than all of us, because of her fiancé, who must know all about it by now. Everything came out! Yes, absolutely everything. And all because of Clementine.

Clementine was spying on us all that night. From where? From the church? Or behind our house, standing out in the rain? No matter how, she watched us the whole night. How she must have shivered!

When she heard the doves singing at dawn, she must have said to herself: 'My hour has come! Now I've got you! Yes, now I've really got you!' And perhaps she had even listened to the antics of Catherine and Zacharia, with her ear clapped to the wall!

I got up at five-thirty as usual and began to wash. Clementine must have heard me and said to herself: 'Now the little one is getting ready and soon Zacharia will also leave . . . then it'll be just the two of us, Catherine!'

I went off to the church to prepare the altar. It wasn't a proper church, of course; just a shed got up with masses of palm-fronds.

Mass began at a quarter past six, and by that time it was almost day. Zacharia came to church also this morning. Suddenly we heard a frightful racket from the direction of our house, a thudding and battering sound which shook the earth all around us, as if a young elephant were trapped in there and had determined to smash the walls which imprisoned him from his native forest. From time to time, this was mingled with oaths, curses and threats uttered in voices inhuman with rage.

The Father went on with the Mass as if he heard nothing. I tried to do the same, but I kept glancing furtively through the wall of branches, only to see the two girls burst out of the house and fall rolling in the dust, locked together like lovers. As they rolled through the dust, now one and now the other would briefly seize the mastery.

All the villagers rushed up to see the two girls fighting. It was now almost daylight outside and everyone at Mass kept squinting out through the palm-screen. Far from separating the wrestlers, the villagers kept spurring them on to new frenzy. The boys doubled up with laughter and the women kept shouting: 'Oh, no! That's against the rules, you're fighting dirty', or else: 'Don't tear off her knickers just to shame her, that's not fair!' or again: 'Stop biting her like that! It's not allowed . . .'

At last the congregation, unable to restrain themselves longer, also surged out into the courtyard, while the Father continued the service as if nothing had happened, but when he turned from the altar he saw the church quite empty. He gazed into the vacancy open-mouthed, looking vaguely about while his ears rapidly turned scarlet. Then he hurled himself into the court, still wearing his ornaments, and bore down furiously upon the crowd, with me panting at his heels.

When we reached the spot I saw that the two girls had stopped rolling about. Clementine was now firmly seated on top of Catherine, who was stretched on her back in an obscene posture. With homicidal rage, Clementine was pouring handfuls of dust into Catherine's mouth, eyes and nostrils, pausing only to pull her hair. She had come to the combat prepared, wearing a stout pair of drawers. But Catherine was caught unawares and undressed, wearing nothing but a linen shift which Clementine had pulled up to her neck, so that she lay there in the dust completely naked.

The Father had to elbow his way fiercely through the crowd to reach them. Then he bent over them and dragged the furiously resisting Clementine off her victim, pushing her brutally aside. He pulled Catherine to her feet and I saw that her face was bitten and scratched all over.

He had recognized Clementine and he gazed at her in astonishment before demanding: 'What does this mean, Clementine? What on earth does this mean?'

Clementine was quite puffed out and all smothered in dust, so she could hardly frame a word, but she pointed to Catherine with an accusing finger and managed to splutter: 'She's . . . from . . . the sixa! . . . She's sleeping . . . with . . . my . . . husband. Yes . . . she comes from the sixa! . . . And she's sleeping with my husband . . . for a whole week now! . . . I swear . . . for a whole week . . . under your very eyes!'

At last the Father understood and he stood rooted with amazement. He turned towards Catherine, who stood there white to her hair with dust, that hair which was still so beautifully black and thick only yesterday. Her poor torn face was lowered in shame and she sobbed bitterly, with great tears rolling down her cheeks. I believe she was most ashamed at having been naked before so many people.

The Father's face was bright red and his hair seemed to be standing on end. He kept looking from Catherine to Clementine, who was glaring with the ferocity of a lioness at her rival, quite ready to spring and devour her. Catherine kept drooping and weeping there, whilst the Father pinched his lips and shook his head in astonishment and indignation.

He caught the two girls by the hand and took them into his house, where he charged the catechist to look after them and keep them from fighting. We went back into the church, but the Father didn't recommence the service where he had left off; he simply offered Communion, announced that the service was over and retired to divest himself of his ornaments . . .

He was still wearing the same black soutane and I wondered why he clung to it, as if in mourning. Is he really in mourning? . . . For whom, then? A relative, perhaps? . . . His father or mother? . . . No, surely he would have told us. He doesn't talk much of them, but if one of them died he would certainly tell us. Since we started on tour we've only had three lots of mail. It was only the first lot which had any letters from France and he didn't wear black that day or the following, but only several days later. So this garment is not worn as a mark of mourning. But it's funny all the same that he's taken this sudden fancy for wearing black.

The Father and I came out of church together and I felt sick to think that Catherine could easily get me in big trouble if she wanted to. The Father dismissed all the bystanders who were stationed between the church and his house, where we found the two girls still in the same attitudes, Catherine woefully drooping and Clementine glaring at her like a monster. The catechist claimed that three times she had tried to fly at Catherine but he had managed to subdue her.

Catherine was weeping no longer, but she looked pitifully sad. She had washed the dust from her face and put on a dress, so she looked quite pretty again except for her scratched and bitten face. She had folded her hands on her breast and sat in a corner frowning and cowering like a terrified dove with its head under its wing. And she gazed at the ground with such persistence and intensity that one would think she was looking into another world, where she saw a monstrous being who frightened and fascinated her at the same time.

At the table the Father sat silently in the greenish light of the rising sun, pursing his lips. Zacharia came in and set breakfast before him with the manner of one seeing and knowing nothing of the matter, lofty and indifferent. He was smartly dressed, as always. Just as he was going out, the Father called him: 'Zacharia, stay there.'

'Why so, Father?'

'I say I wish you to stay there. You know perfectly well that this whole scandal is provoked by you.'

Zacharia grumbled between his teeth that it was no concern of his and he certainly hadn't looked for trouble. The Father must deal with these women as he thought fit, but he, Zacharia, would have nothing to do with it. For if he did, he would give Clementine such a thrashing that the matter would end there . . .

'Listen to him, Father, listen to him!' screeched Clementine at these words. 'Listen to that! Now he wants to thrash me. Can you believe it, Father? Me, his own wife in the eyes of God!'

But Zacharia had already gone out. The Father yelled, furiously: 'Zacharia!'

No reply. After a while: 'Zacharia!'

Still no reply: 'Zacharia!'

After the third command, still ignored, the Father sprang to his feet as if about to hurl himself after Zacharia. That's undoubtedly what he would have done formerly, but instead he slumped back into his chair in the strangest fashion and began swearing in French: 'In the name of God, no! . . . Oh, shit! . . . What a cow! . . . Oh, it's really too much . . .'

Then he fell silent. Gradually he simmered down, smoking incessantly. He ate nothing and drank only a mouthful of coffee. Finally, he began to question the two girls.

Clementine spoke first. She said that for a month or more, at the mission, she had noticed the lustful relations of her husband with this hot little wench, who acted like a bitch on heat . . . At this point the Father cut her short with an angry command not to insult people in his presence . . . Several times she had found her in the Father's kitchen for no reason and could never discover what had brought her there. At that time she had said nothing, and anyway she was pregnant then. Could she fight when she was pregnant? So she said nothing, but already suspected something dirty going on.

Then she gave birth and a few weeks later Zacharia went on tour. In a way, she was glad that this tour would take him away, away from that daughter of Satan . . .

'Clementine!' yelled the Father, 'didn't I tell you not to insult people in my presence? Yes or no?'

'Pardon me, Father, pardon me, I beg. It's only anger that makes me talk like this. Please pardon me, Father . . .'

So, Zacharia had gone on tour. But on going to Mass during the next few days, she couldn't see that . . . who, then? . . . that . . . that . . . Catherine among the sixa girls. She made inquiries and discovered that Catherine had disappeared a few days after the start of the tour.

According to Raphael, whom the Father had wrongly left in charge of the sixa, Catherine had gone to visit her sick mother and would soon be back. An utter lie, of course . . .

And Raphael had lied like this to her! The wife before God Himself of Zacharia! . . . The mother of his family, with a young baby in her arms! Oh, this Raphael was also a loose fellow and the Father would do well to keep an eye on him (here the Father rolled a shrivelled and burning eye).

But fortunately she, Clementine, was a woman of exceptional intelligence. Doubt had entered her heart and there was only one way to expel it; to set off in pursuit and keep close watch on Zacharia, all the closer because she knew her man pretty well!

So she had set off and caught up with us, spying on us without betraying herself. (Would she now bring me into it? My spine froze in anticipation.)

And what had she seen!

Ah, life! What a life it is, after all! One day she spotted Catherine waiting in a little hamlet right on our route. She was waiting in one of the houses there, very smartly got up and overflowing with anticipation. So Clementine had installed herself in the house opposite and from there she had seen that . . . that . . . woman accosting her husband (a warning glance here from the Father).

After nightfall, she had seen a hurricane-lamp lighted in Catherine's house and a little later a tall figure was silhouetted in the doorway. It was Zacharia, and could be none but he! She couldn't attempt to express the anger, shame and pity for herself she had felt at that moment. Only by thinking of her baby had she been able to recover a little courage. Zacharia had stayed a long while with Catherine in that little house; she had heard them laughing together and even singing. Clementine saw them quite distinctly in the lamplight, sitting close together, buttock to buttock (a twitch of protest from the Father) and cheek to cheek. Frequently they embraced each other, like the children of Satan they were. And they must also have been drinking, for nothing else would explain their gaiety. It was quite late when they decided to leave the house, she following them closely in the darkness, and arm-in-arm they arrived at the presbytery. Without a sound, they had glided into the house next door to the one where the Father was still working, for she could see his light. Clementine had gone behind the house, uncertain what to do, and clapped her ear to the wall. She had heard them chuckling and whispering together inside. Suddenly, just as she was wondering what to do, she heard them fall on the bed, groaning with pleasure and wallowing together like two pigs in a swamp. Unable to stand any more, she ran farther off, choking and suffocating with indignation. Then she returned to the hamlet and took refuge with the old woman who had sheltered her. There she turned over many schemes in her head and finally arrived at a plan of action. Fortunately, she now knew all their little contrivances.

She followed us again on the next step, to Teba. That evening, Zacharia and the girl behaved in exactly the same fashion. But, while they were drinking in the hamlet, she went before them to await their arrival at the presbytery. She still didn't know exactly what she would do. Then all at once she decided to attack Catherine at dawn, when everyone else would be at Mass; for she had now realized that Catherine would stay away from Mass in case she was recognized by the Father.

Clementine had stayed outside all night in the rain, with her ear pressed to the wall, listening while the couple indulged in bout after bout of furious fornication (here the Father shrugged and gave a grunt of resignation), but this only strengthened her resolve to fight on the morrow. A woman robbed of her husband can do only one thing, fight. It doesn't matter whether she loses or wins; the important thing is that she fights. And all this was happening only a few centimetres from the Father's own house! (Here the Father pinched his lips.)

At the first notes of the morning doves, she made her dispositions while the two inside, having woken up, audibly made love once again.

The little one had got up first (that was me, so perhaps she wasn't going to drag me into it); he washed and dressed before heading off towards the chapel, all of which she heard distinctly. Then she heard Zacharia stretching and cursing in a low voice: 'What a blight this Mass is every morning! Today I'd as soon go there as I'd swim in a river in all this rain.'

That girl replied to him: 'Are you nuts? If you don't turn up the Father himself will come to check on your state of health.'

'So what?'

'So what? So he'll see me.'

'And then?'

'Shush! Don't talk so loud. Perhaps your master hasn't gone out yet.'

All the same, Zacharia got up and began washing. The Father too, who had risen without Clementine's knowledge, came out of his house and set off for the church, clacking his sandals on the hard ground. Then her husband emerged and went in the same direction, dragging his steps unwillingly like the incorrigible sinner he was.

Clementine waited a moment longer and then burst in, finding that girl still flat on her back, with her legs parted in the most obscene fashion. She rushed at her and gave her a thorough beating. The Father himself could witness, couldn't he, how thoroughly she had punished her? And out in the courtyard, too, had she not beaten her thoroughly?

'All bad women who disturb Christian households should be treated in the same style, shouldn't they, Father? I'm sure if it was always done . . .'

'Couldn't you have come and told me everything instead of fighting?' asked the Father sternly. 'Don't you know that it's wrong to fight like that?'

'And what else could I have done, pray?' protested Clementine, hands on hips. 'Could I have done otherwise, Father? A woman grabs my husband like that and I must fight her. If I don't, she'll do it again! Yes, Father, that's how it is.'

The Father sighed and turned towards Catherine to question her.

Catherine denied none of Clementine's accusations. Still gazing at the floor, she said nothing but 'yes' or 'no' in reply to anything, occasionally just nodding her head. She added only the number of days she had been accompanying us and that it was Raphael himself, the director of the sixa, who had permitted her to follow Zacharia on tour. She said also that she had already slept with Zacharia at Bomba mission, with the connivance of Raphael.

'You see, Father, you see! What did I tell you?' screeched Clementine, when she heard this.

The Father called the local catechist to give Catherine a thrashing. The catechist threw his long bunch of canes across her buttocks again and again, while Catherine wrung her hands and wept and Clementine's eyes burned with a strange brilliancy in watching her writhings.

Then the Father sent the two women back to the mission in the catechist's charge, telling him to watch carefully to prevent them fighting again. This morning's palaver was cancelled because of all this business, which caused great excitement in the village.

We left Teba quite early and the Father went ahead on his bicycle. Zacharia had disappeared and I had no idea where he was, so I walked along in company with the porters, all young boys and girls.

Half-way between Teba and Kondo, we ran into Zacharia. He was sitting in a house and called out to me as I passed. I found him drinking with his friends, for he is known everywhere here. He told me he'd seen the boss (the Reverend Father!) go by on his bicycle, but had refrained from calling out to him. He asked me how things had turned out this morning and I told him everything. When he heard about Catherine's thrashing he got really annoyed and said it was Clementine who should have got it, if the Father knew what he was about. There was an old woman in the room and Zacharia called her to witness: 'Isn't that so, mother?' he asked, 'that stuck-up Clementine is the one who should have been whopped?'

'Yes, yes, of course,' she answered, 'you're absolutely right. It's Clementine who's the guilty one.'

'Did things go on like this in your day?' Zacharia continued.

'Certainly not! In my time the wife had no cause to fight unless the woman her husband was enjoying was also married. Only on that account did she kick up a fuss. But she'd have been quite in the wrong to fight if her husband's little friend was just an unmarried girl like this one.'

'You see, mother,' exulted Zacharia, 'how truly wise our ancestors were! The whites understand none of our wisdom, not even the Father, whom I've been trying to educate for years.'

He offered me some palm-wine and I drank it, because I was feeling rather sorry for myself and rather lost, especially when I thought about Catherine and the bastinading she got this morning.

Someone asked Zacharia: 'The story goes that your clientele has fallen off and that the Father is blubbering over it: is it true?'

'Yes, the clientele has really fallen off, it's a fact. And it's really the Father's fault, for not listening to me. But it's not true that he's in tears over it; far from it. A man, a real man, never cries whatever happens, and the Father is certainly a real man.'

'They say he's talking of giving up this country?'

'Oh, he talks of it, but I don't believe he'll really do it: he's far too attached to the area.'

'So you don't want your empire to diminish, eh?' asked another man.

'But you're wrong there,' said the first, 'for this blessed Zacharia can afford to snap his fingers at all of it now, na so? You could leave Bomba at this moment, you've looked after yourself so well; and you wouldn't soon fall into poverty. Oh, get on with you, you rascal!'

Everyone in the room laughed heartily, including Zacharia. We got up to leave and as we did so Zacharia declared that Catherine was certainly the prettiest girl he'd ever clapped eyes on and that everything was far from finished between them.

Poor sweet Catherine . . . Oh! I mustn't think like that. My! I've been deep enough in already. On the other hand, I'm so deep in now that one impure thought more or less can hardly make any difference. Another Mass tomorrow morning without Communion. But I still won't confess myself to the Father, I simply haven't the courage. He must already be in despair and could hardly stand yet another blow. Perhaps he's still working in his room, for I haven't heard the local catechist come out. All the same, it would be quite easy. As soon as the catechist comes out, I could go straight in and tell him everything. That's what I ought to do, but I just can't make up my mind to it.

A little while ago, being unable to get to sleep, I went out on the veranda and looked at the night. There was a suspicion of moonlight in the corner of the forest, like a trace of sunshine through water, and the darkness seemed to be chewing at the long, slender bodies of the palm trees, for sometimes they appeared faintly and then vanished again. And I felt quite estranged from myself, as if I didn't know myself any more. I don't know what's become of me.

On my right hand, in the depths of the courtyard, the indistinct shadow of the church was floating. It's a small church but very charming, probably the most charming we've seen on the whole journey; all made of brick and with a little clocktower, just like a real church. Apparently, it was built a long while ago. It certainly couldn't be done nowadays; there simply wouldn't be enough money or enough Christians to do it. The church is still standing, however, though the only people at confession were some old Christian mothers and some kids who will surely be polygamists or the wives of polygamists tomorrow . . . Suppose the Father asks me tomorrow: 'Don't you want to confess yourself?' What on earth shall I do? Can I simply reply, no? . . . Oh, I wouldn't dare: so perhaps I shall be forced to confess? But I still hope that he won't ask me. I want to confess to none but Jean-Martin.

The Father came to table very late, well after eight o'clock. The local catechist was there, as well as Zacharia, who was leaning against the wall opposite. The Father ate for a long time without speaking and Zacharia gazed fixedly at him. He didn't seem ill; only exhausted, or rather, feeble, and manifestly discouraged. When I remember the Father of only a few months ago, it seems to me that now I look upon a stranger – out of his element, pensively calm, attentive to everything said around him – exactly the opposite of the Father I knew.

Zacharia coughed a couple of times and asked: 'Father, why did you have that girl beaten?'

The Father looked up at him with an expression of defiance mingled with distrust. He shook his head, wiped his face and said: 'Don't you know, then?'

'No, Father. I really don't see the point of all that severity.'

'Ah, Zacharia,' sighed the Father, as he returned to his food, 'I knew you were capable of many things, but this time you really exceeded my fears, I must confess.'

'How so, Father?'

'Only last night, if you remember, you assured me that you had no wish for a second wife, that you were a good Christian. Don't you remember?'

'Certainly, Father, certainly I remember.'

'Very well, I'll tell you something in confidence. Last night, I actually believed you. I took your assurances for good currency. At first I was doubtful, but in the end I believed you. Imagine that!'

'But you did well then, Father.'

'Ah, you're at it again!'

'Look, Father, I was never married to that other woman.'

'But have you slept with her or not?'

'Yes, Father, indeed I have. But what does that prove? It proves nothing, except that my wife has recently delivered.'

'Poor Zacharia! Why torment yourself? You know very well that I don't believe you.'

'Then you are wrong, Father, for what I've just said is true. What's more, I've always told you the same thing and you have never wanted to believe me. I don't know how the whites manage such things, but we blacks, when our wives have given birth, leave them alone for a good year. That's how it is with us and I can't do otherwise. I know some people who've tried to bring up their babies on powdered milk, but it always turns out badly.'

As he finished these words, Zacharia crossed the threshold and disappeared into the night. Left alone with us, the Father burst into a wild peal of laughter.

Later, I cleared the table, polished his shoes and went off to bed, leaving the Father and the catechist to go through the parish registers together.

I'm still wondering why the Father should have laughed in that extraordinary way. Was it because Zacharia was telling a lie? I don't know whether it's a lie, but it seems to me that my father behaved in exactly the same way with my step-mother. Whenever she had a baby, they stayed apart for a whole year. But my father didn't profit from this by going after other women. He always slept in the house and if any women had come, I'd have seen them . . . Pah, I'm sure Zacharia was lying. Why, Catherine admitted only this morning that they were already lovers at the mission . . .

Kouma

Saturday, 14 February

I've confessed! . . . At last, I've confessed and I feel so good! I'm so happy. I feel just as I do after a good hot bath: all the filth that covered me has slid away on to the ground, and freed of that foul garment, how light and free my body feels in all its movements! My God, how sweet it is!

How many useless tears I shed, too! How, how I wept, as if the tears that fell from my eyes were also the juices flowing from a great wound in my heart. I have never cried so before, except just when my mother died.

Crikey! And I thought the whole day was over. The Father had finished eating and I had finished serving. Then, as he began talking to the catechist and the monitors about the state of things in Kouma, I went out to distract myself by gazing at the night and the stars. Then I went to lie down in my room, but after half an hour I still wasn't asleep. I kept thinking about Catherine and about Zacharia's argument with the Father. So I lighted my candle and began reading *Mamadou and Bineta Grow Up*, from which the dictations are apparently chosen in our certificate examination. Through my reading, I could hear bursts of talking from the Father, the catechist and the monitors, whose discussion lasted four hours. Then I heard the Father's visitors leaving and bidding him good night. When all was still, I closed the book, blew out the candle and wrapped myself in my covers again, trying to sleep. But a few minutes later I heard the Father's door open and the sound of his footsteps on the veranda. He was approaching rapidly and soon his steps were on our own veranda, where his sandals struck softly on the badly-beaten earth. He stopped right under my window! When he tapped the first time I made no response, pretending to be asleep. The second time I was still silent, but I stopped breathing and lay quaking in my bed. When he tapped a third time, calling out my name, I pretended to wake up, stretching myself noisily and rubbing my eyes to make them red. The Father called out: 'Are you awake?'

'Yes, Father,' I replied in a muffled and sleepy voice.

He called: 'Get up and come to my room. Don't rush, though: it isn't urgent.'

Then he went away, flapping his sandals on the ground as before. I got up and dressed slowly. My heart was beating furiously and I wondered what the Father could want with me. I thought: 'Perhaps it's only to polish his shoes. If so, I'll polish them in a flash so that he won't have time to ask me anything.' But I didn't really believe it was that; if it had been, he'd have said as much when he called me at the window. Since he'd revealed nothing then, I suspected he wanted to speak to me of secret matters. Zacharia was snoring peacefully in his room. I went outside and stopped dead on the veranda.

All at once, I knew for sure that the Father had woken me to come and confess myself. If I could have run away at that moment, I would certainly have done so. I looked at the village, which had a closed look like a hostile man. The moonlight trickled over the forest in a yellowish and sticky stream, like unpurified palm-oil. The whole place filled me with dread. I didn't know this country and we were at least a dozen kilometres from the mission, ten of them through thick forest. The air was filled with the howling of chimpanzees and the hooting of owls, darkly menacing to the wanderer. And then, if I did run away, why should I run to the mission? That would be madness; but where else could I go?

I don't know what finally got me moving, but I walked resolutely up to the Father's door and went inside.

He was sitting in a cane arm-chair, reading his breviary, with his shoulders pressed fully against the chair-back. He didn't look up when I came in, but continued reading. I stood upright in the little room, right in front of him, twisting my hands. I wanted to cry, but I fought it as hard as I could; for if it turned out that he hadn't called me to confess, I should be obliged to do so anyway if I broke down. There was a horrid whistling in my ears and I began rubbing my eyes again, just because I had nothing else to do, I believe. I rubbed them frenziedly, as if there had been a big sore in each eyeball. There was a hurricane-lamp burning on the table, together with the parish registers, an ink-well and a bottle of water.

Finally, the Father stopped reading and gazed straight at me for a long while. I kept cracking my finger-joints as I twisted my hands about. Then he said: 'Bring that chair from the corner and come and sit here in front of me.'

I did as he said. I sat before him, never daring to look up in his face, and to avoid doing so I kept rubbing away at my eyes. I was so scared that I felt a terrible pain in my stomach and a sort of rumbling inside.

'Don't rub your eyes like that! Are you sleepy?'

'Yes, Father.'

'Don't you want to confess?'

I was petrified by that question. I stopped rubbing my eyes and looked straight at the Father, but I couldn't see him at all. I had irritated my eyes so much that I saw nothing but a mist shot through with piercing stars.

'Don't you want to confess, eh? It's a long while since you did so.'

That was where I burst out sobbing. I cried so much I thought I would choke. I felt that the Father was shaking his head at me as I heard him say: 'What are you crying for? What have you got to cry about, you great ninny? It's incredible. He's never cried like this before. What's come over him all of a sudden? Tell me, are you sleepy? Is that the trouble?'

Without ceasing in my sobs, I signed with my head that I wasn't.

'You are ill, then?'

Again I shook my head.

'So, why are you crying?'

I made a violent effort to control my weeping, because I was so ashamed of breaking down like that, but I couldn't prevent those great sobs from shaking me.

The Father said then: 'All right, if I understand the matter, you've done wrong and you're frightened of confessing. Is that it?'

This time I nodded my head. He lifted me off the chair and set me on his knees with a heavy sigh: 'Soon, I shan't be able to take you on my knees, you're getting so big. Now, tell me all about it and stop crying. Don't you understand that I'm like Christ and can only

give you pardon? I pardon always, for that is the gift of our Saviour.
Do stop crying! Confess yourself and I will forgive you. Tell me
everything, little one, and stop crying. Now, speak! You can't go on
weeping for ever.'

'I'm ashamed . . . and . . . afraid, Father.'

'Afraid of whom? Of Christ, whom you have offended?'

'Yes, Father.'

'But I have said that He pardons all and will pardon you.'

'Oh, Father, I'm afraid . . .'

'Then it's me you're afraid of?'

'Yes, Father.'

'I've already told you that I am like Christ; that I, too, always give
pardon. In any case, your tears prove that you already regret your sin.
You do regret it, don't you?'

'Oh, yes, Father!'

'You repent of it?'

'Yes, Father, and I promise never to return to it again.'

'Bravo, my boy! Now, tell me all about it. What have you been up
to?'

'Father, to begin with, I suspected nothing. It's true, it really wasn't
my fault in the beginning . . .'

'Then whose fault was it?'

'That girl's, Father.'

'Which girl?'

'The one who fought with Clementine yesterday, Father.'

'What is her name?'

'Catherine, Father.'

'And did you know her before this?'

'Oh, no, Father. Only during this tour, since she began following
us. I was scared to come and tell you, because of Zacharia.'

'Are you crying, then, simply because you were too scared to tell
me that she was following us?'

'No, Father. It's not only that.'

'What else, then?'

To my astonishment I then told him everything in detail, without
hesitation or difficulty. Only it was a bit difficult right at first. I even
told him how often I had thought of Catherine, and that when I let

her get me drunk one day, I had sat on her knees and kissed her cheeks. I told him the whole lot.

When I had reached the end, I fell silent and looked at the Father. He didn't seem at all angry, he just kept pulling at his beard, which has grown very long just now. He spoke to me for a long while in a very gentle, paternal way. And here I was imagining that he'd make a frightful scene, chasing me about and cursing me too, perhaps! How wrong I was! He was so good to me. He advised me to have nothing to do with women, to make sure that they never came near me. He said that men could never be too careful of women. That's true, we can never distrust them enough . . .

At last, he gave me absolution and said: 'Now that you are at peace with Christ, don't cry any more, eh? Go and sleep quietly.'

And he made a little sign of the cross on my brow.

E-e-e-h, how good I feel. I feel light enough to spring in the air, like a full balloon. The Father is really too good to me. What things I let myself imagine beforehand! Thinking he would flare up all red, reproaching my foulness and calling me a child of Satan. Ah, what a fool I am!

Yes, I feel really good. When I think that only a short while ago I was so unhappy, so sick of this journey and this whole business . . . Ah, Zacharia, too, has had a beating! I had a feeling it would happen soon . . .

It was late when we left Kondo and the Father went ahead of us again on his bicycle. Zacharia and I walked side by side. He was holding his pullover over his left arm, which rested on his hip, and whistling gaily as he went along. He seemed quite debonair, as though he had forgotten all the events of the day before. We walked on in the heat, and about half-way between Kondo and Kouma we began passing through a small hamlet. A man suddenly burst out of one of the houses and bore down on us without a word. At first, he was bent forward, as he hoisted his trousers up to his waist, but when he stood up straight I saw how big he was. He called out loudly to Zacharia: 'Now, fellow, show us that you carry a real pair of balls, and that you don't only use them for tickling girls' bellies!'

He threw himself violently on Zacharia and in a trice they were completely enlaced. They fell rolling to the ground, each in turn coming uppermost for a moment, but never able to stay there long.

As the women were in the fields, only a few kids were nearby, while the men just watched the contest from their doorways.

The two men got to their feet again and attacked each other with wrestling holds. Soon they were rolling on the ground once more, each mastering the other from time to time, like the two girls yesterday.

When they got up again, Zacharia had a swollen eye and a cut on his temple, for his adversary struck him with the speed and fury of a madman whenever he had a chance. They were both panting and looking intently at one another. Slowly they moved apart, Zacharia throwing off his shoes quickly and hoisting up his trousers. Then the other man came at him again, trying to seize him in his arms, but Zacharia slipped free. They began boxing, with Zacharia's assailant delivering a flurry of hard blows; the cook was now bleeding badly and his lip too was swelling up. He was hitting back, but the other man had the faster punch. He was even taller than Zacharia, and aimed all his blows at the eyes and mouth. Suddenly, he caught Zacharia in a firm hold, slipping quickly round behind him and pinioning his arms. Zacharia struggled to turn himself or to break free, but he was firmly held and couldn't do a thing. Then the man began to spin him round faster and faster, so that Zacharia's mouth fell open, his tongue and eyes protruded and all the boys started laughing as he hurtled past them. When the man saw that Zacharia was sufficiently dazed by being spun like a top, he tripped him up and sent him crashing on his face. Quickly, he jumped on to his back and began beating him about the head; then he rolled Zacharia over on to his back, sat on his belly, and began raining blows on his eyes and mouth. At every blow, Zacharia grimaced horribly and one of the boys began to shout: 'He's going to kill him! He's going to kill him!'

That cry lashed me like a whip and I ran at the man to try and force him off Zacharia. If I were only a little bigger and stronger . . . the man just shoved me with the flat of his left hand and I was sprawled on the ground, yards away. But I got up, weeping with rage, and ran at him again. Once more, he shoved me off with his left hand, but this time I didn't fall and came running back at him. Then he turned towards me and bawled: 'Listen, you little brat, if you do that again, I'll stick my thumb up your arse-hole and tear you in half!'

All the boys laughed at this, and I could do nothing but weep. The man seized Zacharia by the throat and pressed him head to the ground. With his other hand, he tore open Zacharia's fly-buttons, groped inside and did something that made Zacharia howl like a wild beast and squirm about in agony. But he didn't relax his grip and soon Zacharia broke into dry sobs, while his lips turned back over his twisting mouth and his eyes were shot with blood. Then the man laughed aloud and said to his victim:

'Now at least you will remember, eh? Just remember that the sixa girls are not put there for your pleasure. Will you remember that now? Speak! Will you remember that?'

And all the while, he was laughing. Suddenly, he pinched his lips and Zacharia let out a terrible yell of pain, tears starting from his eyes. Then at last the men came from their doorways, nonchalantly approached, and obliged the man to get off Zacharia, saying that it was legitimate to correct a man but not to kill him.

Zacharia slowly struggled to his feet, weeping bitterly and scarcely recognizable. All the men looked at him with a sort of ironic pity, as one might at a presumptuous child who has finally been punished by a larger child he has foolishly provoked. They said to him: 'There's one thing you've got to get into your heads, all of you who work at Bomba mission: just remember that the women in the sixa are not put there as your wives. They haven't been sent there for your benefit, and you'd better remember it.'

Zacharia was still sobbing when the Father whizzed up on his bicycle. He leapt out of the saddle, letting the bicycle fall on its side, and ran forward with his hair standing on end and his face bright red, crying:

'Who did this? Tell me, who did it? Just show him to me. Where is he, in God's name?'

But the man had disappeared and the Father searched for him in vain. I believe he must have taken to the bush as soon as he saw the Father coming. When the Father came back to us, he stood looking at Zacharia for some time and muttering to himself: 'Oh, the brute! The bastard! If I can just get hold of him . . . the bastard!'

Then he glanced towards the villagers who, having separated the combatants, were still standing around. Focusing on them for the first time, he muttered again: 'Oh, the bastards! The bastards!'

He turned towards them and said in our language: 'And where

were all of you when it happened, eh? Why didn't you stop them fighting? Perhaps you helped him to beat up my cook? Speak up!'

All the men turned as one and made off lazily towards their houses. One of them, without turning back, said to the Father: 'Does it mean that you protect your people, no matter what they've done? So you are all the same? It's enough that a man is cook to one of you whites, and he's sure of protection in all circumstances. Yes, you're all the same, after all!'

And another called, again without turning round: 'Haven't you always preached that a man is punished where he has sinned?'

They all laughed aloud and sauntered off to their houses with the most exasperating nonchalance. The Father shrugged resignedly.

We all set off together on foot. Zacharia was limping heavily and his mouth was twisted with pain. The Father walked gloomily beside him and I carried his shoes. A boy came to tell the Father that we were awaited at the presbytery, but we were delayed because the Father went to the bedside of a dying man to try to induce him to accept baptism *in extremis* – in vain, of course.

When we arrived at Kouma, the people had been waiting a long while. There were green branches, garlands of flowers and bunches of mango leaves all around the presbytery. Zacharia was still hobbling, though he tried to walk upright, and he wore the expression of a condemned man. The children of the school – for Kouma is big enough to boast one – greeted us with the *Marseillaise*. When they had finished singing, the Father patted various children on the head and made a little speech of congratulation. The monitors looked pleased and got their children to sing:

> *France is fair,*
> *Blessed and strong.*
> *We'll live for her,*
> *We'll live as one.*

> *Passing the mountains and the seas*
> *And visiting a hundred climes,*
> *Rejoicing to the edge of the world*
> *You will faithfully sing:*

> *France is fair, etc.*

Zacharia went into the house and I stayed outside with the Father. He listened to this song with a pained expression, as if it embarrassed him; but he always used to love it before and ask for an *encore* every time. How odd that he doesn't like it any more!

Zacharia lay down soon after our arrival and all the cooking was done by the village boys. I got the instructions from Zacharia and then passed them on.

So that was Catherine's fiancé, that cruel and threatening man! He might have killed Zacharia. And, my God! If he knew the things I had done with Catherine, he might have beaten me too! Wow! But he was strong! A real gorilla. But he certainly punished Zacharia. I never thought to see him subdued like that.

All the same, Zacharia is a funny lad. Who would have thought he would cry like a little girl? He's met his match at last and perhaps he'll crow a little less from now on. A good thing, really, and I should be the last to complain of it. Oh! But I ought not really to think like that! We're supposed to be charitable even to those we don't like. Poor Zacharia! To be punished so severely is really unjust. Still, I did try to defend him. It's not my fault if I'm not strong enough yet for that.

At Kouma we visited several houses, even those of men. And we were well received in all of them, for now we're only a dozen kilometres from Bomba and the people already resemble those of the roadside rather than the real Talas.

We got lots of presents: cocoa, groundnuts, chickens and eggs. Later we visited the chief in his fine new house, all built of brick, with a pan roof and a ceiling of bamboo slats. The Father congratulated him on it, for he's only recently completed the work.

The chief is a Christian and was married in church, but rumour has it that he's already taken other wives whom he leaves at their parents' homes, where he visits them from time to time. He may even have children already by these other women.

He was sitting in a low arm-chair with a fly-whisk in his hand.

'You understand, chief,' said the Father, 'I shall forbid you the sacraments if what they say is true.'

'What is it that they say, Father?'

'You don't know?'

'Oh, Father, they say so many things about me! But tell me the latest one they have made up; it should be really interesting.'

'That your wives are scattered all over the landscape and have already born you several children. Is it true?'

The chief laughed heartily.

'Just think, Father, just think! There's not a word of truth in these slanders. I can even tell you the names of those who circulate them; all the jealous and envious ones, and those who hate me for no apparent reason, the fools!'

A silence, then:

'Just ask yourself, Father, is it possible? A man marries women and scatters them all over the landscape! Why should he marry them, if only to chase them off into the bush? He'd have to be mad! No, Father, it certainly is not true! These are the slanders of envious men, who've already tried to discredit me with the Administrator. They failed there, of course, so now they've turned their attention to you . . .'

The Father laughed aloud.

'Father,' said the chief crossly, 'life is not so easy for us. There are always hordes of fanatics about, full of the most baffling resentment. Oh, the idiots! I've long since ceased to bother with them. But you shouldn't be taken in by them. Don't forget that you're an old friend of mine . . .'

As soon as we were outside, the catechist told us that the chief wasn't very highly thought of by his subjects, who accused him of various unsavoury intrigues with the administration . . .

But his house was certainly very decent and the walls were all covered with pictures of boxers, cut out of magazines. One of them showed a huge black boxer almost stepping on the prostrate form of a white man, stretched at full length in the ring. The white referee was pushing the black man towards his corner to stop him walking all over his victim. I believe one of them was called Joe, or something like that; I couldn't be sure which, and there was nothing else written under the photo. I asked the Father later, but he said he didn't know and he believed the fight was somewhere in America. I looked at the photo a long time and I'd very much like to know the black boxer's name. But Joe certainly isn't an African name . . .

The chief gave us excellent presents when we left: a goat, several chickens and some cocoa.

The people at Kouma are good Christians and really love the Father; so our tour will finish well, after all. I believe the Father is quite content at last. Perhaps he won't give up the country now? Oh, at this moment, it's difficult to guess what he'll do. He's so peculiar lately that anything can happen . . .

When we got back to the presbytery, Zacharia had demanded some hot water from the catechist's wife and was taking a bath in a big basin, in his own room.

At about eight o'clock, the Father sat down for his chop. I served him myself, fetching the dishes from the kitchen, for Zacharia was already in bed.

While the Father was eating, in the silent manner now usual with him, one of the monitors reported that M. Vidal was touring the neighbourhood and must still be quite close to Kouma. M. Vidal had told them that the Father was nearly killed by a fellow at Zibi. Was it true? The Father confirmed it, but said it wasn't a serious affair; in any case, he was not afraid to die. Then one of the catechists said: 'Father, you must forgive them, despite their evil hearts. They know not what they do.'

'Yes,' said the Father, 'I know that their hearts are evil and that only faith can heal them. But they have no faith; they believe in nothing and this is what makes me despair. I am useless here and no man has need of me.'

One of the monitors replied: 'All the same Father, there are good Christians here.'

'Yes, there are some,' said the Father, pausing to light a cigarette. 'But so few. So few in all this country, which is the most populous and important covered by my mission.'

They were all silent, while the Father pulled deeply at his cigarette. Then he signed for me to clear the table, though he had eaten almost nothing. While I was clearing away, the Father asked them: 'Did M. Vidal tell you why he is touring the country just now?'

'Oh, Father,' one of the monitors said, 'it's his custom. He goes round to see that everything is in order.'

'Is that all?' asked the Father, insistently.

'That is all, Father.'

The Father hesitated a moment: 'And the road?'

'What road, Father?'

'Didn't he speak to you of a road?'

'Oh yes,' replied the other monitor, 'he did ask us whether we'd like to have a road for marketing our cocoa, instead of putting it all for head.'

'And what did you reply?'

'Oh, that we'd be too happy to have a road, of course.'

'Yes,' said the Father, 'of course . . . But it will cost you dear, your road. You will see.'

'How so, Father?' asked the first monitor.

'How so? Don't you know how a road is made hereabouts? They chase all the people from their homes and force them to work in the most atrocious conditions.'

'But somebody must do the work, Father.'

'Would you be willing to work on the road yourself?'

'But I shan't have to do it, Father. I'm running a school!'

'Are you really a fool, or do you bray like an ass just to make a noise?'

'I don't understand you, Father.'

'You don't? Then you are indeed a fool. Listen to me. Suppose I replaced you with another monitor; then you'd be liable for forced labour like everyone else, wouldn't you?'

'What have I done to be dismissed from school, Father?'

'What a blockhead!' cried the Father, laughing. 'When I think that this boy is a monitor . . . No, take it easy, poor old chap! I've no intention of sacking you from the school. It was just a hypothesis.'

'Ah, now I understand, Father.'

'At last, eh? So, would you be willing to work on the road?'

'No, Father.'

'Can't you understand that your brothers, who will be rounded up like animals for forced labour, are no more eager to go than you are? How is it you can't understand that?'

'We need a road all the same, Father.'

'You really think we need a road?'

'Oh, yes, Father!'

'And just why do we need it?'

'Everyone else has a road now, except us.'

'And so?'

'Well . . . they treat us like savages, like blockheads, because we still live deep in the forest.'

Then the Father burst out laughing.

'It's a pity Zacharia is ill today,' he said. 'Anyway, let's talk no more about it.'

Then they bent over the registers and I went to arrange the Father's bedroom before going to lie down.

I'm not sure what the plan is, but I think we'll be leaving tomorrow morning; unless the Father decides to spend two nights here, as he sometimes does in the larger places. But it's not likely, as he seems to be in a hurry to get back to Bomba.

In any case, we are now at our last stopping place. What a tour! . . . I've been through fifteen days in Hell. Fifteen days in an accursed country, swarming with the ministers of Lucifer. I never dreamt such paganism could exist in a land to which Jesus Christ has deigned to send one of His greatest servants. Almost all the men are polygamists and apostates into the bargain. The younger men all want to go dancing and drinking in the town, rather than go to Mass or confession at Bomba. All the girls have babies before getting married. None except the mothers of families seem to be real Christians. But, who knows, perhaps their husbands will soon stop even them from going to Mass?

I'm more and more convinced that this country has need of a great misfortune . . . There! Those are the Father's footsteps! He's coming this way . . . Oh, he's knocking! He only has to push the door, for I haven't bolted it . . . Now, it's done! . . . And he's knocking at Zacharia's door . . . He's gone in and I can hear them talking together, but I can't hear what they're saying. He must have gone to ask Zacharia whether he's feeling better . . . Zacharia is answering in a strangled sort of voice.

Yes, what these people need is a real chastisement, to restore their faith and show that God isn't joking. Oh, that road of M. Vidal's is a real inspiration of Providence! He really must get on with it. Then we'll see whether the Talas are still proud, whether they still mock at God!

What I can't understand is the Father wanting to leave this place

145

when he's about to reap the harvest of all his efforts; just when the people are really going to have need of him. He says he's afraid of appearing to profit by it! Is it his fault if the Administrator wants to make a road? I don't understand anything any more; it's all too complicated for me. . . .

Catholic Mission of Bomba

Sunday, 15 February

Ouf! So at last we are back in Bomba!

How sad everything is here! . . .

But then, what has happened to me? I am scarcely myself any more. It's almost as if a stranger had penetrated me, slowly taking over and inhabiting my being, to such a point that I scarcely recognize myself.

At the time, the first days of that miserable tour seemed to me like a nightmare. But now it's no longer the tour that I look on as a nightmare, but rather all the preceding part of my life which seems dreamlike, cloudy and insubstantial, like something from which I have awoken . . . Yes, exactly as if I were waking from a long sleep, without quite knowing what use to make of my new day. My God! How bizarre it all is. My eyes open on a colourless world; it neither rains nor shines and I can't even guess what time it is.

Everything has been silent at the mission since our return. The Father arrived ahead of us at Bomba. I don't know whether the sixa director and the other mission employees have yet come to speak with him, but I've seen no one since Zacharia and I arrived. Zacharia is almost himself again; he doesn't limp now but he seems terribly tired.

Just now the sixa girls came into the church in their lines for evening prayer. They were praying very quietly; I stole into the church while they were at it, pretending to arrange something on the altar, and took a look to see if Catherine was among them. But I couldn't be sure, because it was so dark in there. After prayers, they all filed out again and I watched them from the doorway of the sacristy, but still couldn't see Catherine, for by then it was dusk. Anyway, perhaps she isn't here at all. Perhaps she's run away?

I've only spoken to one person, Daniel, the Number One Boy. He was gloomy and withdrawn, as if he'd had a bad fright – or at least a great burden of cares. He didn't say much, but I gathered that he knew all the details of our journey.

'All?' I asked him, in alarm.

'Certainly, all! Someone nearly killed the Father . . . Clementine had a fight with little Catherine over Zacharia . . . Zacharia was beaten by Catherine's fiancé, and so on.'

'Is that all?'

'Strewth! . . . You mean there were other things?'

'Oh, yes, lots of things happened.'

'And . . . were they equally important things?'

'Is that really all you heard? You don't know any more than that?'

'No, no, that's all we were told about.'

What a relief! I was afraid Catherine might have told them about me and her. Daniel was very fidgety during the conversation; then he went off somewhere and disappeared.

After all, I'm quite happy. I think I shall have an easy week, with nothing much to do. Nothing, except to ring the bells at six in the morning, at midday and at six at night. That's not very difficult; the only thing is to be punctual, especially with the morning bell. When I think how I had to do everything on tour – serving the Mass, decorating the altar, serving the Father's meals, polishing his shoes, and so on! How restful it is, after a routine like that, to know that one has nothing to do. Daniel can do it all now . . .

Oh! I must ask Vincent Azo, the school monitor, whether his Mass services are properly organized. I don't know how he divides it among his boys, but often they don't turn up on time, saying they haven't been told, or they live too far away, or something. Then it's me who has to serve the Mass, with no warning at all. I don't want any more of that, so I must go and discuss it with Vincent Azo soon. No more early Masses for me, like on tour. If the tour is finished, so are my duties.

Just as long as Catherine has the sense not to reveal what happened between us. It's true I've confessed, but that's no reason why she should noise it about. But then, who knows if she's still at Bomba? Perhaps she's run off to escape any more trouble; it wouldn't be the first time.

Where can the Father be? And what can he be doing? Maybe he's just sleeping in the Fathers' house. I would go and check up if it wasn't such a long way off – at least five hundred metres! But where has he been all day? I haven't set eyes on him since we got back. Neither have I seen Jean-Martin, the new Vicar, although I've wandered all over the mission. Big as it is, I'd surely have seen one of them if they had come out of their house. Why didn't I think of looking to see if they were at dinner? . . . Yes, I was so happy to be back at Bomba that I did nothing but saunter about. My God! Something big must be happening, I'm sure of it. I can't feel at ease since that blasted tour; I fear every moment that something will happen to me. However, I have at least confessed it all. Ever since that night with Catherine, I've lived in fear . . .

So the Fathers have kept in their place all day? Why, I'd really love to know. Perhaps they've been arguing, or the Father's been giving advice to his Vicar? Or is he packing his bags, really meaning to return to Europe, as he told M. Vidal this morning?

They had another discussion this morning, at Kouma. The second Mass wasn't sung there today. When the Father is cross, he always does that. He turns the High Mass into a Low Mass. All the better for the schoolboys of Kouma: they didn't have to sing! These bush boys sing so badly that they always finish the *Introit*, for example, several notes flat. It's ridiculous, because the *Introit* is so easy to sing. But there was no singing at Kouma, and the Father looked done-up. I don't know what made him like that, for the Kouma people proved themselves real Christians.

Just after this second Mass, while the Father was talking with the catechist and monitors, up came M. Vidal on his motor-bike. He went into the house where the Father was sitting among his people. The Father half rose to shake his hand, saying: 'Excuse me a moment, Monsieur the Ad-min-is-tra-tor. I'm still talking to my flock!'

'Carry on, Father, I beg you!' laughed M. Vidal.

The Administrator went out on the veranda and amused himself by watching the people passing in the courtyard. All the men, on recognizing him, doffed their hats hastily. Then he re-entered the house and stood waiting to one side. He was looking at the Father, and every now and then he glanced at his entourage, as if seeking a culprit.

Soon, the Father said to him: 'A moment more, please, Monsieur Vidal. I'm really very sorry.'

'Of course, Father, of course! I have plenty of time.'

At last, the people went away and M. Vidal took a seat opposite the Father.

'Did you release him, then?' the Father asked.

'Release whom?'

'Why! That fellow the other day . . .'

'Oh, him! I'm so sorry, Father, I forgot all about it.'

'You forgot it? That's very odd.'

'Don't you yourself ever forget things?'

'And what have you come to tell me?'

'I haven't come to tell you anything at all. I've merely come to bid you good morning. Believe me, I was thinking of you all last night.'

'Very kind of you. But why didn't you think of the other chap?'

'All right, Father, all right! Let's put that matter behind us.'

M. Vidal pulled a little notebook out of his pocket and scribbled in it for some time. Then he put it back in his khaki trousers and said: 'This time you can be sure that I won't forget, Father. O.K.?'

The Father shrugged and M. Vidal smiled. Then he asked: 'Anything new, Father?'

'I'm going to Europe.'

'You're kidding!'

'Ask anyone.'

'And when did you take this decision?'

'Oh goodness! Only a few days ago.'

'And could I ask, without indiscretion, just why you're going?'

'I wish you good luck here, my dear Vidal! Because I am a failure, a sacred failure. I doubt if anyone has ever fallen deeper into defeat. So, once again, good luck!'

'Father, is this really true?'

'I believe so. I believe that I am really going, without hope of return.'

'Without hope of return?'

'These good people worshipped God without our help. What matter if they worshipped after their own fashion – by eating one another, or by dancing in the moonlight, or by wearing bark charms around their necks? Why do we insist on imposing our customs upon them?'

Vidal's mouth fell open and he flushed slowly as he gazed at the Father, who turned as he spoke and watched the courtyard slowly emptying.

'I've never asked myself this before. Why don't the Chinese devote themselves to converting all Paris to Confucianism or Buddhism or whatever? Oh, I'm not saying that I've solved the problem. Perhaps I'll never solve it, except by the Grace of God. But all the same, I'm certain that it's a serious question.'

Vidal suddenly spotted that I had poured him a Cinzano, so he swallowed it at a gulp before answering: 'Father, forgive me, but do you think your bishop would encourage you in speculation of this kind?'

'Why do you ask me that?'

'No reason. I suppose he disapproves of you, though?'

'Yes, he disapproves of me. Perhaps he'll try to get me declared a heretic; who knows?'

'And what will you do then?'

'I will go still farther, of course.'

The Administrator clapped loudly and cried: 'Of course! . . . How perfectly you said that! How incredibly French you are, Father. I adore you.'

'Have I no right to form my own opinions on the Christian conversion of the blacks? I've been here twenty years, in any case, I tell you. Twenty years of experience counts for something, my friend.'

They were silent a moment. Then the Administrator said: 'Certainly you have immense experience, no one can deny that. All the same, there are missionaries who have died at their labours, at fifty, sixty and seventy years of age. They didn't despair.'

'They didn't despair, as you say. I'd be happy to know their secret. They must have been saints – with all the constancy and Divine Grace demanded by sanctity – or else incurable idiots, full of dangerous ambition and frustrated drives for power.'

'Hold it, Father, hold it!' cried Vidal with a laugh. 'You're going it a bit strong there!'

And he laughed again, but the Father glanced at him reprovingly and he flushed all over again.

'Obviously,' said the Father slowly, 'you don't understand these things.'

'But I do, Father. I understand them only too well. All the better because these things are of some concern to me also.'

'How is that?'

'Listen, Father, let me tell you everything. The condemnation you've just pronounced extends to us also, we colonialists and officials, heirs of Faidherbe and the great Savorgnan de Brazza. For if the Christian religion doesn't make sense here, it must be admitted that the civilization we're seeking to implant is an absurdity under the tropical sun. Exactly what I've always said to you – we're both in the same boat! Have I said something funny?'

'A boat full of crabs, no doubt!' hooted the Father. 'No, my dear Vidal, no! You are not here to implant civilization. Don't fool yourself about that, or, if you haven't already done so, think carefully about it. You are here to protect a certain and precise category of people, that's all. And you will protect them until the others become too strong and throw them out, and you along with them.'

'I don't believe you, Father.'

'You don't believe that they'll throw you out, one day or another?'

'Perhaps they will kick us out one day, although at present it seems very unlikely. To my mind, they cannot compete with us morally or intellectually, let alone technically. Where I cannot agree with you is when you say that I am here only to protect a precise category of people. We've made mistakes here, admittedly, but that isn't what we are doing, Father.'

'There's no way you can avoid doing it, Monsieur Vidal. If you build a road, for example, isn't it under pressure from certain European merchants, cronies of yours? But all the same, it's the natives who have to build it. Do you know a single native who owns a transport company?'

'They'll profit from it, all the same, Father.'

'How can we prevent that, my dear fellow? Certainly, they will profit from it, but who's fault is that? Not yours, or anybody's.'

M. Vidal looked at the Father with some disquiet, though he took pains to conceal it.

'Look,' said the Father, 'I'd rather not answer to God for colonization; I'd rather not be in your shoes. You tell me that I'm an exception among the missionaries: alas, it's true, and you see how it grieves me. There are only two things I can do now: I can stay in this country along with you, associated with you, and thus assist you to colonize it, with dreadful consequences; softening up the country ahead of you and protecting your rear – for that's how you envisage our role, isn't it? Or else, I can truly Christianize the country; in which case I'd better keep out of the way, as long as you're still here.'

'But that isn't what you said a moment ago; that isn't how you justified your departure then!'

'It is merely my second motive.'

'Listen, Father; why don't you try to explain sincerely how you yourself see the roles of administrator and missionary? Why don't you explain to me how they are opposed? Eh, Father? Why don't you do that? Just as a favour to me.'

The Father said: 'I can't explain it just like that, in the abstract. I've already told you that it still isn't clear in my own mind. I do understand that what I should have done was to keep a very detailed diary from the day I arrived here. Then, in relating the facts to one another and studying them together, I could perhaps have arrived at a theory of my own.'

He fell silent and, resting his cheek on his left hand, began doodling mechanically on the page before him.

'Do you know,' he added after a while, 'I can't even describe my life to you? I don't know, but sometimes it seems to me that I see nothing clearly, that I've almost lost my wits. Oh! It's nothing to do with the climate! I left France with all the ardour of an Apostle. I had only one notion in my head and one ambition in my heart: to extend the Kingdom of Christ. Rationalist Europe, so full of arrogance, science and self-consciousness, filled me with dismay. I chose the disinherited, or those whom I was pleased to regard as such. How naïve I was; for are not we ourselves the truly disinherited? . . . When I arrived here twenty years ago, Christ was not wholly unknown in this country. The German missionaries had been here before us, and I found a population attentive and compliant almost to the point of obsequiousness. I abandoned myself to prose-lytism, never pausing to question my activities. I interpreted their attention as the hunger for Christ and their compliance as a proof that they had found Him. I never stopped to think that I was in a colonized country, or that a subjugated people might have special characteristics. I found myself among men who obeyed the slightest motion of my little finger. I played the aristocrat, throwing them orders which they instantly obeyed. I built schools, churches, houses, almost a whole town at the Catholic mission of Bomba. I didn't even ask myself what all this display had to do with Christ. In a word, I became an administrator like you, Monsieur Vidal. Yes, exactly like you! This lasted a long while . . .'

Now the Father was leafing through the Kouma registers, but I'm sure he wasn't reading anything at the pace he was going.

'It might have lasted even longer, if I hadn't suddenly noticed among them a sort of . . . *volte-face*. I was vexed, I stormed at them, but it made not the slightest difference. They simply weren't the same people any more. I didn't recognize them. And I didn't realize that they'd spotted me, that they'd judged me and decided that I had all along deceived them . . .'

He was still riffling through the registers as he spoke.

'. . . This resistance was especially sharp in the country where we are now, the Tala country. I tried everything with these famous Talas, but to no avail! And yet I couldn't ignore them, for they were by far the most numerous tribe in my care. So I thought up recently a little stratagem of my own. My God! To think what hopes I based on that little idea! I felt my spirits as lofty as Napoleon's when he sketched on the map his plan for the victory at Austerlitz. It was all a pipe-dream! But let me tell you what my scheme was; it was simply to abandon the Tala country for two whole years. Thus they would learn to hunger for me and for the love of Christ. Suddenly I would come among them again like a miraculous vision: they would run upon me, embrace me, and rejoice to have found me again. A splendid victory, you'll agree? Unfortunately, it existed only in my imagination, as with all failures and fond idiots. I had understood nothing of the matter. I hadn't understood that my defeat was already pronounced, like a young man who refuses to admit that the girl of his dreams has scorned him. Only the women seemed to have been affected by my long absence. But how much does that mean? Perhaps as much as the hypocrisy of the roadside faithful, who rush to the Mass, confess themselves, communicate and surround me

154

with attentions? Yet these are the very people who are being decimated by colonialism; a colonialism which yields nothing in ferocity to the plagues which swept our cities in the Middle Ages. Forced labour, conscription, floggings, arbitrary imprisonments – practically the same thing. Are they linked by cause and effect? I don't know, but I can no longer avoid connecting them . . .'

He smoked in silence for a while. Then he spoke again: 'I'm more and more certain that I can pierce this enigma if I think on it deeply enough. Wasn't their adherence to Christianity, a formal adherence at that, simply a defence mechanism; just like that little animal . . . What's it called? . . . The chameleon, which takes the colour of its surroundings to avoid being hunted? Oh! Monsieur Vidal, you don't know these people yet. It's very hard to understand them, as it must be with all oppressed people. Their reactions may strike you as strange at first. They don't stand firm in the face of violence, like the oak tree of La Fontaine, no! They bend, as their experience has taught them to bend. And my roadside Christians bend in becoming Christian for the sake of form. Oh! They aren't fools. They've noticed long ago the tone of deference and superstitious respect with which you colonials speak of missionaries and all religious matters, even though you don't practise your faith for an instant. All the formal aspects of religion are presented to them: its prayers, its genuflexions, its signs of the cross and incantations and saints and crucifixes. What an instrument for the revenge of their outraged humanity! "See how at ease we are with your own deepest mysteries! Why then do you persist in despising us?" '

He paused for a moment.

'. . . Here, by contrast, where the people can stay at peace in their own villages and really choose for themselves – yes, I said, choose – they stay Christians for a few months, just to try the thing out and satisfy their curiosity. Then, without regret or nostalgia, they leave it aside and return to their old ways . . . I've also noticed the agreement with the colonials which all the missionaries here seem fated to fall into; this is a real betrayal of the Africans. I say "fated", but is it really so inevitable? I just don't know, but I'd dearly like to know. All I know is that you protect us and that we prepare the country for you, softening the people up and making them docile. The saddest thing is that I'm completely trapped in my European race and my white skin. That's what they're always throwing in my face. Here-abouts, whenever I rebuke the people, they say to me: "Oh! After all, you are just a white man . . . And Jesus Christ, was he not also a white?" meaning: "You wear a soutane only to impose on us more effectively." At least they have understood that you are all here to impose on them, eh, my dear Vidal? Oh! It's far from easy . . .'

Here the Father gave a high-pitched laugh.

'Of course, Father, of course!' cried the Administrator. 'Of course it isn't easy. But are you not exaggerating the difficulties in just the same degree as your hopes were exaggerated? You demand that these poor people should absorb Christianity in less than half a century. Aren't you asking too much? Look how long it took us. We mustn't forget the ages it took us, and all the persecutions, the barbarian invasions and . . . and . . .'

'Are you sure that it's exactly the same thing, Monsieur Vidal? There was perhaps some resistance among us, but nothing in comparison. It was really very superficial resistance, whereas here it is more serious and more profound; it's a spiritual resistance. How can you get a man here to sincerely adopt the principle of monogamy? Sexual abstinence and sexual purity are totally unknown among them. Just take one thing against which I have fought uselessly for years, the unmarried mothers. As you know, the girls begin going with boys at a very early age, fourteen or even thirteen. So, of course, everything happens as one might expect and they have babies. Well, I've never succeeded in getting the people to realize that this is a disgrace to the family. To their mind it's a most fortunate event, above all if the child happens to be a boy.'

M. Vidal couldn't help laughing.

'You are wrong to laugh, Vidal. All the same, to have laboured for twenty years, to have given the best of oneself, to have hoped so much and to finish like this – you'll admit it's hardly fair . . . No, to my mind, it's not at all the same thing. Among us, the soul was prepared: once the seed was sown, it sprang up immediately. But here . . .'

'Might it not be that we merely adapted Christianity to suit our own stomachs, Father? Why not, eh? In Christ's conception, it was to be a universal religion, wasn't it? And Christ was no fool. He must have known that everyone in the world doesn't have the same morality. It's like food: we all eat food, black and white alike, but we don't eat it with the same sauce. Do you see what I'm driving at? Why not present a Christianity that is suited to the blacks? A Christianity . . . well, perhaps, in which polygamy is permitted . . . and where sexual chastity is not regarded as the chief of all virtues?'

The Father contemplated him in silence for a moment and then threw up his eyes, as if the young man had uttered a piece of great nonsense.

Now M. Vidal rose and stood with his back to the room, looking out into the sunlight. He stayed like that for some time, like someone who has been hurt and who fears to show his anger, or simply his sorrow. Then he looked at his wristwatch and said: 'Noon!'

'Don't feel obliged to stay,' said the Father.

'I don't feel obliged to stay; I want to stay.'

'Fine. Then, come and eat with me.'

'Soon, Father. For the moment, let us talk. That's my great passion!'

'Haven't you had enough of it?'

'Oh, Father, you misjudged me entirely, if you only knew.'

'And you too, my dear Vidal, you misjudge me equally.'

'Don't laugh at me, please. You are really someone important to me, a pledge of security, a barrier against solitude. Just to know that I can see you when I want to is a great reassurance to me. Now, without you . . .'

M. Vidal was still talking with his back turned.

'Try to make some friends,' said the Father.

'Ah, those! If only you knew them. Empty, puffed up with their own conceit . . . and their wives! . . . I can't tell you.'

'Try nevertheless to make some.'

'I have tried, Father. I have tried for the whole two years I've been amongst them; but it doesn't work . . .'

'I don't see why.'

'Look! You cannot become a gangster: you must be born one.'

'How severe you are!' exclaimed the Father, with a chuckle. 'I'm beginning to be sorry about some of the things I said to you. You are so young! We never know what effect our words may have on the young. But is that the whole story?'

'What are you trying to say?'

'Well, Heavens above . . .'

'Ah, you mean the Africans? But, Father, I don't even know their language! And anyway, you have failed there yourself . . .'

'You will perhaps succeed. All things are possible.'

The Administrator shrugged and turned towards the Father. He stood in silhouette, hands in his pockets.

'Father, do you know what I'm telling myself at this moment?'

'What is that?'

'That we shall cut very sorry figures in the eyes of future generations.'

'Why should it be so?'

'We are missing the chance to do something really big, with those very same blacks whom we hold in our hands like little children; it will be our fault if they entirely ruin their destiny.'

There was a pause, then, suddenly: 'Father, do you really believe they are the sons of Ham?'

The Father, who had been gazing at the registers, raised his astonished eyes upon him.

'Why do you ask? They don't look any more like the sons of Ham than any other race. But, suppose we admit that they are his sons, what difference does it make? Christ came here precisely to rectify all those ancient crimes, my good fellow. He said: "The curses of the past are over." He has mingled us all in the same love.'

'Oh! Stay here, Father. Your place is here. Don't leave these people you love so much to be devoured by the Bolshevik monster.'

'The Bolshevik monster? . . . But, my dear Vidal, what are you after now?'

'And what do you suppose, Father? That the propaganda of the Communists will spare this country? Oh! Don't deceive yourself. According to our informers, there are already certain subversive groups in the towns who follow Marxist–Leninism and I don't know what-all. To my mind, the best weapon we have against that thuggish philosophy is Christianity. And don't forget that time is short, Father. Everything changes so quickly nowadays. Cook up some kind of Christianity for the Africans, it doesn't matter what, but don't go away and leave us.'

The Father laughed aloud.

'Oh, my dear Vidal, I don't know how much credence to give to your informers. Marxist–Leninist groups of subversives here! Oh! Come on, don't mind my laughing! Even if it were true, you must once-for-all get this into your head: I will not be a sort of gendarme to watch over your moral order. It's no concern of mine . . .'

'No concern of yours! Just wait till the Communists come here! If you're still allowed to say Mass in your church then, do you know what fortune I'd pay you?'

'A bunch of grapes, of course! But, in the meantime, my worries are quite different. Anyway, why should Europe, after two thousand years of Christianity, be swept along now by the Communist attack? Can you explain that, eh? No, I'm going. If we really have to adapt Christianity for Africa, then I'll be more useful back home than I will here.'

'One thing I'm sure of; we shall certainly hear more of you.'

'Thanks. But I'm not sure it's so certain.'

'Oh! Yes it is, Father. You're in the grand tradition of Abelard and Lamennais, of all those who refused to get sunk in a routine.'

'If only that were true!'

'You are something still more than that; you're quintessentially French. I believe that's what makes you so fascinating to me.'

'You're talking nonsense.'

'Perhaps . . .'

M. Vidal began pacing up and down the little room, while the Father buried his nose in the registers, as if wishing to talk no more. Suddenly, the young man stopped, reached once more in his pocket for his notebook and stooped over the Father, who was still reading busily.

'Just have a look at this, Father, please. Take a look.'

'What is it?'

'My fiancée!'

'Ah!'

They gazed at the photo together for a long time: the Father looked amused, while M. Vidal flushed and kept wetting his lips with his tongue.

'She's sweet!' said the Father at last.

M. Vidal scribbled on a piece of paper and offered it to the Father.

'Perhaps I shan't see you again before you leave. Please take this, Father.'

The Father took the paper and read: 'Avenue Mozart . . . Number . . .'

'Yes, that's her address. Go there and you will see her. Tell her that you know me and that we're the best friends in the world. You will tell her, won't you, Father?'

'But of course, my dear Vidal, with the greatest of pleasure.'

'Thank you. Tell her that we spoke together just a few days before your departure and that you shook my hand. Don't forget, Father.'

'Certainly not, old chap.'

'Tell her, too, that the cannibals haven't got me yet and there's a good chance they never will; they've seen enough of me now to know that they risk a fearful belly-ache if they chop me.'

They laughed together.

'And say that my skin hasn't turned black, despite all this sun-shine, but it isn't my fault. So she must just force herself to give up dreaming of having coffee-coloured children.'

'Because she . . .'

'Oh, yes! She loves coffee-coloured children.'

'That can be arranged.'

'Just what I told her. Plenty of black men in Paris! But no, there's only one Negro she wants, and that's me! Plenty of water must flow before I become a cannibal, though.'

They both chortled away for a long while.

'And when will you be married?'

'Married, Father?'

'But, of course! Aren't you engaged?'

'Oh, yes! . . . We are engaged. Too much engaged and for too long. But . . . put yourself in my place, Father.'

'Thanks! But I'm afraid I can't.'

'No, seriously. What good is it getting married if one stays in Europe and the other with the cannibals?'

'Is her health too poor to come out here?'

'Do you see her living here, in good health?'

'Why ever not? She wouldn't be the only one, after all.'

'Don't say another word, Father, I beg you! You make me

ashamed. She wouldn't be the first? A merry company she'd keep, I assure you! Daughters of grocers and butchers and provincial chemists! Those sluts would go anywhere, just by scraping up a million little economies every two or three years.'

'And she?'

'The daughter of a Bar President!'

'Ah!'

'No less.'

'Then you can expect to be Governor-General, old fellow! After which, you can get yourself made chief adviser to the Ministry of Colonies. Isn't there a message for your father, too?'

'My father can stuff . . . I beg your pardon.'

'Oh, there's no need.'

'My father! What a menace! It's all his fault that I find myself in this hole. A real fanatic for colonization, he is! From the arm-chair, of course. He knows the name of every little ass who's carried a musket or pitched a tent in any corner of the world. Knights of civilization, he calls them. Long-range commercial travellers, says my mother, just to contradict him. It was Vietnam one minute and Senegal the next. So, I scarcely had a chance, you see!'

'But who forces you to stay here?'

'And what could I do in Europe now, with no proper training? . . . Not counting the taste for power which I've acquired. And, after all, it will be a "good experience" . . .'

'Nothing for your mother?'

'You won't see her, Father.'

'I'm sorry.'

'I don't mean that she's dead. Just that they're divorced and she's gone to live in the provinces, in the East.'

'Shall we go and eat now?'

'No, Father. If you'll excuse me, I must be going now. Safe journey! Don't forget us! Write and keep me in touch with your studies.'

'I won't forget, my dear young fellow. Keep your pecker up! Don't lower yourself too much, and don't isolate yourself too much, either.'

'Farewell, Father. When I come to France, I'll certainly look you up.'

'*Au revoir*, then, Monsieur Vidal.'

The Father ate quickly and then went outside to supervise the porters, who were busy with the many presents we've received on this last stage. Apart from last night's presents, a whole lot more were brought to Mass this morning: sacks of groundnuts and cocoa, hordes of chickens . . . The Father divided the loads among several porters, including women. He had lost that worried and tormented look he wore while talking to M. Vidal. He looked alert, full of vigour and even gaiety. He must always be absorbed in some task which demands all his energies, or he will suddenly turn gloomy. When a big youth found his load too heavy, he tapped him on the shoulder and exclaimed: 'You should be ashamed, my lad! Look what your old father can do!'

Then he lifted the load himself, holding it at arm's length and at the level of his shoulders, almost without effort, before letting it drop. He laughed aloud and the young man laughed with him. The Father tapped him on the cheek and the young man swiftly lifted the load on to his head.

'You see?' cried the Father in felicitation.

When we were getting ready to leave, at about two in the afternoon, the two monitors led their pupils out into the courtyard. Standing in neat rows, they began to sing:

> *Through the dark night creeping,*
> *Hand-in-hand,*
> *We hear the great world sleeping,*
> *Hand-in-hand.*
> *A star in heaven lights our path,*
> *Hand-in-hand.*
> *A star in heaven shows our path,*
> *Hand-in-hand.*

Then they began filing off with the song:

> *When we were young children,*
> *Just to vex grandmother,*
> *We would snatch her snuff-box*
> *One time or another.*

How sweet to the heart at last
Are these memories of the past!
How sweet to the heart at last
Are these memories of the past!

One of the monitors shouted: 'One, two! . . . One, two! . . .' as they swung away.

It was now very hot and the Father put on his helmet, which he seldom wears. Many people came running, pagans among them, to hear the children singing and watch them march in their smart uniforms.

After the parade, the Father patted three or four boys on the head and distributed among them the few little images he had been able to find in our boxes. Then he said: 'My boys, I am very happy and proud for you. I don't know if I'll ever see you again, for I'm going back to Europe, to my own country, to rest for a while. Your Father is an old man now, you know. For nearly twenty years I've been among you and I am tired, like any father of a family who grows old. It breaks my heart to think that perhaps you, who love me so much, will never see me again. But remember that I shall think of you always, even if I don't have the joy of seeing you. Nothing could ever make me forget you. I shall speak of you to the young children of my country, those of your own age, and I'm sure they will love you also, even without meeting you. I'll be sure to tell them how clever you are and that you sing like angels. Obey your monitors always, love them and respect them; they are well-instructed people who will also instruct you well. Good-bye, my dear children! And may Jesus Christ watch over you.'

He then bade good-bye to the monitors and catechists, but I couldn't hear what he said to them, as I was standing some way off and there was now a lot of noise in the courtyard.

At last we began our journey, followed by crowds of schoolboys and other older admirers for a good kilometre. Gradually our cortège dwindled until only the three of us were left, for the porters had already gone ahead. Zacharia walked along with a bored and indifferent expression, while the Father pushed his bicycle beside us. He seemed about to speak to Zacharia, but he changed his mind and, mounting his bicycle, called out to us: 'Try to walk a bit faster: it looks as if it might rain.'

Then he sped off, disappearing round the bend of the path as though his white soutane had suddenly been gobbled up by the high green waves of the forest.

Some hours later, just as Zacharia and I reached the road, we saw a lorry coming towards us. It was loaded high with big logs, which stretched right out behind, for the driver had left off the trailer. They often do this on Sundays, when the bosses are unlikely to notice, for they consider the trailer a nuisance. But the bosses don't like it, because the extra weight is bad for the back end of the lorries.

As the lorry rumbled towards us Zacharia thumbed it down and I was amazed to see it stop. The driver greeted Zacharia gaily, I believe they must have been old friends, and invited him to ride in the cab. I perched myself just behind, between the back of the cab and the logs. We didn't quite catch the Father, the lorry being so heavy, but we got to Bomba without mishap. It didn't really rain, only a light drizzle for a few minutes . . .

In another week I have to go back to school. What a prospect! The monitor of my class is sure to take it out on me and shame me in front of everyone. He always calls me 'the Touring Boy', as if it's my fault that I have to tour so much. Anyway, for the moment I have a whole week of holidays.

I suppose my father has a point. All the same, it would be useful to go regularly to school and improve my French. For instance, I would have understood better all the discussions between M. Vidal and the Reverend Father. It's true I remember every word they said, but I didn't really understand what they were driving at. They seemed to be saying that the Catholic religion isn't really meant for Africans. But if that were true, we couldn't go to Heaven, for it says in the Bible: 'Without the Church, there is no Salvation.' Yet the Father has always told us that Heaven is open to everybody who deserves it, black or white. My God, it's all too complicated for me! . . .

Catherine . . .

It's amazing how I can't forget her. And every time I think of her, a great wave of blood floods my heart and gets me all hot again. I suppose I'm still afraid of her because of what she did to me that night. Yes, that must be why I flush so hotly when I think of her. I always do that when I'm frightened.

Oh! I'll never manage to forget Catherine, though I know I shouldn't think of her. Where can she be now? Has she really run away? In any case, this affair is sure to turn the mission upside down. Raphael can scarcely get out of it without blame . . .

Just so long as Catherine doesn't drag me into it! I don't believe she will; she was so sweet to me, so very sweet . . . I still remember that morning and always will. I woke up half-stunned and my legs would scarcely carry me. Then Catherine washed and dressed me like a mother with her child, and at the end she kissed my cheek!

Catherine . . .

THIRD PART

How wonderful it would be if men were driven by the desire to fertilize the earth, rather than to gather in the harvest! That's what I want to say and I know how stupid it is. Almost as if one had faith in humanity and suspected it of altruism!

Maxim Gorky

Bomba

Now it's all started again, as I knew it would! I dreaded it.

It reminds me of the appearance of the full moon in September, when my mother was still alive and I was very young. She said to me: 'Look at that moon. Isn't it larger than all the other moons? As if it were swollen? Well, that's because it's with child! It's carrying the baby which it bears every year, just at this season: the rains . . .' And, in fact, the appearance of that moon provoked a series of rains which didn't stop till near Christmas. Just like that accursed tour, which has brought on a whole series of catastrophes. But I know so little of this new kind of season that I wonder not only when it will finish, but whether it will ever finish. Why did the Father have to go on this tour himself? If only he'd had the excellent notion of letting his Vicar go, perhaps we'd have avoided the whole business?

So Zacharia has fled! Yes, he's vanished from Bomba and there's no longer a cook by the name of Zacharia. What a creature, all the same! He went without a thought of bidding farewell to the Father, of even shaking his hand. He left him as one might a casual acquaintance, encountered on the path. That's his friendship, not even a handshake! He knew that the Father would have shaken his with goodwill, and that he'll probably never see him again. And that's after a dozen years of working together!

Yes, it seems that Zacharia has been at the mission for a dozen years. The Father took to him from the first and never went on tour without him. Zacharia should have been sacked on countless occasions, but the Father always turned a blind eye to his misdeeds. Apart from his habitual generosity towards Zacharia, he gave him a house so large and comfortable that it made the monitors jealous. But he still went off without a word of farewell. Just because the Father sent for him to answer to the charges of ill-treatment brought by his wife.

This woman Clementine, who's always moaning about something or other, arrived early in the afternoon, waving her arms in the air and howling like a drenched chimpanzee. Her nose was bleeding and her mouth was so full of blood that she spattered everyone when she spoke. Her dress was all torn behind and she cried out to everyone she met: 'Where can I find the Father? Do you know where he is? For God's sake, tell me where I can find him!' When she saw me, she flew upon me and grabbed me like a doll and kept shouting: 'You at least must know where he is. You must know. Tell me where I can find him . . .'

We went together through the mission, searching for him, and found him at last in the garage. Clementine stammered out her story. Zacharia had brought Catherine into their house, without her knowledge. Then they fell upon her and beat her till she bled, both of them at once. She was sobbing so much that she could hardly speak. She kept sniffing at the blood which poured from her nose, or spitting it out on the ground. I really had to feel sorry for her. The Father heard her story without speaking, then set off for his office with us trailing behind. As soon as he got there, he sent one of the workmen to call Zacharia and tell him to come at once to the office.

A few minutes later the fellow came back puffing. Zacharia had refused to come. His very words were: 'I've had enough! I won't be mucked about any more by anyone. I've had enough of this blessed prison and I'm clearing out. As for Clementine, she can hang herself wherever she finds a good hook! Let her not dare to follow me. If she does, God alone knows what I'll do to her!' I expected the Father to jump up and go straight to Zacharia's house. He did nothing of the sort. He went inside his office and sat down, as if expecting that Zacharia would come after all. At first he tugged his beard, then he began smoking, cigarette after cigarette. Clementine was sobbing quietly on the veranda.

At about five o'clock, he sent the same workman to repeat his message. Once again, he came back puffing. Zacharia had gone. His neighbours confirmed that they had seen him leaving.

The fact was that Zacharia didn't have many possessions at the mission. Everything he had acquired, he had carried to his native village, where he was said to own a big property. This village was far away from Bomba.

When he heard that Zacharia had really gone, the Father jumped up, shaking his head with surprise or with anger. He crushed a cigarette in the tray and went outside. Seeing Clementine still sobbing on the veranda, he said to her: 'Go and sleep, Clementine. If there is anything you need, come and see me.'

Then he went to see his young Vicar, Jean-Martin.

I stayed on the veranda and thought about Zacharia's conduct. That's his friendship! Yet I can hardly believe he's really gone. It's as though they'd come to tell me he was dead – that wouldn't be any harder to believe straight away. I wonder why? Zacharia is such a strange fellow; he gives such an impression of vitality and force, which for a long time I confused with actual muscular strength. But I was disillusioned that day when he was humbled by Catherine's fiancé. All the same, I'm used to having him around.

The Father and his Vicar talked for a long while. I could hear their voices as I stood on the office veranda, which adjoins the Father's house. When they came down, they entered the office and the Father sent me to fetch Raphael, the catechist-director of the sixa The sixa was almost a kilometre away, right on the other side of the mission. All the way across I was questioned by everyone I met. Most of them were workmen who would normally be going home by this time, for it was nearly six o'clock, but instead of leaving they stood about in groups, talking in low voices. Mingled with them were various people who had come for confession, but who seemed equally disinclined to leave the mission.

All of them turned as they saw me and called: 'Where are you rushing off to, sonny?'

'To call Raphael,' I replied.

'Is it something serious, do you think?'

'I don't know.'

'Do they want to question him about that business?'

'They didn't tell me anything. They just said: "Go and fetch Raphael."'

'What did Fada say when he hear Zacharia gone?'

'Nothing.'

'Na true?'

'He just gave a sigh.'

'He no get angry?'

'He's never angry now.'

'He no get sad?'

'Oh! A little.'

Raphael got up with a worried look when I summoned him. He followed me like a little dog which wants to slink into the earth. If he hadn't been so tall, I'm sure he'd have tried to hide behind me. When we got to the office, I stationed myself on the veranda so as not to miss a thing. After a long hesitation, Raphael went inside.

'Raphael, my boy,' said the Father, 'why is it you haven't come to see me since I got back? Eh, Raphael, why didn't you come to talk to your old Father, returned from a long journey?'

But Raphael stood there like a stump.

'Say something, my boy. What's the matter with you?' asked the Father. 'What has happened? Have you some little sin on your conscience?'

Still Raphael said nothing. He stood there stupidly, twisting his hands about like a kid. The two priests looked at him curiously. It was getting dark and the Father went to light his Aida pressure-lamp. Then he said: 'Raphael, I've heard lots of things about you. First of all, I want the truth; then I'll consider what to do. Go and call that girl Catherine. As for you, I'll send for you this evening, or tomorrow, or another day.'

Raphael shot out like a bird released from a trap. It was getting cold on the veranda, so I walked behind the office and came into the ante-room at the back. It was a little place that no one used and where I wouldn't be noticed. It was a smart idea of mine to hide there. Otherwise, the Father might have seen me in the midst of his inter-rogation of Catherine and sent me away, out of earshot.

Catherine arrived soon after Raphael's departure and I saw her creep nervously into the light of the lamp. The Father went out on the veranda and called the assistant cook, Anatole. Then he took from the cupboard the stoutest cane he could find. Anatole came in with his sleeves rolled back to the shoulders. He was a strong lad and he took the cane without a word, knowing just what the Father wanted. Catherine, who also knew, stood awaiting his first stroke. Then he began, cutting her by preference across the buttocks. After each blow, she rubbed the place furiously with her hands. While she did this Anatole waited, for the Father didn't like girls to be hit on the hands. As soon as she stopped, Anatole hit her again and Catherine began to twist about and to stamp with her feet on the cement floor. She was trying hard to stop her tears. I felt miserable watching her suffer like that and tears came to my eyes too.

Finally, the Father signed to Anatole to stop. Catherine kept twisting to and fro, while the two priests looked at her. When she had calmed down a bit, the Father yelled at her: 'You're a wicked girl! The Devil is in you. You have come here and corrupted my sixa with your filthy conduct . . .'

Unable to check her sobs, Catherine shook her head in vigorous denial.

'Aren't you ashamed of your lust?' cried the Father. 'After the scandal in Tala and the correction I gave you there, could you not give up seeing Zacharia?'

'But I haven't seen him again!'

'You're lying!'

'No, Father. It's the truth. I swear it's the truth.'

Her sobs were deeper than ever.

'The truth . . . The truth . . . I haven't seen him . . .' she kept sobbing through her tears.

'You didn't see him this afternoon?'

'No, Father.'

'No! Then where did you fight with his wife? I suppose you're going to tell me you didn't fight with her today?'

'Yes, Father, I did fight her. But I didn't see Zacharia. I swear it.'

'And where did you fight?'

'Near the cemetery, Father. Between the church and the cemetery.'

'You're lying, it was in Zacharia's house.'

'No, Father, that's not true. Someone's been telling you lies. We fought by the cemetery. One of my friends in the sixa saw her in church and came to tell me. I went and hid in a bush near the cemetery and waited for her . . . All the sixa girls were there, Father; they can tell you. It was Raphael who separated us, and he's already given me a thrashing to punish me . . .'

The Father turned to Anatole: 'You're a cousin of Zacharia's; do you know anything about this?'

'Yes, Father; I was there.'

'What happened, exactly?'

'As this girl says; they fought near the cemetery. Catherine got the better of it, I think. But I saw Clementine go back to her place, bad woman. Then, for no reason, she attacked Zacharia, saying it was he who had incited his mistress to ambush her. But Zacharia knew nothing about it and he was annoyed, so he gave her a drubbing too. It was only after this second drubbing that she came running to you . . .'

'Ah, I see!' muttered the Father, frowning deeply. 'She lied to me as well. That's what they all do! Why did you go and attack Clementine?'

'I had to get my revenge, Father. She really shamed me that first time, just because she caught me unawares. Put yourself in my place; you must see that I had to take my revenge. But I haven't been seeing Zacharia, I swear.'

'Good!' said the Father, pinching his lips a little. 'Now you must tell me everything that happened between you and Zacharia, from start to finish. I want all the details, nothing left out. You see the cane in Anatole's hand. I can tell you one thing, he knows how to use it. Just understand that?'

Still crying a little Catherine began blurting out her story.

From the time she arrived in the sixa, Raphael had given her a horrible job to do. This was to beat the clay in preparation for tile-making. With four or five other girls, she was set to pound the clay in a rough mortar, using a big stone which needed both hands to lift it. They worked like this every day, from morning to night. After a whole week of it, the other girls in the gang kept muttering that they ought to have been relieved by another gang. Normally, this was done every two days. Catherine knew nothing of the rules, but when her fiancé came to visit that Sunday she complained to him about it. He was a smart fellow and went straight off to see Raphael, to whom he gave five hundred francs, or so he told Catherine afterwards. From then on, Raphael seemed to take special care of her. He found her a new job, which was to sweep his house and to do his cooking for him, at such times as his wife wasn't present. As Raphael's house was within the sixa compound, just beside the girls' dormitory, she was practically unoccupied and very contented with her lot.

In this way she spent almost all day in the catechist's house until, one morning, Zacharia chanced to call on his friend Raphael and found her all alone there. He joked with her and they laughed heartily together. After that, he came to see her every day, always bringing her some present such as meat, fish, boxes of sweets or loaves of bread. Catherine was very grateful for these presents, because her fiancé lived far away in the town and hadn't much time to visit her, especially as he worked for a white man. Also, her parents were far off in their village and took little interest in her, now that they had pocketed the bride-dowry. Hence, she had no one else to bring her food or gifts, and would have been really unhappy at the sixa but for Zacharia. He came every day to see her and was always full of jokes and laughter.

Now, one night, when she was already sleeping in the dormitory, her day's work being finished, Raphael came in and asked the girls who were still awake: 'Where is Catherine, the girl who works in my house?'

'She's over there, asleep,' they told him.

Catherine had awoken at the sound of her name, always enough to rouse her, but she feigned sleep while she listened to the catechist's approaching step. He shook her and said: 'Wake up, Catherine! Why are you sleeping at this hour? Are you awake? Good. I'd like you to come over and do something at my house.'

She got up and followed him. Raphael pointed silently to one of the rooms of the house, where a hurricane-lamp was burning. Still half-asleep, Catherine walked in and found Zacharia smiling at her from the bed. Catherine tried to run out again, but Raphael blocked the door and said sternly: 'Where the hell are you going? Get back in that room!'

She was frightened and confused, hearing Raphael say again: 'For the last time, get back in that room!'

She hadn't the courage to disobey him . . .

That was how they became lovers. Catherine now spoke hesitantly, admitting that what she had done with Zacharia was wrong. But she hadn't really any choice, for if she refused Raphael would send her back to the heavy work, loading her with painful difficulties, insecurity and suspicion. She had gradually come to understand that everyone in the sixa had to dance to Raphael's tune if they were to avoid suffering; it's true there were a few recalcitrant girls there, but their position was most unenviable. So she had resigned herself to this irregular liaison with Zacharia, hoping to keep it secret until her marriage. In this way, she hoped in her heart to lose nothing by it; she would live in peace at the sixa and in the end she would be married without scandal.

From then on, she slept regularly at the catechist's house, in a room reserved for her. Zacharia came often to sleep with her, either all night or for a part of it.

This had gone on for a fortnight or more, she couldn't be certain. Then one of her friends in the dormitory warned her that it had leaked out and everyone in the sixa was chattering about her affair with Zacharia. One girl in particular, called Monica, was obsessed with the subject, harping on it like a *voyeur* and accusing Catherine of sleeping with the cook just to get the leavings from the Father's meals. Catherine was bitterly offended and determined to have it out with this girl Monica, but her friend restrained her and advised her to be very cautious about the whole thing – she said that Monica was motivated by jealousy. Catherine pretended to agree with her, but she soon sought out Monica and thoroughly beat her up. There was a scandal about this, but Raphael did his best to hush it up . . .

Here the Father interrupted her narrative: 'Listen, why did you say that Monica was motivated by jealousy?'

'That's what they told me, Father. I know nothing about it.'

'You know nothing about what?'

'That . . .'

'Yes, what?'

'She was also Zacharia's girl, long before me.'

'Who?'

'Why, Monica, Father.'

'Is that all you know about it?'

'Well . . . yes, Father.'

'Do you want another whipping?'

'Oh, no, Father!'

'Then what do you know about all this?'

'Zacharia gave her up because she smelt bad.'

'She smelt bad?'

'That's what they told me, Father.'

'And how long did their affair last?'

'I've no idea, Father.'

'Make a guess.

'I don't know . . . some weeks, perhaps.'

'And do you think that after sleeping with a woman for weeks, one could give her up on the pretext that she smelt bad?'

'It does happen, Father.'

'Are you making fun of me?'

'Oh, no!'

'Look here, wouldn't Zacharia have known right away that she smelt bad?'

'But, Father, she didn't smell at all when they began their affair.'

'And suddenly she began to smell?'

'Just so!'

'If you push me too far, I'll have you thrashed so that you'll never forget it!'

'It was because . . . she had the disease, Father.'

'The disease!'

'Yes, Father, the disease.'

'God in Heaven, what a race! Has it no name, this disease?'

'Yes, Father, but . . .'

'Quickly!'

'Father . . .'

'Will you speak or not? Do you want to be flogged to death?'

'Oh, no! It's the . . . the . . .'

'The what?'

'The syphilis, Father.'

'Syphilis! . . . Do you have it, too?'

'No, Father.'

'Syphilis! Why on earth didn't you say so?'

'But, Father, when you say "the disease", it's always the syphilis that you mean.'

'Yes, that's true. And where did she contract it? In my sixa?'

'I don't know, Father.'

'In your opinion?'

'Here.'

'Syphilis in my sixa! That's beyond everything! Are you sure it's syphilis this girl has?'

'It seems so. I'm a newcomer here and don't really know, but that's what they all tell me.'

The Father mopped his brow with a handkerchief while the Vicar, who a moment before was half-smiling, suddenly turned gloomy again.

'Look at this cane,' said the Father. 'You see it well?'

'Yes, Father.'

'I command you to tell me the name of your friend.'

'My friend, Father?'

'Yes, the girl who has told you all this.'

'She knows it all because she's been here longer than I, Father.'

'Her name! Tell me her name? Is she married already?'

'No, Father.'

'So, is she still in the sixa?'

'Yes, Father.'

'Her name?'

'Marguerite, Father.'

'Marguerite, Marguerite . . . There are millions of Marguerites in the world. Do you want to drive me crazy? Do you want another thrashing? Marguerite who?'

'Anaba. Marguerite Anaba.'

The Father quickly wrote the name on the paper in front of him.

'Did it never occur to you to come and tell me all this?'

'You wouldn't have believed me, Father.'

'What makes you think that?'

'I hear you've been told things before and didn't believe them.'

The Father frowned deeply and cried: 'Go on!'

'How, Father? . . .'

'With your story.'

'Well, Zacharia and I stopped seeing each other for a while, so as not to provoke another scandal. I went back to sleeping in the dormitory . . .'

'You missed it, eh?'

'What, Father?'

'You missed not sleeping with Zacharia, didn't you? Be honest for once in your life. Didn't you long to see him again? Speak, then!'

'Yes, Father, I did miss seeing him.'

'And why? Just why? You knew you were doing wrong; you've just said so yourself. Why did you wish to see him again?'

He turned towards the Vicar and murmured in French: 'Of

course, she doesn't know! They are all eaten up with lust! Ah, what a race!'

Jean-Martin gave an embarrassed smile. The Father was really angry now and kept shrugging his shoulders. 'Go on!' he roared at Catherine.

Although she no longer saw Zacharia, nor slept at Raphael's house, Catherine was still not put back on the hardest tasks . . .

Now her narrative got more and more hesitant, so that the Father yelled at her again: 'You want the cane?'

Catherine trembled all over and said quickly: 'No, Father!'

'Go on, then, quickly. Otherwise . . .' And he pointed to Anatole, who was flexing the cane expectantly in his hands. Then Catherine began speaking swiftly and without pause.

For more than a week she didn't see Zacharia at all. Then he came to tell her that he was going on tour with the Father. He asked Catherine to go with him, but she refused, fearing that the sixa girls would whisper it about and perhaps get it to the Father's ear. That evening, however, Raphael sent for her and told her firmly that she must agree to go. She agreed, though with great reluctance.

'And your fiancé?' leapt in the Father.

'My fiancé?'

'He could have come to see you during your absence. What would you have done then?'

'He hardly comes any more, Father, because his white man gives him less and less free time. But even if he had come, they would have explained my absence one way or another. It's always easy enough to explain such things.'

'Continue!'

'That's all, Father.'

'How do you mean, "that's all"?'

'There's nothing more to tell, Father. I followed Zacharia on tour – you know the rest. His wife got wind of it and came after us; we fought . . .'

'Yes, yes, I understand.'

The Father was leaning right over the table, frowning and jiggling his knee. Suddenly he said: 'All right! Now get out!'

Catherine went cautiously away, walking backwards.

The two Fathers were silent. Meanwhile, Anatole kept bending the cane across his thigh. Then Father Drumont said to him: 'Send for the girl Marguerite Anaba.'

Anatole went out. I was still hiding quietly in the ante-room. I saw the Father get up and go to the cupboard, from which he took a big register. As he sat down beside the Vicar, he exclaimed: 'Ah! What a people! What do you think of this, eh, Father?'

'I can scarcely believe all the things that girl said.'

'I don't blame you. You who are staying here should remember this always. I couldn't give you a better initiation than this interview. Believe me, it's no sinecure to be a missionary in this place. What a race!'

They both smoked in silence.

Anatole returned, pushing Marguerite Anaba before him as if she were a goat. She stood in the little circle of light before the two priests, with her eyes obstinately lowered. She was an odd-looking girl, this Marguerite; strongly-built as a boy, despite her short stature; wearing an ugly dress over her bandy legs; her head mown like a meadow and her toes turned inward in the strangest fashion.

The Father looked at his register and barked: 'Are you Marguerite Anaba?'

'Yes, Father; Marguerite Anaba, daughter of . . .' Here she gave the names of her parents, her village, her tribe, her mother's tribe, her paternal grandmother's tribe and many other details, none of which were demanded of her. I saw at once how aggressive this girl was.

'How long have you been in the sixa?'

'That's the sort of question I detest.'

'What?'

'I said, that's the sort of question I detest.'

'Is this girl mad?'

'Oh, no, Father, no, I'm feeling fine. But as soon as you knew my name, you had only to look at your own register to see exactly how long I've been in the sixa.'

The Father was taken aback for a moment, but then he turned to Anatole and said: 'Teach her to answer properly.'

The assistant cook brandished his cane and sought out a good position. Then he brought it swishing down in a great arc to strike Marguerite's bottom with a dry, hollow crack, like the sound of a mango falling on hard earth from a tree-top. Marguerite gave neither sound nor sign. Now Anatole began beating her swiftly and with all the energy of his first stroke, and at every crack I shut my eyes, shaking all over as if I had myself been hit. Still Marguerite made no sound or gesture, but stood there rigid as a stump. After twenty strokes, the Father signed to Anatole to stop. Only then did Marguerite carry her hands to her buttocks and rub them slightly. The two priests watched her in silent curiosity.

'Didn't that hurt?' demanded Father Drumont.

Marguerite grimaced indifferently.

'Perhaps you'd like to try a bit more?'

Still she made no reply, but stood there looking downwards at the floor. The Father signed slightly to Anatole, who again took up his post and gave her another resounding thwack. Marguerite hadn't noticed the Father's sign and wasn't expecting this renewed assault, so the first blow made her tremble. From now on, every stroke made her kick about; she rubbed furiously at her buttocks and tears brimmed in her eyes, but she still didn't cry. Again, the Father signed to Anatole to stop. Now the Vicar was shifting about in his chair and frequently swallowing his saliva.

'Now I hope you'll reply to my questions without any more nonsense,' said the Father, glaring into Marguerite's face.

But Marguerite, though still twisting with pain, made no reply. Then the Father demanded: 'How long have you been here?'

'A year, Father.'

Now she began crying and her voice was broken with sobs.

'Why for a year? Why aren't you married?'

'It's a long story, Father.'

'Let me hear it.'

'I'd been here for three months and my marriage had been announced on two successive Sundays. It was to be announced once more and I would be married in the week following the third Sunday. I was so happy about it. But one day . . . yes, it was the Tuesday morning, always an unlucky day for me, I went to get my morning task as usual. That day, I was given the unusual job of going to the catechist Raphael's house. I had swept it out and was about to sweep the kitchen when someone came to say that the Reverend Father wanted me. I ran here and found you in the office. Raphael was standing behind you. You asked me: "Is it true that you've already been married, to a polygamist?" I was about to say that it wasn't true, when I noticed that Raphael was signing to me to say yes. I didn't understand what he was at, but since the catechist was pushing me that way, I said it was true. Then you said that my marriage must be delayed, as was customary whenever the former wife of a polygamist was to be married in church.'

'And wasn't it true? Are you not the ex-wife of a polygamist?'

'Certainly not, Father.'

'Then why did you tell me so?'

'I've just explained to you. I was scared.'

Marguerite wiped her eyes, but soon she began weeping again.

'Scared of whom?'

'Of the catechist Raphael, Father.'

'Why?'

'Why? But, Father, it's he who is in charge of us. He would give me an awful life if I disobeyed him. He is my master.'

'What? Raphael is no more your master than I am.'

'Oh, Father, there's one thing you don't seem to understand at all. In giving Raphael the sixa to direct, you as good as said to him: "Here are your wives: they belong to you. Do with them as you will." '

'I said no such thing!'

'It may be so. In any case, that's how he understood you. He is the big chief, with a village full of wives. Any other man would be the same in his position, it's natural. And when anyone has complained of him to you, have you ever believed in the truth of their complaints?'

The Father silently teased at his beard. The Vicar made a wry face and looked at Marguerite. Then the Father said: 'Why did Raphael want to delay your marriage? What was his motive?'

'I don't know, Father. I have no means of knowing.'

'Why do you think?'

'I can't tell you.'

'Do you want another taste of the stick?'

'No, Father!' cried Marguerite, shaking all over.

'Then don't force me to use it. Tell me what Raphael's motives were, and be quick about it.'

Fluttering her eyelids nervously, Marguerite glanced at the two priests in turn. Then she lowered her gaze once more and murmured: 'I don't know, Father, but . . .'

'But what? Will you get on with it?'

She said that Raphael had come to call her from the dormitory on the night of the same Tuesday. He led her to his house and there he told her that he knew her fiancé quite well; he wasn't at all the right man for a girl like her.

'You say this happened during the night?'

'Yes, Father, the Tuesday night.'

'And was his wife not there, if he was entertaining girls from the sixa during the night?'

'She's never there, Father. You scarcely ever find her living with her husband.'

'Why not? I'm certain you know the answer.'

'I don't concern myself with other people's lives, Father.'

'You don't, eh? Come on, talk! Why is his wife not there?'

'I've just said that I don't know the reason.'

'So you want the stick, after all?'

'It seems to me that the director always finds reasons for sending his wife away.'

'Marguerite Anaba, you've been in the sixa for a year?'

'Yes, Father, a whole year!'

'And what do you think of Raphael's conduct in general? Is he a good Christian?'

'Yes, Father. He goes to confession twice a week and takes Communion every day, and he always joins us at prayers . . .'

'That's not what I'm talking about.'

'Ah?'

'For instance . . . is he a good husband?'

'A good husband!'

'Yes . . . Come now, you know what I'm driving at.'

'Oh, yes! He's a very good husband: he gives his wife everything she wants.'

'Everything?'

'Yes, Father. Raphael has plenty of money.'

'Indeed?'

'Of course! But you must know that, for it's you who pay for him.'

'But what I pay him is very little, almost nothing.'

'Well, Father, I just don't know.'

'Go on with your story.'

'He took me to his home that night . . .'

'So that's it! Then he takes other women apart from his wife?'

'Who, Father?'

'Why, Raphael! Speak up, or it's the stick again for you!'

'Well . . . I think he does have girl friends.'

'From the sixa?'

'Sometimes, yes.'

'And other girls also?'

'Yes, Father.'

'Go on.'

Raphael had insisted that Marguerite's fiancé was not right for her; he was ugly, poor and ignorant. Marguerite said nothing, wondering what the catechist was getting at. Then Raphael said: 'I'm sure you'd like to marry someone better-looking, richer and more educated, a better man altogether! You're so pretty, and that counts a lot!' Still Marguerite said nothing, but she thought he was talking sincerely and began to reflect that she would indeed prefer a better man. Raphael said: 'Exactly! I know a young man who's so keen on you that he's ready to kill himself; he told me so himself. He's rich, too, and well educated and everything . . . Wouldn't you like to marry someone like that?' Still Marguerite hesitated and the catechist cried: 'Come on, tell me! I assure you he's rich and clever . . . everything you could want . . .' Then Marguerite dared to say: 'Do you think he'll really marry me?' Raphael pooh-poohed her doubts: 'But of course, my girl, haven't I said so? And I'm a bit like your father now, aren't I? A father doesn't deceive his child.' She was still hesitant, so the catechist added: 'Listen, you shall see him tomorrow. He's coming specially for that, to see you and say he wants to marry you.' 'Does he know me already?' asked Marguerite. Then the catechist laughed and said: 'Do you imagine that you live in a hole? Tons of men see you every day, my dear, even when you don't notice them. When you come out of church on Sunday mornings, what do you suppose all those men are standing about for? To look at you!' Marguerite replied that she would give him a definite answer when she'd met the young man.

'The next day?'

'Yes, Father. For I couldn't see him until the next day.'

'There's something I want to know first.'

'Yes?'

'Where did you sleep that night?'

'I don't remember now, Father . . .'

'You want a thrashing?'

'Oh, no, Father!'

'Come on, then! Tell me where you slept that night.'

'Umm! . . . At Raphael's house, Father.'

'Yes! And in what room?'

'Er . . .'

'Speak, girl!'

'I'm trying to, Father. But I can't remember any more . . .'

'That settles it! Teach her to reply, then!' cried the Father, turning to Anatole.

Anatole took up a good position and began thrashing Marguerite afresh. She twisted like an earth-worm under his blows and screamed out: 'I'll tell you, Father! I'll tell you!'

Nevertheless, Anatole continued his beating until the Father signed him to stop. Then the Father yelled: 'Now, talk!'

Marguerite stammered through her sobs: 'Fada, you're torturing me unjustly. You must know what goes on here, what's always gone on right here in the mission. You must know that every girl in the sixa sleeps with someone here or someone from outside. Why are you torturing me like this? Why are you persecuting me? Anyone can tell you these things if you ask them; why do you pick just on me? I'm no more guilty than anyone else . . . When I came to the sixa, things were already just the same as they are now. You can't blame me for bringing bad morals here. You're unjust . . .'

Hot tears were pouring from Marguerite's eyes and she kept stamping on the floor as she spoke. 'If you want to know, every girl in the sixa is sleeping with someone or other. Everyone, do you hear me? And more often with two men than with one. And as for syphilis, it's your own Boy who is spreading it. Yes, your Number One Boy, who keeps going from one girl to another! Of course, he never admits that he's got it! As for Raphael, it's he who arranges and ties up and re-ties all these liaisons, just as he wishes, because he makes money by it. All the men pay him to supply them with girls from the sixa. And Raphael himself sleeps with all of us, before passing us on to others. That's how it is! What more do you want? Yes, that night I slept in Raphael's room, in his bed, with him! Why don't you ask Raphael about it? There's plenty he can tell you: how much money he's made by his filthy intrigues, how many girls have left the sixa pregnant on the eve of their marriages, and even the names of his most faithful clients. Why don't you try beating him, eh? Why don't you submit him to all this interrogation? . . .'

'Enough!' roared the Father, his face scarlet and his hair in eruption.

Marguerite stopped at last, sobbing uncontrollably. She wept a long while, and the two priests sat there watching her until she subsided.

Then the Father spoke to her in a gentle, paternal voice: 'Marguerite, my daughter, listen to me. All right, I won't question you any more about the others. But tell me the rest of your own story.'

She dried her eyes, looked up and spoke in a forceful tone: 'That Raphael, your catechist, your right-hand man, uh! I utterly detest him. I hate him, do you hear me, Father? I could kill him. Everything that's happened to me is his fault. But for him, I wouldn't be dragging on here in the sixa, a poor girl with no husband and no prospect of one. The young man he cracked up to me, do you know who it was, Father? Nicholas! Your own monitor in charge of the first-years.'

So, Marguerite must have been pretty naïve not to realize that they were fooling her. When she met Nicholas, he made no precise proposal of marriage, but he did propose briskly that they should sleep together right away. She didn't refuse him, sure that he would soon take her to wife. Every evening, he waited for her behind the old church. With Raphael's connivance, she would slip out of a concealed gap in the sixa fence, cross the bush in darkness and join Nicholas there. Then they would cross the cemetery and go into his house.

'Ah, that boy! How easily he deceived me!' she cried, bursting afresh into sobs.

The priests were still gazing at her. Father Drumont was frowning deeply and his whole face seemed to be trembling. The Vicar was gaping, overwhelmed with astonishment. Anatole stood a little to one side, bending his cane across his thigh as if pining to use it again.

Marguerite resumed her story.

Her former fiancé had come to see her. He wondered why the marriage had been delayed and wanted to see the Father Superior about it. The first time he came, Raphael told him that Marguerite had failed her catechism exam and that was the sole reason for the delay. She didn't dare tell him the truth, for she was stunned by the complexity the whole affair was assuming. Raphael dissuaded the young man from seeing the Father, urging that this would only put the priest in a rage and achieve nothing. The next time he came, Raphael told him that Marguerite had given him up and was bent on marrying another. Naturally, the summonses that the Father sent to the young man's village never reached him, for they were sent through the local catechist, who took care to suppress them at Raphael's request. Raphael kept insisting that the man should be kept away from the Father for a while, because the latter was in a great rage with him. No one could dispute this, because Raphael always posed as knowing all the Father's secrets.

Thus the Father's messages didn't reach the ex-fiancé until he'd already been told that Marguerite didn't want to see him any more. Then, his own pride prevented him from making any more effort to see her. Never having seen the Father, he never discovered what had happened at the sixa. If he could have seen him, he would have convinced the Father that Marguerite had never been married to a polygamist. Then, perhaps, everything would have come right after all? . . .

Meanwhile, she had continued to see Nicholas every night – or as often as she could manage it. Things went on like this for months. Then one day she told him she was sick of the sixa: if they were going to get married, wasn't it time to start the formalities? For weeks he evaded the question. When she finally cornered him, he told her flatly that he'd never marry her. She got angry and shouted; he became plausible; it wasn't his fault; it was all the fault of his clan who insisted on him marrying a girl of their own choice. Nicholas had gone there specially and argued with them; to no avail, they still insisted on his marrying the girl they had selected. Only then did Marguerite realize that this Nicholas was a rascal who had been abusing her all along. She knew well enough that young men nowadays paid precious little attention to the marriage plans of their clans, or even of their families. Those days were gone . . .

'After that, I stopped seeing him. I tried to get back my former fiancé and make peace with him. But I learnt that he'd already made a civil marriage with someone else. And he says he'll never send his new wife to the sixa, for someone else to enjoy. He says: "I've got the point now", to anyone who'll listen to him.'

Marguerite was visibly fighting her sobs again.

'And Catherine?' asked the Father, when she had calmed down a little.

'I warned Catherine because I like her a lot. She was my closest friend here, almost my sister . . . When she arrived she was put into my dormitory, so I initiated her and looked after her. I taught her to look after herself, for she was still a bit soft. There was only one thing Catherine really understood, fighting. Once she starts on that . . . Anyway, she was very unhappy at first, really miserable, because they put her on all the hardest work, as they always do with the new ones. She was visibly wasting away, for she really isn't used to toiling like that. You see, Father, Catherine is really much more like a town girl, not one of us. So, because I finished my tasks early and was often back in the sixa before her, I used to cook for the two of us. Then Catherine had nothing to do when she got back except eat. I also split my supplies with her, because she had none. Hardly anyone ever came to see her.

'But one day she got mixed up in an affair as complicated as my own. So I took sides with her.'

The Father turned towards the young Vicar with a grimace and a sorry shaking of the head. Jean-Martin swallowed two or three times and returned his silent, communicative gaze. At last, the Father turned to Marguerite and said: 'All right. You can go.'

Then, turning towards Anatole: 'Get chop ready now.'

Marguerite went trailing out, with Anatole close behind her. I slipped out of the back door as quietly as possible. Then I came back to serve their dinner, because the Number One Boy said he was sick and went to bed. I believe he was scared to confront the Fathers after what they'd heard about him, which he must already have learned from Anatole.

They ate in silence until the coffee came. Then the Father exclaimed, as if to himself:

'Perhaps that girl is right . . . She's right, I ought not to have questioned her about the others. From now on, I'll interrogate each girl on what concerns her alone.'

'Certainly,' said the Vicar; 'certainly, but how will you extract the truth from them? There's no precise evidence against them, so how can you force them to speak? They'll proclaim their innocence.'

'Leave that to me, Father. I know them all right; I'll make them talk!'

After a pause: 'Ah! But think of it! What a race!'

'God! What a story!' echoed the Vicar.

They sat silently, face to face, gazing into the black depths of their coffee cups.

Then the Vicar asked: 'What do you plan to do after this?'

'I don't know . . . Yes, I do. Above all, I plan to return to Europe.'

'To rest for a bit . . . Yes, you must.'

'Oh! Perhaps for good-and-all. But before that, I must drive myself on to know everything. For twenty years I've known nothing in reality. After a story like this, I feel that I'll go back having learnt something useful, at least.'

They sat there till ten o'clock. Then the Father rose and said to his Vicar: 'Good night, Father!'

'Jesus Christ be praised!' replied Jean-Martin.

Left alone there, I cleared the table, swept up and went to bed . . .

Daniel still hasn't come back! His bed is empty and there's been no sign of him since I came in. I used to wonder where he went off to like this. Now I know; he must be with the girls. And he said he was ill this afternoon! . . . He's got syphilis, and it's he who's spreading it through the sixa, from girl to girl!

I should have suspected something, because the two girls who were recently told off to prepare the Boys' meals have been doing it with a care and willingness unusual with sixa girls. Of course, they were feeding their men! How blind I've been all along.

Syphilis! . . . I wonder what it's like? It sounds terrible. And if Catherine has it too, perhaps I . . . Oh! She mustn't have it. No, I'm sure she hasn't . . . If she had, Zacharia would have dropped her; a scoundrel like him, who knows everything that happens in the mission . . .

'Wow! What a story!' as the young Vicar says.

'What a race!' as the Father adds. True enough, we are a hell of a race. And perhaps we really are accursed, as the Bible says?

I'm certain nothing like this ever happens in the Father's own country . . .

Bomba

When I think of the severity with which I judged the Tala during our fortnight's journey! I thought of them as real monsters. How unjust I was! Or rather, how naïve.

Now I begin to comprehend all the disquiet, the torment and the anguish of dear Father Drumont. Now at last I understand the meaning of all his conversations with M. Vidal. Yes, as for these roadside Christians, are they really any better than the Tala tribe? Does their faith plunge deep into their hearts, like the roots of a forest tree? Or does it just spread on their skins, like the roots of those other trees which spread their roots on the flat ground?

The Father doubts the sincerity of all his roadside converts. And now, after yesterday's confessions, and still more after today's, I believe he's right. For most of these girls, these employees of the mission, are the daughters of roadside families. And what shall we learn tomorrow, if these interrogations continue? What lies in store for us tomorrow?

I'm beginning to wonder myself whether the Christian religion really suits us, whether it's really made to the measure of the blacks. I used to believe it firmly, for didn't Jesus Christ say to his disciples: 'Go and announce the Good Tidings to all the peoples of the earth?' But now, I'm not so sure. All the same, He did say it: 'Go and announce the Good Tidings . . .' I'm sure He said it! Doesn't the Bible say so?

But was He definitely including us? Oh God! If we aren't aboard the good ship of St Peter, there's no salvation for us! If that's really the case, the blacks will never get to Heaven . . . Ugh! See how I drivel on. I mustn't let myself think like that, or I shall lose my faith entirely.

Yes! Daniel, the Number One Boy, and Raphael have both disappeared! . . .

I don't believe Daniel has been back to our room since I noticed his disappearance last night. Or, if he did come in for a bit, it must have been while I was asleep. I keep wondering when he finally decided to bolt. Perhaps last night . . . I should have been more alert and looked to see if his boxes were still in the room when I came to bed.

As for Raphael, the last anyone saw of him at the mission was last night, at about nine o'clock.

In any event, both of them had vanished this morning. The whole mission was searched – the church, the gardens, the sawmill, the garage, the brickworks, the farms, the sixa and even the school. The Father was certain they had fled to avoid being interrogated. But the Vicar thought there might have been an accident and it was he who directed the search throughout the mission. Father Drumont kept trying to persuade him to call it off: 'They're no fools, those two scoundrels!' he said, shrugging his shoulders, 'I'm sure they've bolted. Don't tire yourself out any more, Father. What accident could possibly happen to those two? And to both of them at once? We'll soon hear news of them, believe me. Don't rush about any more . . .'

By midday, completely exhausted, Father Jean-Martin Le Guen called off the search. Then Father Drumont hit on the idea of going to Daniel's and Raphael's houses to check if their things were still there. Of course, they weren't. The Superior came back hooting with laughter and seized his Vicar by the shoulder, saying: 'You see, Father? Perhaps you think a little accident has befallen their things also?'

Then the two priests went into the dining-room.

By tomorrow, I'm pretty certain some others will have imitated the example of the two fugitives. For this afternoon Father Drumont recommenced his inquiries and many men about the mission were compromised, including five or six monitors, the chief brickmaker, both the sacristans and even some of the bigger schoolboys.

I couldn't eavesdrop on these interrogations, because I hadn't the time. With Daniel gone, I'm the only steward-boy at the mission just now. The Father still hasn't decided whether to take on another one. And even if he did, I'd still have to supervise everything until the new boy got used to the job. As it is, I scarcely have a minute to myself.

So I couldn't follow the interrogations in person, but Anatole, who saw everything because it was he again who thrashed all the girls to make them talk, has told me all the details.

Early in the afternoon, the two priests took up their posts in the office. They lined up all the girls on the veranda and called each one in turn. As soon as one came in, the Father would get up and close the door. Then he'd call on Anatole to give each girl an initial thrashing of fifteen strokes. Those who weren't sufficiently subdued by that, were given an extra ten lashes for good measure. There weren't many who weren't eager enough to talk, after that.

Anatole said to me with disgust: 'How pathetic these girls are! Even the hardest of them only need their arses tickled a little with my cane to make them begin farting out their nastiness. Never trust a woman with your confidences, I assure you, old chap. She'll deliver up your secrets at the first cut of the stick! Agh! How pitiful they are. They offered the names of everyone who'd slept with them, even up to ten years ago! What do you think of that? No, honestly, old fellow, you should have been there. You'd have been edified, believe me. Every male in the mission was mentioned today. Every one! Do you hear me? Except you and me, of course. And do you know what? There were even schoolboys, too. Yes, schoolboys! Mind you, I'm not really surprised. All the little brats who keep hanging around the sixa must be there for a good reason. Talk about a brothel! And there was I, slashing away at their fat arses, flabby as mud. My cane really seemed to sink into their rotten flesh. Oh, how I detest the little mice! How I despise them! I'd like to spend my whole life thrashing them . . .'

'Was Catherine questioned again?'

'Who?'

'Catherine! You know, Zacharia's sweetheart.'

'Ah, that chick who came yesterday! The one who followed you on tour? What a little hussy! Fancy doing that a few centimetres from the Father's own bed!'

'Yes, but was she questioned again?'

'Oh, no! They had no time for going over yesterday's ground

again. There were over fifty girls lined up on the veranda! And remember, there's still another twenty to be questioned tomorrow.'

'It's funny, there they were on the veranda, and even outside. What was to stop them running away?'

'Ah, ah, ah . . . Hee-hee . . . Don't you know the answer to that, my dear lad? Why, this morning, as soon as he knew that Raphael had disappeared, the Father rushed off to the nearby villages and came back with three catechists. Only bush catechists, of course, but real tough fellows, believe me . . .'

He fell silent, busy with the pots which were boiling on the stove. But suddenly he burst into a laugh so huge that it made me shake all over.

'What's up?' I asked him.

'Oh, nothing. Just that Catherine you were speaking of, old chum. Her name reminded me of something really funny: they've all got syphilis! Dirty little hens, all the same . . .'

'All of them? No!'

'Didn't I just say so?'

'Catherine too?'

'No, not her; nor another five or six of them. It was a scream; they were all betraying one another: "She had it before me! If I hadn't gone with a boy she'd been going with for ages, fool that I was, I wouldn't have caught it . . ." Do you know what?'

'No! Tell me about it.'

'Listen, then, old chap; just listen. Ah, ah, ah! Listen. It seems that one of them had such a sore between her legs and smelt so terrible that her companions chased her out of the dormitory one night. Don't you remember? That one who disappeared about three or four weeks ago, the one they looked for everywhere and couldn't trace. Remember?'

'Y-e-s . . .'

'Well, that's her!'

'And she had a sore?'

'Yes! A huge one, between her thighs!'

'Why between her thighs?'

'Why? God, don't you understand anything?'

'No! I don't . . .'

'That's syphilis, you chump! Yes, syphilis! When it gets bad, it makes a sore like that and the victim begins to stink like anything!'

I was horrified and turned cold all over. I could scarcely stand up and felt really sick. I ate nothing this evening, for fear of vomiting.

The Fathers ate in silence until I brought their coffee. Then the Vicar spoke up carefully: 'Excuse me, Father, but don't you think you might just as well stop these interrogations?'

The Father Superior looked at him a moment and went on smoking.

'After all,' continued Jean-Martin Le Guen, 'it's pretty revolting. Anyway, I certainly can't listen to any more of these horrors; I really can't stand it. Surely you'll stop them now, Father?'

'Oh! I don't know . . . I think I'd rather press on now.'

'But why, Father, if you'll excuse me?'

'Why? Oh, Father, I don't really know any more. How often do we know exactly why we do things?'

A pause, then: 'I long to know everything. And, after all, it does have its instructive side for us.'

'Of course, Father. But don't you think you know enough already for that?' After a while, he continued: 'What I'm saying is for your sake, Father. I've already explained that I personally can't stand any more of these sessions. But you have lived here for decades, putting up with this foul climate, too. Your nerves are already shot to pieces, although you mayn't realize it. All these unsavoury stories could really disturb your mind and make you seriously ill. Give it up now, Father, I implore you!'

'I'll think over what you have said, Father. But I shall postpone a decision till tomorrow.'

They were silent again, while Father Drumont gazed at his own smoke-rings swirling towards the ceiling and Le Guen played nervously with his coffee-spoon.

At last, the Father Superior said: 'Look at the density of the darkness tonight, Father. You who are a poet.'

They both turned towards the black square of the big dining-room window.

'What does it suggest to you?' the Father Superior asked.

It was quite dark outside, without a trace of a moon.

'I haven't really asked myself that yet, Father. I'm still at the stage of discovering everything, you see. And here everything overwhelms me, so that my intellectual and poetic faculties are numbed. For instance, I haven't yet fitted the night into my general view of the world. But I shall, I shall . . .'

Father Drumont look at him from the corner of his eyes and grinned.

The Vicar continued: 'What could such a night suggest? Let's see what I can find by tomorrow: by then, I shall certainly have found a metaphor.'

They both laughed quietly, between their teeth.

'And meanwhile?' asked Father Drumont, in a teasing voice.

'Meanwhile . . . Let's see, let's see . . . Yes, let's see . . . Oh night! . . . Night of Africa, what do you resemble? . . . Night black as pitch, deep as ocean, dense as a tropical sea, immovable as . . . as a scarecrow! Unfathomable night, what wrecks does your breast gather in? Ah! Father, I've found my metaphor. What this night suggests to me is a great ocean of pitch!'

'That much I expected to hear – an ocean. You couldn't have left that out. It's quite an obsession of yours, Father.'

'It seems so.'

'As for me, I find it more like a sponge.'

'What? A sponge!'

'Yes, certainly. But I keep asking myself what a coloured sponge might be made of; a black sponge. Do you know?'

'Let's think . . . leave the sponge aside and put in its place . . . seaweed!'

'Seaweed?'

'But of course! A submarine seaweed. Why not?'

'And is that black, a submarine seaweed?'

'Well, it certainly isn't pink!'

Again, they laughed softly together.

'Thanks to poetry, I shall one day sing your praises,' offered the Vicar.

'Poetry, how you seize us all!' cried Father Drumont.

After a moment, the Vicar exclaimed: 'That sponge of yours was an excellent notion; don't you think so, Father?'

'Thanks. Of course, you know that I . . .'

'I'm serious, Father. It's never too late to be a poet.'

'Perhaps you're right; but I should have become one when I first arrived here, not when I'm about to leave. If I hadn't lacked that special intuition which only poets have, I might have understood the Bantu mentality – improbable as it seems – before it was too late. And that would have saved me a multitude of errors!'

'Errors?'

'Yes, of course. I'm thinking especially of what's been cooking up here, under my own lid, as it were. How shall I put it? Under my own protection! A real brothel!'

'Oh, Father!'

'Oh, excuse me. But the memory of this will never leave me; I'll drag it with me through life like a stomach cancer or a lung-scar. Let's talk no more of it; I've no wish to demoralize you.'

After a moment, he asked: 'Do you know what the weather is like now in my own country?'

'Ah! yes, in Provence . . .'

'No, in the Comtat Venaissin, Father. Don't be stubborn!'

They both laughed.

'O.K.,' said the Vicar, 'the Comtat Venaissin. We're in February now, aren't we? The sky is of a curiously pure and transparent blue. The Mistral blows often and there's plenty of sunshine. The weather is soft, except when the Mistral blows. The air is so light! . . . Of a lightness that is . . . Provençal! Oh, forgive me!'

'Tell me, have you ever been in the Midi, Father?'

'No, never. Why do you ask?'

'One would believe you'd been there.'

'You see, Father? Another virtue of poesy. I've been there only in imagination. I've always dreamt of your country and its sunshine. I've looked with envy at all the English, Belgian and Dutch tourists who flock through Brittany, all going to the Midi or returning from there. They all speak of Provence as an earthly paradise. Yes, how I envied them and how privileged I thought them!'

'They were, Father.'

'Perhaps . . . in a way. But the really privileged are we ourselves, don't you think? Despite all our annoyances, it's we who'll have the fascinating stories to tell.'

'Stories which we'll often lack the courage to recount.'

'And all the more delicious for that! Like a song one holds in one's head to be sung only to the chosen listener . . . Like an undeclared passion . . .'

'Watch out, Father! You tend towards the profane! Take care that your love of poesy doesn't land you into a defrocking.'

They laughed softly once more and, still chuckling, rose to bid each other good night.

I feel quite at ease. Only one girl could have betrayed me, and she didn't. Catherine didn't give me away! All the same, she's a brave girl, this Catherine. Anatole imagines that I have nothing to reproach myself for, like himself . . . As for that, why is he so innocent? Perhaps because he is really so? In any case, the interrogations aren't over yet. But he doesn't seem to have any fear of being dragged in, judging by the boldness with which he thrashes the girls. Perhaps he really is the only man here who hasn't been mixed up with a sixa girl. Why is that? He's always been an odd one, solitary and taciturn. And it may be that he's a genuine Christian? Otherwise, why should he be the only one like that? . . .

Bomba

This evening it seems to me that I'm witnessing the end of the world, the Last Judgement. Everything is completely topsy-turvy. Even in my dreams, I've never glimpsed such a turn of events as today has brought us.

There's no longer any school here, nor any sixa, nor any staff, nor any mission, nor anything! The mission of Bomba has ceased to exist. It's true that the church and the other buildings still stand, but what for? Bomba, the real Bomba, the Catholic mission itself, has gone. There's no one left within it but the two priests, the assistant cook, the three visiting catechists and myself. The sixa girls are leaving tomorrow morning, when the Father Superior has sworn to throw them all out.

Not a single mission worker turned up for work this morning. In amazement, Father Drumont sent Anatole and I to look for them: 'Go and look in their houses and see if they are there.'

All of them were empty, except those of the very few workers who were married. There, the wives said to us: 'My husband has gone. He said nothing to me, except to pack all the things and follow him as fast as possible.'

'But where did he go?'

'I don't know.'

'But didn't you just say you were going to follow him?'

'That wasn't what I meant. I am to go back to our home, to my husband's village, that is.'

'Why did he leave like that?'

'I don't know. He said nothing, except that I was to pack everything and go back to our place.'

By ten o'clock these wives had also gone and everything was silent around the mission.

When Anatole and I told all this to the Father Superior, he simply said: 'This makes it easier for me; otherwise I'd have had to chase them all off, the swine.'

Apparently, they'd all been compromised in yesterday's interrogations.

The schoolchildren played all morning in the courtyard, because there was no monitor in charge of them. The Father went to them at about ten and told them all to go home to their villages, but they didn't leave immediately; they hung about in little groups around the courtyard, wondering what could have happened.

As soon as he came back from the school, the Father jumped on his motor-bike, the one with the side-car, and left the mission. Neither Anatole nor I knew where he had gone. Early in the afternoon he returned, followed by a van which halted in front of the Fathers' house. A white man got out, wearing a doctor's coat. I instantly recognized M. Alfred Arnaud, the town doctor. There were also four medical assistants in the van, all wearing their white coats. Curious to know what all this could mean, I heard the Father say to Doctor Arnaud: 'It's over this way, doctor.'

They went over to the sixa, followed by the four medical assistants carrying all kinds of instruments and apparatus.

After nearly a quarter of an hour, the Father came walking back on his own. I was getting more and more intrigued. Why had he left all those medical people over in the sixa? I went over to talk to Anatole, who's getting very friendly with me nowadays – last night he came to sleep in the boys' room with me. He exclaimed: 'That's funny! The Father has given up his interrogations and now he's gone to fetch the doctor from the town. There's something fishy there, believe you me.'

'This doctor has already visited the mission several times.'

'Yes, but that was just to look after one of the priests. This time, they took him straight to the women. Why? . . . That's why I say there's something fishy about it, old chap. You wait and see!'

About six o'clock, the Father told me to light the Aida lamp in the office. The doctor and his black assistants were still over in the sixa. I went over to the office and began lighting the lamp with great caution, because those things scare me stiff. While I was still there, the Father entered. followed by the Vicar and Doctor Arnaud, while the assistants filed past and climbed back into their van. I went to my usual hiding-place in the ante-room and watched everything from there.

The doctor sat down facing the two priests and began: 'Well, Fathers, I see you're waiting to hear my report. Here it is.'

He also wears a long black beard, over a khaki uniform shirt with epaulets. He began reading from a sheaf of papers, which he deposited upside down beside him as he finished them. I can still remember most of it: above all, I remember that he kept calling the sixa 'the women's camp'.

'Report by Dr Arnaud on the Women's Camp

'I shall begin with the general hygienic conditions of the camp, inside and out. I must tell you, Reverend Fathers, that they are seriously defective.

'As soon as I entered the camp, I was struck by the sordid look of the surroundings, with the bush ramping inwards over everything. Neither the courtyard nor the borders of the houses had been swept. Everything was covered in rubbish: bits of food, clothing and all kinds of filth all over the place.

'In the course of a necessarily brief survey of the interior of the camp houses, I observed that both their disposition and upkeep were an offence at once to good sense and – more serious still – to the regulations promulgated by the competent authority in this Territory; that is to say, the Service for Mobile Health Units and Prophylaxis.

'GENERAL DISPOSITION OF THE CAMP

'The houses are scattered at random, without regard to north or south, to inadequate or excessive light, or to either dryness or humidity. The mat roofs, riddled with nailholes, let in the rain. The brick walls are interrupted with large openings which are not fitted with any sort of shutter. Consequently, the occupants are exposed to all the violence of the weather. Bearing in mind the abrupt fall of temperature which, in this country, always accompanies the setting of the sun, one can easily imagine how debilitating these conditions are likely to be to the human organism.

'I will omit the details in order to tell you how shocked I was by the paucity of beds, of which I observed two kinds.

'First – this is true of most of the houses, isn't it? – there were beds of a type so primitive as to defy description. Nevertheless, I will say that they were largely made of dried banana-leaves – or of some other straw which I couldn't recognize – and sustained on banana trunks. When I approached these strange beds to examine them more closely, I lifted up the various bits of old and insalubrious cloth that covered them, only to find the woodwork pullulating with what – in Europe – we call fleas, bed-bugs, lice, etc. I couldn't identify these creatures precisely, not having the necessary instruments with me for studying them.

'The proper beds – I mean those that can strictly be called such, you understand? – right, now for the proper beds. These are made of barely-smoothed planks, without mattresses, and are scarcely less primitive than the others. In place of mattresses, they have only a series of palm-branches cut open and laid across them like railway-sleepers. A glance under the covers revealed exactly the same swarming of pests as covered the beds that lay right on the ground.

'Apart from this, the sunlight pouring through the large openings I've already described revealed an atmosphere loaded with dust and filth to the proportion of 75 per cent – at a rapid guess, you understand?

'I looked in vain for any building which might serve as a dining-room or a kitchen. At last, I found a humble thatched shed at the far end, all cluttered up with native vessels of the crudest type – clay pots, wooden bowls and plates. When questioned by my assistants, the girls, who were standing apart and watching us, asserted that each of them had to do her own cooking and feed herself. I refrained from making any investigation into the sources of food for the camp, as this lay outside my terms of reference.

'I saw no showers or baths and was at a loss to see how the girls could wash themselves, but here again I contented myself with noting the matter for the attention of the Reverend Fathers.

'I observed the same discretion in matters which concerned the human conduct of the camp. But I cannot refrain from mentioning the crushed and hunted look on the faces of these girls; nor their red and calloused hands, their torn skin, often quite deeply gashed, and their emaciation – all save a few – which clearly spoke of the heavy labours, exceeding the strength of their sex, to which they were exposed in the depths of the forest.

'I pass now to the question of venereal disease, since that was the original object of my inquiry.

'I must tell you right away that as soon as I announced I was going to examine them one by one, fifteen of the girls ran away. Your people couldn't recover them, but I took their flight as evidence of their venereal condition. None the less, it's regrettable that I couldn't identify exactly what disease they had, nor how advanced it was, nor yet what curative measures should be taken.

'After the flight of these fifteen subjects, I was left with thirty-seven, which proves that I should have examined fifty-two (I hope my mathematics are correct?). Anyway, of these thirty-seven, only eight are entirely clear. You'll find all the details in this notebook, which I will leave with you. Among the remaining twenty-nine (right, again?) there is general infection, though it varies in degree and in kind.

'To begin with, two of them have gonorrhoea, one chronic and the other normal. How did I know? Nothing easier! I didn't even need my microscope to identify the Neisser gonococcus, given their vaginal effusions, the stains on their underwear and the fetid odour of their genitals.

'The chronic case was also easy to identify: pains in the pubic area, irregular periods, more abundant white effusions, etc.

'In both cases, I was convinced that the virulence of the disease had been increased by the negligence of the sexual hygiene practised by these girls, a negligence which I attribute to the poor toilet facilities of the camp. For native women, as I have reason to know, are usually conspicuous for the care they exercise in this matter.

'Secondly, the syphilis.

'God above! I counted no less than twenty-seven cases of it. Once again, I had little need of my instruments to ascertain the facts, save when testing the eight girls who were free of the disease. Here, I examined the blood and the spinal fluid by application of the five classical techniques: the Border-Wasserman, the Kline, the Hecht, the Meinicke and the Kahn tests. I also tested the proportion of pallinindine in the blood and the spinal fluid. But, for the rest, I scarcely needed my instruments, except to use my microscope to reveal the pale syphilis spirochete in a few doubtful cases.

'Remarkably enough, the disease hadn't reached its tertiary stage in any of these cases, which points to their having acquired it quite recently. The presence of chancres and swollen ganglions in the groin was alone enough to point to the primary stage.

'The secondary was indicated by pink rashes, mucous patches on throat, the tongue, the tonsils and the anus, the headaches complained of by the subjects and the consistent hoarseness.

'So, twenty-seven cases of syphilis. Eighteen of them in the primary stage and only nine in the secondary. None in the tertiary. This again points to an epidemic within the women's camp. And it is borne out by a comparison of the syphilis rate in the female population at large and that occurring in the women's camp of your mission, which is infinitely higher. I don't know how long most of the women stay here, but it seems to me likely that they were all free of the disease when they entered the camp.

'Reverend Fathers, you will find all the details in the notebook I am going to leave with you.'

Doctor Arnaud here fell silent. The two Fathers were slumped in their arm-chairs, completely overwhelmed. After a pause, Doctor Arnaud demanded: 'Have you any instructions to give me about how I am to cure these young women? Shall I treat them here, or send them all to hospital?'

Father Drumont jumped as if awakening from a dream. 'Excuse me, Doctor, what did you say?' he asked. 'Ah, yes! Well . . . really, I haven't considered the matter yet. All so complicated and novel to me, you see!'

'Then, Father, you have only to write to me with your decision. But if you will permit me to advise you, you'd better decide quick.'

He got up to leave. The Father Superior also jumped up and made a vague gesture of amity, saying: 'You're going, Doctor? But surely you will dine with us first?'

'Actually, Father . . .'

'But, of course, of course, of course! You will give us this pleasure all the same.'

They ate rapidly, for the doctor had a harassed look and his face was lined with worry. Father Drumont said to him: 'You're really concerned about something, Doctor.'

'Yes, Father, it's my hospital. I've left a boy there, you see . . . he may be dead at this very moment.'

'As bad as that?'

'Ah, yes!'

'What's the matter with him?'

'Oh, there's no shortage of diseases in the country. What with the fevers and the snake-bites . . . Such misery everywhere! What they need here is a doctor every five kilometres! Instead of all this rubbish: these forest-fellers and . . . and . . . Greek merchants and administrators. Ah! What a crew. I wonder what the hell they're doing in this beastly country. As if the people were not plagued enough already. They're a real pest . . .'

Father Drumont called to Anatole and told him to give some chop to the assistants. They descended silently from the lorry and trooped after him, still wearing their white coats. They must have eaten well, for they were all licking their lips when they passed back again.

After Doctor Arnaud's departure with his party, the Vicar Le Guen asked the Father: 'What are you going to do now?'

'God in Heaven! I'm going to report to the Bishop. Yes, I'll be there from tomorrow onwards. I shall also show him the doctor's report.'

'And what do you think he'll say?'

'Him? One can never know what he'll say about anything or any development.'

After a while: 'Have you noticed something?'

'How do you mean, Father?'

'The only girls still uncontaminated are those who've only just joined the sixa. When I reflect that this has been going on for years, perhaps, or even for dozens of years! This epidemic is a local phenomenon. That was what the white man meant to say.'

'Don't worry about it too much, Father, I implore you.'

'How can I stop doing so? Tomorrow, I'll pack all those girls off to their villages, or anywhere else they choose to hang themselves in! Poor defenceless creatures . . . prey to the first predator that comes along – poor black girls.'

After a while: 'You know, Father Le Guen, I'm going to tell you the whole truth . . .'

'To what purpose, Father? Better go and rest a bit.'

'Yes, yes, yes! I'm going to tell you everything. Perhaps that will relieve me. The guilty party in this whole affair is me. Do you hear? Me!'

'Father!'

'Yes, listen to me. And above all, don't imagine that I've suddenly gone crazy. I'm as sane as can be. The last time I set foot in the sixa, it had only just been built! Do you get me? That's almost twenty years ago now. I told one of my catechists then to make the rooms more comfortable – more habitable, indeed! And I supposed that he had done so. Since that day, I haven't set foot inside the place. Twenty years! Do you understand me?'

The Vicar gazed at him open-mouthed.

'What's so surprising about it? I acted like everyone else: is that what astounds you? Father, if you stay long here, you'll meet lots of other missionaries of my generation. Well, the day when you catch the Superior of a mission going to inspect his sixa, write to the Pope and ask him to canonize this living saint.'

He got up and began pacing about, arms behind his back. He continued: 'The native girl, the docile little black girl, what a perfect machine! No need to grease it, even. No need even to go and see if it's growing rusty in the little garage where we've chucked it. A really unmatchable machine! She looks after herself all alone, do you hear, all alone! Above all, don't go and pull her out of the garage in the morning. What an asinine idea! No, she'll run out of her own accord and come to ask you: "Give me some work to do." Who has been able to invent the equal of that?'

A pause, then: 'The worst of it is, you understand, the worst is that we found things like this. For the natives had discovered long before we came that their women were perfect machines. They're no more stupid than we are; get rid of that idea at once, if you've got it. So we came along, we, the messengers of Christ, we, the great civilizers. And what do you think we did? Give woman back her dignity? Oh, certainly not that, Father! Oh, no! We kept her in her ancient servitude, but turned it to our own profit . . .

'Exploiters, foresters, Greek merchants, administrators . . . Yes,

Doctor Arnaud, a regular load of rubbish. But you forgot one element in the rubbish-heap: the missionaries. Or perhaps you left them out in simple charity, in simple pity for us? . . . Good night, Father.'

'Good night, Father.'

And they both went up to bed right away.

How strange it all is! I keep wondering what decision the Bishop will take tomorrow.

But I must get to sleep now. I have to rise early in the morning, because I'm the only boy left in the entire mission.

Bomba

Thursday, 19 February

My God! How fast everything happens now!

The sixa girls have now joined the exodus. The Father has chased them away, just as he promised his Vicar last night.

He called them all together after Morning Mass and assembled them in front of the office, where he was waiting with Father Le Guen. They were shepherded by the three catechists he had summoned from the bush. Father Drumont came outside and the Vicar watched from the window. He spoke to them sadly, scarcely raising his voice: 'Go back to your villages. I'm ashamed of you; you have dishonoured my mission. I don't wish to see you again. Go.'

Some girls began moving off immediately, calling gaily to each other: 'That's just what I've been longing to hear. Now he's said it, and there's nothing to keep me here.' Or else: 'Why did I wait for this dismissal, anyway, before returning to my village? It's funny, really. Why on earth did I hang on here?' They quickly packed their things and left the mission, sometimes one by one, sometimes in little groups.

But there were other girls who remained a long while in front of the office, crying and lamenting. These exclaimed: 'I have no family now and no homestead to return to. The only home I have is the mission!' Or else: 'How can I go back to my village now? I would die of shame. Everyone will hoot at me, after all the rumours about us and the sixa. How can I ever go back?'

This painful scene was played out right in front of the Father's office and lasted a long while. At last, he came rushing out, brandishing a long stick and threatening to beat the girls with it. They scattered about the mission, still weeping, filling the air with their cries.

Just after nine o'clock, without taking his lunch, the Father jumped on his motor-bike and set off to see the Bishop, just as he had planned. He must be there by now, although it's quite a way from Bomba – more than fifty kilometres.

When all the girls had gone, the three bush catechists also returned to their villages. There was no one in the whole mission but the Vicar, Anatole and myself.

The schoolboys came back this morning, but the Father once more sent them off to their homes. None of the old employees of the mission has reappeared. All their little houses are silent as the tombs in a cemetery. Strange to remember how, not long since, the noise of activity continued far into the night, like a great wall of human warmth surrounding us. Whichever path you took from the mission, you were sure to come across friends and acquaintances.

But tonight everything is cold, quiet and as unknown as the virgin forest. If you cry out, the echo of your voice returns to you, as if you were calling only to yourself.

None of this makes any impression on Anatole. He's really a very odd fellow. This morning, after the Father had left, he chased up the few girls who were still weeping here and there about the mission and beat them off with a cane. He came back very pleased with himself and calling out: 'Well, my dear, at least I was able to get in a few last lashes on their backsides. They won't forget me in a hurry. Fancy kicking up a row like that! What do they think this is? They say they've no families or homes to return to . . . Did you ever hear such impudence? Just because they spend their time taking lovers at the mission!'

I saw Catherine going off. She was smartly dressed, as she used to be when we were on tour. But I didn't dare approach her or be seen talking to her, for she was with a group of girls who all left while the Father was still here. I just stood close to the way she must pass. She saw me and gave me a friendly wave. I waved back and she cried out laughingly: 'Look after yourself, little one!'

'You too, my sweet!' I called back.

'Will you come and see me when you get a chance?'

'Where can I find you? I don't know your village.'

'My village? Don't you know where Zacharia lives, then?'

'I think I could find my way there. Why? Are you going to join him?'

'What? You mean you don't know? We're going to get married.'

'No fooling?'

'Exactly so, my little one.'

'But Zacharia has already had a church wedding.'

'So what?'

'What about his wife?'

'Why should I trouble about her? You'll come and see me, won't you?'

'I'll do my best.'

'Don't fail. I'll be very nice to you, you'll see!'

And she went off, still laughing aloud.

Bomba

Phew! I'm really whacked out. We've been working all afternoon. Thank goodness the Father has called in some labourers. I've never worked so hard in my life, but now it's almost over.

Funnily enough, the Father didn't stay long at the Bishop's – scarcely two days. Usually he stays there at least a week.

He reappeared this afternoon and his bike was followed by two big lorries, both crammed with singing labourers. As soon as he stopped, he greeted the Vicar and handed him a letter. Then he gave orders to the workmen and instantly they began loading the lorries with all our furniture, kitchen stuff, church ornaments and so forth. The Father asked Anatole and I to lend them a hand as well, so we were at it until six o'clock. Then Anatole went to prepare the chop and I to lay the table . . .

My God, how weary I am!

The labourers kept it up until really late, and they went off with practically everything that could be moved.

During dinner, the Vicar suddenly asked the Father: 'Have they finally decided what to do, up there?'

'No. Only that the mission should be abandoned for a year or two.'

'Does that make sense?'

'I wonder. Anyway, that's what they usually do in such cases.'

After a pause: 'It's a way of indicating that everything's gone awry.'

'Will you sail soon for Europe, Father?'

'Don't talk to me about sailing,' laughed the Father. 'You'll give me sea-sickness before I even start. It looks as though both of us will be enjoying the Bishop's hospitality for some time, in any case. I still don't know the date of my actual departure. But don't worry! I'll give you plenty of warning, if you want to send any messages to your parents.'

'Exactly.'

'Well, you'll have plenty of time for that.'

Clementine came in, looking very tear-stained and bedraggled. Both priests trembled at the sight of her.

'Jesus Christ be praised, Father,' she cried.

She spoke in a whining voice and bore the modest, discreet, resigned expression of a humiliated woman who, having been soundly beaten by her husband, has cooled her anger, recognized her fault and come to beg his forgiveness.

'Ah! It's you, Clementine,' said the Father. 'I haven't seen you since I came back, poor woman. How's that?'

'I came to see you, Father, but you were so busy. So I decided to come back this evening.'

The Father grimaced in an embarrassed way.

'It seems you're leaving, Father?' she asked.

Father Drumont sighed: 'Yes, I'm leaving. We're both leaving.'

'Oh! . . .'

After a short silence, Clementine asked: 'What am I going to do now, Father?'

She gave up the struggle against her sobs and the Father waited until she calmed down again before saying: 'Naturally, you will go back to your husband.'

'My husband, Father?'

'Certainly, my child, your husband.'

'A polygamist?'

'What?'

'Don't you know that he's going to marry that other girl?'

'What other girl?'

'That Catherine, of course! Everyone knows about it.'

'Zacharia? . . . I should have known it would end like this.'

All three were silent for a while, then the Father turned to Clementine and asked: 'What do you yourself think of doing?'

'Going back to my own people, Father, in my village.'

'Are your parents living?'

'Oh, yes, Father.'

'And they'll help you to bring up the children?'

'They are Zacharia's children, Father. He's sure to claim them sooner or later.'

'And suppose he wants to take you as well?'

'I shall refuse, Father.'

'The Church, my child, does not forbid you to stay with your husband, even if he becomes a polygamist.'

'I know that, Father. But I can't do it . . .'

The Father went up to his room and came back with some banknotes. Offering these to Clementine, he said: 'Here's a little money, all that I can offer you. Never forget God, and accept your sufferings as a penitence. Good-bye, my child.'

'Good-bye, Father.'

She trailed slowly out.

Father Drumont sat silent for a long time, resting his chin on his hand. Then he looked up at the Vicar, sighing and shaking his head: 'Ah! Well . . .'

They bade each other good night and both went up to bed.

The Bishop's labourers all slept in the sixa. It wasn't easy to feed them, as we had only the Fathers' food supply in the kitchen. The Reverend Father Superior had to go scouting round the neighbouring villages with one of the lorries, to buy whatever he and Anatole could find. The labourers cooked for themselves and had quite a party over there.

Anatole came to sleep with me in the boys' quarters. Soon he asked me: 'Do you know if they're both going?'

'Yes, both of them.'

'Is someone coming to replace them?'

'Perhaps; but not for a month or two.'

'What are you going to do, then?'

'I don't know. Go back to my village, perhaps. And you?'

'Oh! I'll find a cook's job soon enough. In the town, for example, with a Greek trader. I'll stay there until someone comes to re-open the mission. Those little beasts of the sixa have really shoved us up the creek, all the same!'

'Do you think it's all because of them?'

'Of course I do. If it hadn't been for all that filthy business . . . But don't you think so yourself?'

'I don't know. It may be so . . .'

How tired I am tonight!

Sogola

Sunday, 22 February

So, that's the end! He has really gone and I'll never see him again. I
I can't stop weeping. The dear Reverend Father has really gone.
God! I can hardly grasp it. Now, under my father's roof in my own
village, I must search my conscience tonight, as he taught me.

Never again will Bomba see Father Drumont, the man who
founded it and built it up! Many people wept this morning. We may
not be good Christians, but we loved the Father truly. And the proof
of it was in the tears shed for him this morning by men and women
alike.

There was a real crush at High Mass this morning. Everyone was
full of curiosity, because of all the rumours circulating about the sixa.
Father Le Guen officiated and I sang with one of the schoolboys.
After the Evangelist, it was time for the sermon. Then Father
Drumont came slowly through the church and mounted the pulpit.

In his usual way, he waited until everything was silent in the
church. The coughers gradually subsided and everything was quiet.
Then, without even taking a text from the Gospels, the Father began
his sermon. 'My dear children, brothers and friends, I have very sad
news to give you. You all know something by hearsay about the
events of the last few days. I shall say nothing of them, though they
made me weep like a child at the time. But now for my news! I am
am going back to Europe, to my own country! I shall leave today,
immediately after Mass. But before leaving you, perhaps for ever,
there are many things I want to say to you: fearing only that you
may not understand them. For when a father is worried about his
child, what good does it do to reveal his cares? It may complicate
everything, or the child may not understand his concern. In any case,
these are only my own ideas, private and obscure as yet, since God
has not yet lighted them with his generous glow. I still hope that He

may soon do so; and until then I shall not cease to think about these things. All my thoughts are fastened on you. I shall never forget you and shall pray for you every day. Pray also for yourselves; don't let my long labours to extend the Kingdom of God among you be in vain. Ask Grace of our Lord Jesus Christ. And beg that His Mother, the blessed Virgin, may intercede with Him for you.'

He kept breaking off, swallowing his saliva, as though nervous or embarrassed. He went on: 'I don't know what the Bishop will decide about the future of your mission. I don't know when he will send you a new priest, for my Vicar has already been assigned to another mission. But whatever he decides, have no unjust thoughts towards your Bishop. His decision, whatever it be, will be guided only for your good, you may be sure. Remember your own faults, your unchristian conduct and your women, who have turned my sixa into a den of satanic practices. So, if your Bishop decides to punish you, accept it as a penitence deserved by your sins. And, for the future, strive to live better. Oh, yes! I know how difficult it is for you. Nevertheless, it cannot be impossible. Our Lord Jesus Christ has excluded no man and no race from His Kingdom. He will remember Africa also, for how could He forget you? A man is a man, and every man can become a good Christian by his own exertions. It matters not that customs and habits vary from land to land.

'I shall perhaps return to you, perhaps not; as yet I cannot be sure. But, in any case, your Father is an old man now. True, his hair is not yet grey; true, he needs no stick to lean upon as he goes. Yet he is still old, a man who has worked all his life and who now longs for repose. Be sure that I shall never cease to pray for you, never cease to ask God to enlighten me on your account. In the name of the Father . . .'

He descended swiftly from the pulpit and the Mass resumed its hesitant, melancholy way as if it had no wish to end.

As soon as it was over, the Bishop's labourers began ransacking the sacristy of all its precious objects, placing them in boxes which they bore away to the lorries. They left only what could be neither carried away nor stolen.

The Father told me to get ready. I gathered up all my books, my vestments and sacred images into little bundles which the Father ordered to be loaded also. Then he doled out some little images at random to all the children who were gathered near the Fathers' house. A crowd of adults stood farther off and watched everything we did. The women were all tearful, and some wept aloud.

After lunch, the Father locked up everything himself, leaving only the church. He called three of the Bishop's people and showed them the boys' quarters, saying: 'From now on, you will look after the mission. I have no special charge for you. Just see that nothing is stolen.'

Then he handed over to them all the remains of the food supply.

At about two o'clock, we set off. The Father pushed his way with difficulty through the crowd of women and children who had gathered. Surrounded by their tears, he quickly bade farewell to the bush catechists. I looked vainly for my father's face among them.

The first lorry carried the Vicar, some of the labourers and Anatole, whom they were to drop off at his village on the way. Then came the Father and myself, on his motor-bike and side-car, followed by the second lorry with the rest of the labourers.

My heart was very full when we started out and I feared every moment to burst into tears. I was careful not to look at the Father.

When we got to my village, all the boys came running with cries of: 'Look, there is Jesus Christ! . . . Jesus Christ!'

My father and step-mother had not come to the last Mass, because of an epidemic in our place. He came now and told the Father that he knew everything about recent events at Bomba but still couldn't believe he was really leaving.

'We aren't all like that! You'll come back to us, won't you, Father?'

'I don't know – perhaps I will. But at present I really don't know.'

My step-mother's eyes were so full of tears. All the boys swarmed round us like flies, except the few who were sick. The Father distributed a few more images to my brothers and some other boys. Then some big louts came up demanding images, but the Father said he had none left. He instructed the labourers to unload a few other boxes, as well as my loads, and they carried everything to my father's house. Then Father Drumont pointed at them and said: 'These are for you, my dear Denis.'

He thrust a hand into his portfolio and pulled out some

banknotes which he counted into my father's hand, saying that they were all for me. I don't know how much was there, I didn't notice.

At last, he said to my father: 'Be good Christians, all of you; your wife, your children and yourself. Never forget your prayers. Farewell!'

'Farewell, Father,' said papa, while the priest patted the heads of all the children.

'Farewell, Father!' cried my step-mother in a tearful voice. 'And greet your own mother for me!'

'I shall indeed!' called the Father, as he walked back to his motorbike.

I watched him swing on to the saddle and observed all his gestures, knowing that I was seeing them for the last time. But I couldn't open my mouth or make the slightest move. I was glued to the earth.

Then the Father seemed to cry to me: 'Little Denis, aren't you coming to embrace me for the last time? What! Is this how you leave your old Father? You know that I've had only one son, and that's yourself! Come, come and embrace me! Don't you know that I'm going far away and shall never come back to you? And even if I did, you'd have grown up by then. You could never be a boy in my mission again!'

I came forward and stood close to him, overcome with tears. It was as if my heart were cast adrift within my breast and I must soon die. I could do longer distinguish reality from nightmare.

'Don't cry so!' the Father called to me.

I heard him as if through a curtain. My eyes and soul were alike brimming with tears. To think that I could not keep from crying at such a moment! It makes me miserable now.

Then the Father said: 'I'm leaving you, it's true, but I leave you in good hands. For Christ will never leave you, you may be sure of that. He is always with you and must ever remain so. His eyes are ever fixed on you. And He loves you more than I or any mortal can! So don't cry like that: you will cause pain to your Eternal Father and to Christ Himself. Dry your tears, my little Denis . . . Look at me: do you think it pleases me to have to leave you like this?'

But I still kept on howling.

'I shall think of you always, remember that. I shan't forget you. And I'll even write to you, quite often. And I'll send you photos,

photos of my parents, my brothers and sisters, and myself. I'll tell you all the local news of my country. Think of that. Won't that please you, eh?'

'Yes, F-father,' I managed to stammer.

'You see! Now, smile a little. Stop crying and give me a smile, so!'

He lifted my chin and I tried to smile, but I'm not sure that I succeeded.

Then I heard him start his motor and I turned away, unable to watch him go. With my eyes fast shut, I heard the engine move off and, little by little, disappear in the distance.

When I opened my eyes, I saw my parents right behind me. So perhaps they had been there all through my farewells?

The Father has gone and will never return. What would he come back here for, anyway? We loved him so little . . . As if he were not one of us . . . for he was not one of us . . .

Sogolo

It's now three weeks since the Father left! Three weeks . . . all twenty-one days of them. And I still haven't had a letter from him. Didn't he promise to write to me? Perhaps Jean-Martin has had news of him? But I don't even know which mission he's gone to, or I'd certainly go and ask him for news of the Father.

This morning I could stand it no longer. Before it was daylight I fled from home, wearing all my best clothes, as I did every Sunday in the old days. Although the night was barely over, it was already hot outside.

I went on foot, for the mission isn't really far from Sogolo, barely twelve kilometres. And since I walked on the main road, I had nothing to fear, despite the darkness. As I went along, my heart was full of anguished anticipation, as if I really expected some big surprise on reaching Bomba.

I got there just after dawn and stayed right up till noon. I went everywhere: to the church, where I prayed; to the sixa, where I looked in every corner for Catherine's sweet face; to the school, now silent and empty as death; to the gardens, already invaded by the bush.

At every moment, I expected to hear the Father's grave, deep voice calling to me. There wasn't a sound anywhere. Not a whiff of smoke. Only a great silence, as though the cemetery had gradually invaded the whole mission. Bomba had the look of an abandoned village.

I chatted with one of the watchmen, who told me that no priest had appeared there since the departure of the two Fathers. On the following two Sundays, the faithful had flocked to the church expecting a Mass, but had gone away disappointed. The sacristy was taken over by rats and lizards.

'Nothing has been stolen?' I asked him.
'No, nothing at all.'
'And no one has tried?'

'No one.'

'Not even to spirit away a few oranges or paw-paws from the gardens?'

'Listen, little one, not a soul has been here since you departed; neither by night nor day.'

After a while, he continued: 'The one thing that's given us concern is the flock of sheep and goats you left here. At first we thought that the Bishop would send for them fast enough, but he didn't. And God knows there are plenty of them, with only three of us to watch them! There's always one of them ill, or another who's breached the fence and run off somewhere. Honestly, we don't have a quiet moment with that lot. And there's the courtyard to keep clean, too. I really wonder how you managed to collect such a horde of them.'

'Oh! They were presents given to us on tour.'

'You're not kidding, boy? By God, there's still some generosity around here, then!'

'Where do you come from, yourself?'

'Oh, from near the Bishop's place. And around there they certainly don't give any presents to priests nowadays, believe me, tour or no tour!'

'But why not? Don't they believe in God any more?'

'Oh, yes . . . a little, that is. No, lad, it's nothing to do with that. It's just the proximity of the town. Don't you know that towns make people avaricious?'

'Ah?'

'Of course, because in towns everything costs money, don't you see? So people have to become avaricious.'

It was evening when I got back to my father's compound. He wasn't unduly surprised at my absence and didn't ask me much about it. Since I came home this time, he doesn't supervise me much, scarcely bothering whether I come or go. He seems to regard me as an adult now.

I think more and more of visiting Zacharia, just to see Catherine again . . .

Oh! And I've just heard that they've started cutting that new road M. Vidal was always talking of, the one through the Tala country. The reports speak of a real reign of terror – even women are being driven into the labour gangs. There are rumours that they're going to round up men as far away as this, although we've already made our own road! How unjust! Everyone here is protesting already and saying they won't go. But how can they resist the soldiers when they come? And they're sure to take me as well, despite my age. My father says I shouldn't stay in Sogolo. I'm remembering the advice which Anatole gave me one evening! To go to the town and get a small-boy's job with one of the Greek merchants . . .